HEXSLAYER

Other books from Jordan L. Hawk:

Hainted

Whyborne & Griffin:
Widdershins
Threshold
Stormhaven
Necropolis
Bloodline
Hoarfrost
Maelstrom
Fallow
Draakenwood

Spirits:
Restless Spirits
Dangerous Spirits

Hexworld
The 13th Hex (prequel short story)
Hexbreaker
Hexmaker
A Christmas Hex (short story)
Hexslayer

SPECTR
Hunter of Demons
Master of Ghouls
Reaper of Souls
Eater of Lives
Destroyer of Worlds
Summoner of Storms
Mocker of Ravens
Dancer of Death
Drinker of Blood

HEXSLAYER

Hexworld 3

JORDAN L. HAWK

ISBN: 978-1976236365

Edited by Annetta Ribken Graney

Chapter 1

"No! Stop! I haven't done anything wrong!" the man shouted as a swarm of police officers dragged him out the open door of a tenement.

Jamie tugged on the reins to slow his wagon. The coppers wore the blue uniforms of the regular police force, and wouldn't likely welcome his help, given the rivalry between them and the Metropolitan Witch Police. Even so, he guided the MWP wagon to the curb, beside the police hacks and wagons already partially blocking the street.

The prisoner threw his head back, arms bulging as the police struggled to wrangle him down the steps. "No!" he repeated, frantic. Desperate. "My wife is back in Illinois—she needs the money I've been sending her—we have children. I can't let you take me!"

"Watch out!" one of the coppers yelled. "He's going to shift."

"Hold him, boys!" shouted a familiar voice. A moment later, Jamie's uncle, Inspector Hurley O'Malley, mounted the steps with a piece of paper in his hands. He reached through the knot of fighting men, slapped it against the prisoner's skin, and said, "Be bound to your human form."

A look of shock passed over the prisoner's face. Then the fight seemed to go out of him. He slumped into the arms of the police officers.

Jamie knew of hexes that could force a familiar into their animal shape, but he'd never heard of one to prevent them from taking it. True, he wasn't as accomplished as a real hexman like Detective Kopecky, but he knew more than most witches. If nothing else, it seemed the sort of thing the MWP would use if they had it.

"Mr. Luther," Hurley said. "You're under arrest for violating the Pemberton Public Safety and Security Act."

"But I haven't done anything," Luther protested weakly. "I'd never hurt anyone."

"You're an unbonded lion familiar, not under the official supervision of a witch," Hurley replied. "That's breaking the law. It's the Menagerie for you."

The familiars' prison. The man's legs crumpled beneath him, and the coppers had to all but carry him to the wagon. Its doors slammed shut, and it pulled away from the curb.

Jamie shook his head. What was wrong with the fellow? If Mr. Luther had just followed the law, he wouldn't be in trouble now. The MWP might have offered him a place, or one of the private security forces looking for the muscle a lion could offer. He'd brought this on himself, really.

One of the coppers noticed the MWP emblem on Jamie's wagon and shot him an unfriendly look. "What're you gawking at, fairy?"

Jamie's face flushed, hot with anger. But then Hurley spotted him and called, "Hold your tongue, Captain O'Byrne. That's my nephew, Jamie MacDougal."

Damn it. He should have kept driving, or hurried off before he could be spotted. But Hurley was already beckoning him over, and it was too late.

Not that he didn't love his uncle. He did. That wasn't the problem.

He climbed down from the cart—slowly, because he had to watch how his wooden left leg came down. He had only a slight limp when he walked, but he felt the curious eyes of the uniformed policemen on him as he approached. They must all be members of the Dangerous Familiars Squad. Certainly they'd been picked for their size, every last one of them much taller and bulkier than either Hurley or Jamie.

"Good to see you, lad," Hurley said, clapping him on the shoulder. As an inspector, Hurley dressed in a suit rather than a uniform, his badge prominently pinned to the lapel. "What are you doing here?"

"Just left another illegal hex vendor at the Tombs." Cocking his thumb in the direction of his wagon, he said, "They're expecting me back at the Coven…"

"Surely you can take a few minutes." Hurley turned to his men with a big smile, and Jamie's heart sank. "Boys! Meet my nephew, Jamie MacDougal. The Rough Rider. That's right—Jamie here fought in Cuba alongside Roosevelt himself."

Expressions of shock gave way to grins, and hands thrust forward desperate to shake his. Their words of praise washed over him like a wave, its action slowly scouring out a hollow place behind his breast bone.

They expected him to play the hero. To boast about the Spanish he'd killed, to laugh off the misery as though it had been nothing. To mouth platitudes about the men who had died beside him, but to keep a smile on his face as he spoke of them. At times like this, he felt as though a pane of glass cut him off from those around him. From the world.

"Thank you," he said. "But I really do have to be going."

Hurley nodded. "I'll see you Sunday, Jamie. All right, you lot, let's get back to the station."

Jamie hauled himself into the driver's seat, relying on the strength of his arms and the leg that remained whole. An October wind raced down the street with the sunset, chilling his hands as he took up the reins. Saint Mary, he was glad winter was on its way. He'd loved summer once, but Cuba had changed that, as it had changed so much else. After hours lying in the glare of the sun, the fires begun by artillery shells baking his skin and fever roasting him from the inside, he'd lost his taste for heat.

Leaving his gloves in his pocket, he clicked his tongue at the horse and started back to the Coven.

Nick's shoulders stiffened when he spotted three policemen, led by a man clad in sober black, through the glass window of Caballus.

He didn't say anything to Kyle behind the bar—didn't *need* to say anything, because Kyle knew the routine by now, as they'd had these visits on the regular for the last few months. Nick crossed the room, using his body to block entry even as the door swung open. Thank God he'd inherited the build of his Samoan grandfather, tall and broad enough to make even the meanest drunk think twice about taking a swing.

"Can't you read the sign?" Nick demanded, before any of the four men on the stoop could speak. "It says *Familiars Only*. Find somewhere else to do your drinking, coppers." He turned his gaze onto the man in the black suit, its white collar gleaming in the streetlights. "That goes double for you, Reverend Ingram. I'm sure there's a dozen dive bars that would love to serve you a glass of swipes."

Behind Nick, the saloon's patrons had gone still. One or two would probably try to slip away unseen out the back, whether they had actually done anything to warrant the attention of the police or not. After the passage of the Pemberton Act, no feral could feel safe with a copper in sight.

Ingram wrinkled his nose in distaste. "They're here to answer a complaint I lodged. It seems to me a foul smell is coming from this building. Like a bunch of animals in a pen."

Nick kept his hands from curling into fists only with effort. The reverend probably hoped he'd throw a punch. The reform newspapers panted after Ingram and his organization, the Heirs of Adam. Any violence on Nick's part would end up plastered on the front page as more proof ferals were nothing but out of control animals.

One of the coppers tried to shove past Nick. But he'd chosen his position well, feet secure on the floor, stance wide, and didn't move so much as an inch. The much smaller man stepped back after a moment, trying to look casual, as if he hadn't been pushing as hard as he could against Nick's shoulder.

"Are you the landlord of the tenement above this saloon?" another copper demanded. He spoke with an Irish accent through a thick mustache. A sergeant's badge gleamed on his lapel.

"Why do you want to know?" Nick countered.

The sergeant fingered the handle of his nightstick. "It's a feral colony. Got to make sure you ain't housing dangerous ferals, don't we now?"

Nick ground his teeth together. "There aren't any dangerous ferals here."

"You sure about that?" the sergeant asked. "No felines larger than a house cat? Bobcat, tiger, anything like that?"

Nick forced his face into stony impassivity. "No."

"No bears? What about wolves? Crocodiles or alligators?"

"No."

"Don't forget eagles," Ingram said.

"Right." The sergeant nodded. "Any eagles here?"

Nick's heart kicked against his ribs. It was just a coincidence.

But Wyatt was already an hour late.

"No." Nick shook his head slowly. "No eagles."

"So you say." The sergeant narrowed his eyes. "I think we'll take a look around. Just see for ourselves." He glanced at Ingram. "We have to check out the smell complaint, after all."

Fur and feathers. Did they know something? Or was it just the usual police harassment?

"Show me your warrant," he said.

The sergeant's eyes narrowed. He looked Nick up and down, taking in not just his size, but his brown skin and the black hair he wore to his shoulders. "Now you listen here, feral. We can do this one of two ways. The first is, you stand aside and let us take a look around. Give us your keys, let us search the apartments and determine whether there's any criminal element here. The second way—"

"The second way is you come back with a warrant." Though there was nothing for the coppers to find in the tenement, he'd be damned if he let them into the rooms of his fellow ferals. Even if the coppers didn't wreck the apartments and steal anything of the slightest value—and they would, no question—it would be a betrayal of the people who depended on Nick to keep them safe.

And that was the one thing he'd never do.

He saw the calculation flash through the sergeant's eyes. The coppers could probably overpower Nick, even if he took on horse form. But he'd get in a few good hits himself, first, and he silently swore the sergeant would be the one to take them.

After Ingram, anyway.

It ought to be obvious, even from the sidewalk, that there wasn't much of value either in the saloon or the apartments above. Most of the ferals here were barely hanging on. When the only thing anyone cared about was your magic, it was hard to find work doing anything else.

Apparently, the sergeant decided it wasn't worth it. He spat casually on Nick's boot, then stepped back. "I'll be keeping an eye on you."

Ingram bridled. "What about my complaint?"

"I think an apology is in order to the good reverend, for disturbing his evening, horse. Why don't you make it in the form of a donation to his fine cause. Say twenty-five dollars." The sergeant grinned, showing his teeth. "He'll be taking that now, in cash."

Every instinct screamed at Nick to drive them off his doorstep, slam the door, and to hell with the consequences. Paying bribes to the police was one thing—that was just part of the cost of owning a saloon. But to give his hard-earned money to an organization that wanted to see familiar-kind in bondage, or gone altogether...

Consequences. There were always consequences. If he didn't go along, he'd bear some of them, but the innocent souls in his cellar would pay an even higher price.

"Kyle," he said, without turning around. "Get the money out of the cash box."

"I wonder how you can afford such a generous donation," Ingram murmured. "In fact, I question how an animal like you is able to run this establishment at all. It isn't as though a familiar could do it on their own. Someone else must be instructing you what to do."

Bands constricted around Nick's chest, cutting off his breath. Caballus and the tenement had been built on the bones of his dead dreams, and for a wild moment he almost thought the headlines would be worth the opportunity to take out his fury on Ingram's self-righteous face.

Instead, he swallowed his anger, letting it sour his belly. "Go to hell." He took the money from Kyle and flung it at Ingram. It scattered across the pavement; two of the police officers immediately fell to the ground and began to snatch it up. Ingram would be lucky if he received half of it from them. "And take your bribe with you."

"It isn't I who will be visiting the pit, feral." Ingram peered past him to the other familiars in the saloon, and raised his voice. "Repent, all of you! For the Serpent was the first familiar, and Eve the first witch, and their sin denied us all Eden. Get on your knees—"

Nick slammed the door in his face. "Only one reason I get on my knees," he said with forced levity. "And I sure as hell wouldn't touch *his* unwashed prick." A smattering of startled laughter rewarded him. "People wonder why I don't go to church."

"Protestants," said an Irish otter from one of the back tables. "The true pope—the one in Belfast—recognizes the Holy Familiar."

"Oh no, you papist, I ain't going to be blamed for the likes of the Heirs of Adam," protested a raccoon familiar. "Besides, you lot have got —what—six popes, all of whom have excommunicated each other?"

"Seven, but who's counting?" asked the otter with a wink.

Nick glanced over the saloon. Despite the brave attempts of the otter and the raccoon, the rest of his feral customers exuded fear.

Well, of course they did. They weren't stupid. They could read the newspapers. Between the Pemberton Act and the reform groups targeting anything that smacked of magic, there was a lot to be afraid of these days.

They were meant to be safe here. Of all the places in New York, Caballus was the one place they ought to rest easy. Now Ingram seemed determined to ruin even that.

But he hadn't yet, and wouldn't if Nick had anything to say about it. "Next round is on the house," he announced. It hurt, since he'd already lost his earnings to Ingram, but he'd make do. "So order the good stuff."

As the customers let out a ragged cheer, he nodded to the raccoon to get on the piano. Within seconds, the cheerful strains of "My Wild Irish Rose" mingled with the calls for drinks.

"You're going to get yourself killed," Kyle murmured, when Nick stepped behind the plank that served as a bar to help him pour. "Or bankrupted."

"Probably." Nick shrugged.

Kyle handed over a beer, then leaned in closer. "Wyatt's late." Worry showed in his eyes, as golden as those of his cat form. "And the package he was supposed to pick up is in our cellar."

"My cellar," Nick corrected. Because if things went wrong, he'd swear up and down to the police Kyle hadn't been involved. "I own the building; the goods are my responsibility." He checked the clock on the wall behind the bar. "As soon as the rush is over, I'll step down to get some more booze and look in on the package. Wyatt might yet show up."

"You believe that?" Kyle asked.

Nick hesitated, then shook his head. "No. I really don't."

Chapter 2

Nick clomped down the stairs into the saloon's cellar. Boxes, barrels, and kegs crowded most of the space. The rest was taken up by various things tenants had left behind over the years: broken chairs, cooking utensils, children's toys, and small tools. He maneuvered through the stacks, careful not to knock anything over with his broad shoulders, until he reached the cellar wall.

Who had created the hidden door, he didn't know and didn't much care. The lower part of Manhattan was riddled with tunnels, especially near the docks. His stretch of West 28th Street wasn't near the water, but some enterprising smuggler had taken inspiration and put the door in long before Nick had acquired the property.

The memory of Ingram's implication—that a familiar couldn't possibly own a business—scalded him a second time. Some days, Nick would stare at the book shelves in his apartment, and his breath would catch in pain over what was gone. Everything his dad had wanted to pass down to him: the anatomy texts, the thick tomes on disease, the books on pharmaceuticals. All sold, gone along with so much else into buying Caballus and the tenement.

Nick pressed on the correct brick and was rewarded when counterweights shifted and part of the wall popped out. He grasped the edge and swung it open, revealing the tiny room where he'd hidden the package meant to be passed on to Wyatt.

Fearful eyes fixed on him—three human, and two in animal form. A tiger stood nearest the door, ready to pounce if need be. When the tiger saw Nick, he shifted back into human shape, as did the bear who had positioned herself to block access to the two youngest ferals.

Last November, a bunch of idiots decided to go on a killing spree at a society wedding. A handful of nobs died as a result—no loss there, really. But the survivors had money, and connections, and political power. The attackers had been ferals, angered over the treatment the law allowed witches to visit on so-called dangerous familiars.

If that had been the end of it, Nick wouldn't have given a damn. The nobs could look after themselves, as far as he was concerned. But the attack resulted in hysteria, and in politicians falling over themselves to prove they were Doing Something.

What they'd done was pass the Pemberton Act, named after the state senator who wrote most of it, with the back room help of purity groups like the Heirs of Adam. All "dangerous" familiars in New York state now had to either be bonded to a witch, or under a witch's supervision. That meant working for one of the larger corporations or the MWP—and never mind the ring leader of the attack had been employed by the fucking MWP to start with.

Though that hadn't been entirely forgotten. The fact an MWP officer planned the massacre resulted in a "compromise" written into the act, giving the authority to enforce it to the non-magical police. Hence the assholes who had just showed up on his doorstep to threaten him.

Familiars who saw the writing on the wall had abandoned the state in droves. If they had the means. But it wasn't easy for the ferals covered by the act to leave the city without being spotted by some train conductor, or ferry captain, or just the damned coppers keeping watch for anyone trying to run. If they were caught, they'd be hauled off to the Menagerie.

"Where's Wyatt?" asked the tiger. Conrad, that was his name. "We've gathered our things. We're ready to go."

Nick rubbed his face. "There's been a delay."

Conrad's yellow eyes sharpened. "What happened?"

"I'm not sure yet." Nick glanced over the room, making certain there was enough bedding for everyone. "Wyatt didn't show up, but the coppers did."

Conrad paled. "The police."

"I think it was just a coincidence. Just looking for an excuse to harass ferals, as usual." Nick stamped a foot and shook his head, hair flying. "I'm going to find out what happened to Wyatt."

"What are we to do?" asked one of the young ferals. The girl wasn't more than fourteen, if that. Fear trembled in her voice, but Nick could tell she was trying hard to put up a brave front.

He crouched in front of her, to be more on her level. "You're going to stay here, where it's safe," he said, meeting her gaze. "Anyone wants to hurt you, they've got to come through me, first. And I make a pretty good wall."

He winked, saw her relax marginally. "All right," she said, giving him a little smile.

Nick rose to his feet. " If we're lucky, you lot can move on with Wyatt tomorrow. If we aren't, it might be a few days." He took a step back, into the doorway. "No one is going to find you here, even if the coppers come back with a search warrant. You saw yourselves how hidden this door is from the other side, so there's no reason to be afraid. Do you have enough food for tonight? Enough water? All right, then. I'll be back as soon as I can."

He swung the door shut, making sure it latched. At least they could open it from their side, if he ended up hauled off by the coppers on some trumped up charge.

He had to find Wyatt and get them out of here. Despite his words, too many things could go wrong.

The problem was, he didn't know where to look for Wyatt. A different familiar brought groups of ferals to Nick. They stayed in the cellar for a day or two, then Wyatt came by and led them to a ferry that would take them out of the city. That was the only time he and the eagle regularly met face-to-face. If they needed to communicate, they hid messages in a rocky crevice inside the Cave in Central Park.

Sure, he'd had a few drinks with Wyatt, talked to him a bit, getting his own feel for the man even though Nick's contacts said he was safe. Couldn't be too careful, after all. But a part of being careful was keeping as much personal information from one another as possible, in case one of them was taken by the coppers. Nick had no idea what part of the city Wyatt lived in, or if he had friends, or family, or anything else.

Nick hadn't had time to check the Cave today. But maybe he should. There might be a note telling him something had gone wrong, and when he could expect Wyatt to show up.

"I'm going out," he called to Kyle once he emerged back into the main room of the saloon. Kyle only nodded; he knew better than to ask questions.

Nick stepped out onto West 28th Street. It was getting late, the sun long gone. The frosty air nipped at his cheeks. The Seventh Avenue El lay within spitting distance, but no sense spending the money when he could just run.

Nick shifted into horse form and shook himself. A couple of passers-by stared in surprise at the sight of a huge, black horse loitering on the sidewalk. He ignored them and instead trotted down the street, making for Seventh Avenue and the park. With any luck, he'd find Wyatt had left him a message saying there was a minor delay, and the ferals would be out of his basement by tomorrow.

"We've had a call, MacDougal." The witch who manned the switchboard overnight stuck her head out the door leading to the stables, unwilling to step outside into the chilly breeze. "A body in Central Park, near Playmates Arch, with some sort of hex drawn around it. Kopecky and Rook are already on their way."

Jamie looked up from the notebook where he'd been practicing his hexes. A small stove provided heat, and a hexlight sat on the table for illumination. The air smelled of hay and of the horses in their stalls behind him. "Thanks."

The other witch—or potential witch, as neither of them had bonded—hesitated a moment, as if debating saying something further. Jamie levered himself up and turned his back on the woman. "Central Park's a fair ways," he said, before she could speak. "I'd best get going, so as not to make the detectives wait."

She took the hint and shut the door. Alone again, Jamie let out a sigh of relief.

She probably thought he was crazy, sitting out here by himself on a cold fall night. Chief Ferguson had even stopped by one evening last winter, to remind Jamie he could pass the time indoors. He'd thanked the chief, but stayed in the stable.

At least no one had asked him why. He wasn't certain he could explain why spending time with the horses was easier than with his fellow coppers. The horses didn't ask Jamie to recount the Battle of Las Guasimas, or what it was like to fight beside Roosevelt, or any of the other questions people felt entitled to ask once they knew about his brief stint with the First Volunteer Cavalry.

The wagon wasn't a fast conveyance, but the streets were largely clear of traffic at this late hour. Not empty—this was New York City, after all. There was always an open saloon, or a twenty-four-hour restaurant, or a pool hall ready to provide a bit of late-night entertainment. Not to mention the brothels and street walkers.

The park itself was quiet, though. This time of night, no carriages clattered along its drives, and no bicycles whizzed merrily down its trails. An owl flushed from a tree, flew low across the drive in front of the wagon, and vanished into the darkness. The hooves of Jamie's horse echoed eerily from trees and rocky outcroppings. Even a short distance in, it was easy to forget the city pressing at the park's borders, to feel as though he'd been transported to the country. The smells differed as much as the sights: the cidery scent of fallen leaves, the rich tang of soil and stone. Even the air was easier to breathe, though that might be due to the park's Great Hex.

The architects of Central Park had meant it to be a place where the city's inhabitants could enjoy healthy air and sights, just like the countryside. Where women and children could get fresh milk from the dairy, and even those outside the park could benefit from clean, pure water from the reservoir. So they'd used the paths and buildings to craft the Great Hex, inscribed across the very landscape of the park. The world felt different, as soon as you crossed the boundary; the city noises falling away, the air lacking the perpetual haze of coal smoke, the plants thriving.

A cluster of hex lights revealed the gathering of police atop Playmates Arch, throwing the shadows of the dark iron railings on the path below. MWP Detective Dominic Kopecky and his familiar Rook stood gazing down at what looked like a hex painted in blood on the paved surface of the arch. Dominic tugged absently at a vest that lay snug over a belly gained from spending most of his time behind a desk. Rook was a slender shadow in the night: brown skin, black hair, and a dark suit.

Bill Quigley, the liaison between the MWP and regular police, surveyed the scene with his arms folded over his broad chest. When Jamie drew up, Quigley glanced at him. "MacDougal. They've still got you driving the wagon, have they?"

"Aye." They'd worked together before, and he knew from experience that Quigley wouldn't hesitate to help him load the body. Corpses tended to be difficult things to move, either stiff as boards or utterly limp.

As Jamie climbed down from the cart, someone from beyond the illumination of the hexlights called out to Rook. Rook frowned and glanced at Dominic. Some communication seemed to pass between them, even though Rook was in human form. Rook left the group gathered around the body, vanishing altogether into the shadows.

"It's a bad one," Quigley warned as Jamie approached.

"I've got no choice but to look, if I want to get him in the wagon."

"Aye." Quigley winced. "Just...ready yourself."

The dead man lay sprawled on his back, his head turned to the side. His throat gaped from a slash so deep the bone was visible. The killer had opened his abdomen as well, perhaps seeking more blood to paint the grotesque tangle of hexwork around him.

Open eyes stared sightlessly at Jamie. Pale yellow eyes, like those of his eagle form, set in a face Jamie knew almost as well as his own. A thin golden chain yet hung around his neck, below the slash, a pendant dangling from it.

It couldn't be him.

Jamie closed his eyes tight. This was it—he'd finally gone round the bend. He was suffering an unexpected attack of soldier's heart, seeing the face of a dead comrade instead of what was actually in front of him.

"Told you it was a bad one," Quigley said sympathetically.

"It...it ain't that." Though it was. Jamie forced his eyes open, willing himself to see reality this time.

But nothing changed. The face still belonged to Wyatt. The man he'd loved.

Quigley put a hand to his arm, and Jamie realized he'd begun to sway. "MacDougal? Jamie? Your color don't look so good. Maybe you ought to sit down for a bit?"

"Describe him," Jamie said hoarsely.

Quigley frowned. "What?"

"Tell me what the victim looks like." Now Quigley and Dominic both stared at him as though he'd lost his mind.

Quigley decided to humor him. "Um, pale yellow eyes. Dark hair. Has some kind of necklace on. Scar on the chin."

Nausea rose in Jamie's belly. He fought it back, but nothing would stop the horror that turned the blood in his veins sluggish. For a moment, the air around him didn't belong to a fall night in New York. It was hotter, thicker, filled with the scents of the jungle. Despite the breathless air, they crowded against each other in the two man tent, hands on each other's cocks, while Eddie smoked and sat guard outside. The pendant dangled in front of his eyes, as Wyatt pressed him down into the blankets.

"Wyatt," he whispered.

"You know this familiar?" Quigley asked in surprise.

"Aye." This wasn't happening. This *couldn't* be happening. Better if Jamie was having an attack of soldier's heart, because then at least this grisly scene wouldn't be real. "Wyatt. He was in my unit. He and his witch died in Cuba."

Beyond the ordinary gaslights that illuminated the carriage drives and bridle paths of the park, there shone another set of lights, one that shouldn't have been there. These lights didn't flicker, but instead put out the cold, clear radiance of hexlights.

Nick slowed to a walk, then shifted back to human form. A group of people gathered on Playmates Arch. Even as he watched, an MWP wagon rolled up.

Damn it.

It might not have anything to do with him. Wyatt hid the notes in the Cave, farther into the park, within the lightless confines of the Ramble. If Nick had any sense, he'd take back his horse shape and trot along, past something that was likely none of his business.

He drew closer, sticking to the shadows. The hexlights illuminated the road over the arch more clearly than gaslight, and as he drew nearer, he recognized one of the MWP coppers.

Rook. His little brother.

His brother, who had joined the MWP years ago and now lived fat and happy as some witch's pet. Who had given up his freedom, as though Nick wouldn't have sacrificed anything—everything—to protect him.

Rook might be tame now, but at least his presence meant Nick wouldn't be grabbed as the nearest convenient suspect, accused of whatever crime had taken place on the arch, and have a confession beaten out of him.

"Rook!" Nick called.

Rook turned; even if he couldn't see Nick in the darkness, he'd clearly recognized Nick's voice. Rook glanced at his witch—asking permission, no doubt—then made his way over.

"What happened?" Nick asked.

"Good to see you, too," Rook said with false cheer. "I've been doing fine, thanks for asking. Dominic is doing well, too. We moved into a better apartment, not that you knew what the one before it was like, since you never come to visit."

Nick stamped his foot. "Quit your squawking and answer my question."

Rook rolled his eyes. "A murder." He paused. "Actually, you might be of some use, for once. You know half the ferals in the city. Do you want to tell me if you recognize this one?"

Nick's impatience drained away, replaced by dread. As Rook had said, chances were good he knew whatever poor bastard had died here. Even if it wasn't Wyatt.

Wyatt, who was late, when he'd never been before.

Nick stepped closer to get a look at the face. His gorge rose at the sight—someone had butchered the poor bastard. The face was unmarked, though, and…

Damn it.

Maybe he hadn't known Wyatt well, but he'd liked what he'd seen of the fellow. A cheerful sort, when it came to dealing with scared fugitives, always laughing and joking while never belittling the danger. But when it was just him and Nick, the mask slipped away.

Haunted, that's what Wyatt had been, though Nick never asked by what. There was a sadness in his eyes, accompanied by a sort of quiet regret.

Now he was dead, throat cut and body torn apart. Who would have done such a thing, and—more urgently—had they done it because he was part of the smuggling ring moving dangerous ferals out of the city?

"Wyatt," said one of the coppers. His voice sounded shaky, as though he struggled not to either throw up or cry. "He was in my unit. He and his witch died in Cuba."

The man who had spoken was one of the MWP witches. Handsome, even though his face had gone the color of milk. Black hair, green eyes, and a plump mouth that looked made for sin. His uniform hung a bit loose on his frame, as though he'd lost weight recently.

The world twisted in on itself. Knowledge settled in Nick's bones, his blood. In the space against his heart, as though he'd swallowed a thorn.

This man, whoever he was…was Nick's witch.

Chapter 3

Jamie walked into the Coven the next morning, his mind still reeling. Quigley had tried to talk him out of transporting Wyatt's body to the morgue last night. But Jamie insisted; it was the last thing he could do for the man he'd once loved.

The man he'd failed.

Even so, Quigley, Dominic, and Rook accompanied him, obviously not wanting to leave him alone in his grief. Through the haze of disbelief and horror, he'd appreciated the gesture. Before he left, Dominic and Rook gently asked him to come see them at the Coven so he could answer their questions about Wyatt, whenever he was ready.

Jamie hadn't slept a wink once he'd gotten home, his mind churning. Nothing made sense.

Over a year ago, the army had declared Wyatt dead, along with Eddie. They'd been assigned a special mission after the fall of Santiago. What the mission had been, he'd never learned, only that it had cost their lives. He'd mourned Eddie, alongside the other men he'd known who had died in Cuba.

But Wyatt...Jamie felt as though the familiar's death had broken something inside him. Over and over, he'd wondered if everything would have been different if he'd been with them. If he hadn't been hit by the artillery shell at El Pozo. If he'd made it to Kettle Hill and San Juan Heights, and through to the other side.

If he'd been with them on that special mission, filling in as their hexman, since the real one had been accidentally left behind in Tampa.

Could he have saved Wyatt? The question haunted his nights, drowning out even the pain of his leg. Except apparently Wyatt hadn't needed saving after all. At least, not then.

Saint Mary, Holy Familiar of Christ, give him strength.

He made his way slowly up the stairs to the detective's area, careful to place his wooden leg fully on each step before trusting his weight to it, and using the railing for an extra bit of leverage. Witches and familiars flowed around him, arguing or laughing as they passed. A Sharp-shinned Hawk almost clipped his hat with a wing, and a cat dashed between his legs.

Dominic and Rook shared a desk near the large windows. Dominic had been a hexman before bonding with Rook, and his expertise meant he spent most of the time behind the desk comparing various hexes, rather than working the streets. Though the desk included a perch for Rook, right now he was in human form, huddled close to Dominic as they peered at something together.

Bands tightened around Jamie's chest, and his stomach rolled over at the prospect of what was to come. He couldn't avoid answering their questions. But maybe...maybe he could get some answers of his own.

Dominic glanced up as he approached. "MacDougal, isn't it?"

"Aye, sir." Most of the detectives didn't pay him much attention. He was the fellow who drove the wagon, nothing more. "Jamie MacDougal."

Rook hopped out of his chair and pulled it away from Dominic's side. "Have a seat." Before Jamie could object, Rook shifted into crow form and flapped up to the perch on the desk.

Jamie took the seat. Dominic shuffled some papers, then looked at Jamie. "Before we begin, I'm sorry for your loss."

Jamie swallowed convulsively. "Thank you."

"We've sent for Wyatt's military records, but they haven't arrived yet." Dominic paused. "The Police Board spoke to Governor Roosevelt this morning. He's extremely insistent that there must have been a mistake. None of his men would have deserted."

Desertion. Christ, Jamie hadn't even thought about that. If Wyatt had been declared dead, if he'd never reported back, that made him a deserter, didn't it?

The Wyatt he'd known would never have done such a thing. Jamie would have bet his life on it.

And yet. "It was him. I swear it."

"I believe you," Dominic said. "Someone else has also confirmed

Wyatt's identity."

Someone else? Wyatt had come to New York, not bothered to let Jamie know he was alive, but had revealed his identity to someone else?

"But, as we don't want trouble from Governor Roosevelt, Wyatt will officially be an unidentified eagle familiar," Dominic went on. He opened a notebook and took out a pen. "Now. When did you last see Wyatt alive?"

Jamie swallowed thickly. He felt himself reeling, as he had in the days after losing his leg, certain none of it could be true. "After Las Guasimas." The ambush Roosevelt had led them straight into. "The First Volunteer Cavalry had three witch and familiar pairs: an eagle, a cougar, and a dog. Wyatt's witch was a fellow named Eddie Brookes." Jamie hesitated, uncertain what sort of details Dominic actually wanted. "Their hexman got left behind in Tampa, along with the horses. Ever since I joined the MWP, I've been practicing drawing hexes. Simple ones that might come in handy, nothing advanced like yours," he added hastily. "I'm no hexman, but Eddie had no skill at it at all, so I ended up working with them. Which turned out to be a good thing, since our supply of everything, including hexes, was terrible."

He could still see Wyatt's pale yellow eyes, the color of white wine in a clear glass. His smile. Jamie tried to remember the taste of his lips and couldn't.

Jamie cleared his throat, realizing he'd lapsed into silence. "We were busy after the battle—making and charging new sleeping hexes for the wounded who needed surgery, that sort of thing. So we didn't have much time to talk." He'd been so relieved to see they'd come through unscathed. "But I was injured on the march after."

The hell of it was, the shell hadn't even been aimed at him, but at the artillery guns on the hill above. Maybe if it had happened during a battle, face-to-face with the Spanish, he would have felt more like the hero everyone seemed to think he was. Would have boasted and bragged about how he might have come away with a third of his leg gone, but the other fellow had fared worse. Instead, one moment he'd been fine, and the next lying on the ground, his leg a welter of shattered bone and blood. If there had been any sort of warning, he couldn't remember it.

"You said Wyatt was supposed to be dead?" Dominic probed.

Jamie nodded. "Aye. I didn't find out until I was already on the hospital ship, on the way home. Eddie died on some sort of special mission, after the surrender. I don't know what it was. His body was shipped back to Arizona and buried there. But Wyatt's body wasn't recovered. It didn't really seem odd, though—he was an eagle, flying over the jungle, where snipers would sit in trees. He would never have been found under those conditions. I never imagined, even for a second, that he would desert, and neither did anyone else. I don't understand what happened. Wyatt wasn't a coward. He would have rejoined the unit, not run away."

None of this made any sense.

Dominic took notes in his neat hexman's hand. "You didn't know he'd returned to New York?"

"Nay." Bitterness coated the word, despite his attempt to keep it down. Wyatt had been here, alive, and hadn't even tried to contact Jamie.

Rook croaked softly. Dominic winced, then glanced at Jamie. "You were…friends, though."

"I thought so." But he'd also thought Wyatt would never abandon their fellow Rough Riders. "What happened to him, Detective Kopecky? The hex…"

"We're trying to figure that out," Dominic said, closing his notebook. "Did he have any family you know of?"

"Aye. Well, sort of." Jamie pressed his lips together. "He didn't like to talk about it, but his mother belonged to one of those churches that believe all familiars are touched by the devil. Wyatt left, though he had a brother who stayed behind. I don't think he'd talked to either of them in years."

"I see." Dominic reached into his desk and took out a slender gold chain, bearing on it a small pendant. "This was the only thing of any value on Wyatt's body. Since it doesn't sound as if there's anyone else to give it to, would you like to have it?"

Jamie nodded dumbly. Dominic dropped the necklace into his hand. Jamie ran his thumb over the familiar shapes inscribed on it: a bow symbolizing Diana, Goddess of the Hunt, set within a tangle of hexwork. The activation phrase was inscribed on the back: *Guard and guide me.*

"I figure the old gods look more kindly on familiars," Wyatt had said, when Jamie asked. *"As for why Diana, well, I hunt with my talons, and she hunts with her bow."*

"It's a hex," Dominic said. "Not charged at the moment, according to Tom Halloran. Any idea what it does?"

Jamie shook his head. "Nay. Wyatt said it was 'a little something extra, just in case.' In case of what, I don't know. You really don't recognize what kind of hex it is?"

"I'm certain I could figure it out, given the time." Dominic shrugged. “It looks like some sort of variation on a hexlight. It could be recharged, since the necklace is gold, but it likely isn’t anything with much power. If you want me to dig into it, though…”

“Nay, that’s all right.” Jamie’s hand closed over the necklace. The gold felt cool against his skin. “Have you been able to find his apartment? Or flophouse, or wherever he was staying?”

Dominic shook his head. “No. We’ll likely send one or two of the unbonded familiars around to ask questions, find out if anyone recognizes his description. But given the size of the city, and the fact we’re meant to be focusing on the campaign against illegal hexes, I haven’t much hope.”

Jamie tried not to let his disappointment show. Maybe if he could have seen the space where Wyatt spent his last days, talked to any roommates, this would all somehow make more sense. Or even any sense. “Did you have more questions?”

“Not right now.” Dominic turned back to the pile on his desk. “Please tell me if anything comes to mind, though.”

It was a dismissal. Jamie started to stand, when Rook suddenly jumped to the floor and took human form. “Fur and feathers, just what we didn’t need,” he said to Dominic. “Here comes Nick.”

Nick stood at the foot of the stairs leading up to the Metropolitan Witch Police headquarters. The Coven, they called it.

He’d gone inside a couple of times before, when one of the ferals under his care had been attacked. Strode up the stairs, shouldered his way through the hallways, and found his brother so as to lodge a complaint. Showed the witches he wasn’t afraid to walk among them as a proud feral.

But today he hesitated. His witch was inside.

His witch—what a stupid way to put it. The witch who was most compatible with his magic, that was all it meant. Familiars deluded themselves, thinking everything would be all right if they could just find their witch. Their witch would give them a place to belong, a person to rely on.

But witches didn’t give. They took and they took, nothing more. They dangled a promise of food and safety, of money…in exchange for everything a familiar had to give. Body, soul, and magic. The chance to live a life they wanted, instead of trailing behind their witch.

He’d never bond, no matter how many laws the politicians passed. Better to rot in the Menagerie. Witches had already stolen enough from him: his father, his mother, even his brother. Every dream he'd ever had. But they'd never take his soul.

The moment he'd seen his witch—the witch—had been a shock, visceral as hunger or desire. He'd not expected it to feel that way, and ended up spooking like a colt, stammering an answer to Rook's question about Wyatt's identity, then shifting into horse form and galloping back to Caballus as quick as he could.

In a way, though, it was a relief. He'd spent more than half his life wondering when the day would come. When he'd turn a corner, or board a train, or look across a crowded thoroughfare and spot the witch his magic recognized as best able to channel it. A part of him had feared that day. Not that he wouldn't want to bond, but that, if it were the right person, he might be tempted to give in and bond after all.

He snorted aloud. That was one fear taken away. The witch was a copper, and thank God for it, because it meant Nick wouldn't have to worry about any temptation to bond with him. Now he could stop looking over his shoulder and concentrate on far more important things.

Like the ferals in his cellar.

Had Wyatt been killed because he was in the wrong place at the wrong time? If he'd come to the park to leave a note for Nick, the murderer might simply have attacked him at random.

But if the killer had chosen Wyatt because he worked to get ferals out of the city before the coppers caught up with them…that was bad. Nick could handle himself, but everyone else might be in danger, from the ferals in his cellar to whoever captained the ferry Wyatt would have guided them to.

He couldn't risk attracting attention to any of Wyatt's contacts, unless he knew for certain he wasn't putting them in danger. The only way to be sure was to come here and talk to his brother.

Nick squared his shoulders and made his way up the stairs, pushing through the throng of reporters who normally gathered there, hoping for any scrap of news to print ahead of their competition. "I'm here to see Rook," he told the witch at the desk inside—and kept going, without waiting for the woman to respond.

His nerves drew tight, surrounded by so many witches. If they knew one of their own was his witch, at least some of them would think Nick ought to be forced to bond. He put his shoulders back, straightened his spine, and fixed a scowl on his face. Between his size and expression, a path cleared before him as if by magic.

Thankfully, Rook was at his desk, along with Dominic. But a third person sat there, and when he turned to watch Nick's approach, Nick cursed under his breath. Because of course it was his damned witch.

The fellow looked even better in the daylight. His dark hair was mussed, as though he hadn't slept well, and the flesh around his green eyes had gone puffy with exhaustion. But he was still devilishly handsome, if one liked the slender, pretty types. Which Nick most assuredly did.

Now was not the time to be thinking with his cock. Nick glared at the witch, then turned his attention on Rook. "Who killed Wyatt?"

Rook folded his arms over his chest and stared defiantly up at Nick. At one time, it had been the two of them against the world. People had remarked on how much Rook looked like a smaller version of Nick—a comment Rook had enjoyed when they were boys, when he'd still admired his older brother. When he'd still trusted Nick would keep him safe.

Before he'd sided with the damned witches.

"Sorry," Rook said. "You're going to have to read the newspapers like anyone else."

Nick glowered, but Rook was immune to intimidation. "You must have an idea. What about that hex?" The memory of Wyatt's body flashed behind Nick's eyes. The initial cut had been deep, right through the trachea, carotids, and jugulars. Then the abdomen opened beneath the ribs, perhaps in search of the great veins in the torso. "It was drawn in his blood, wasn't it?"

"I can't share details with civilians, Nick." Rook cocked dark eyes at him. "If you want to know, join the MWP."

"Did you know Wyatt?" his witch asked.

No, *the* witch. Not his.

Nick glanced at him. So close, he saw that the man's right eye had a patch of brown amidst the green, covering about a third of the iris. *Heterochromia;* the word floated up from the depths of his brain, where he'd consigned the knowledge his father had passed on. It added interest to a face that might have been forgettably pretty otherwise.

The man blinked, and Nick realized he'd been staring. And forgetting to scowl while he was at it. "None of your business, witch," he said, his tone extra rude to make up for the momentary lapse.

The witch frowned. "Wyatt and I served in the army together. If you knew him, I'd like to talk."

"If you knew him, we'd all like to hear about it," Dominic put in.

Rook nodded. "If you have any information that would help the investigation, now would be a good time to mention it."

Even if Wyatt hadn't been killed for smuggling ferals out of the city, one question would lead to another, and the coppers would come back to Caballus with a warrant this time.

The ferals hiding in his cellar were his responsibility. As were those living in the colony under his protection. He couldn't bring the police down on any of them.

"No." Without saying goodbye, he turned and left.

He would just have to look into Wyatt's death himself.

CHAPTER 4

"WAIT!" JAMIE CALLED. "Hey, you! Nick, wasn't it? Wait!"

He'd tried to hurry after the familiar, but the blasted steps had slowed him, first inside, and now again in front of the Coven. For a moment, he thought he'd lost Nick—but no, there he was, towering over everyone else in the crowd thronging the marble stairs.

At his shout, Nick turned. His brows lifted, his nostrils flared, and for a moment Jamie thought he'd simply turn and leave.

Instead, he folded his arms across his chest, set his stance wide, and waited for Jamie to catch up.

"Thanks for waiting," Jamie said, tilting his head back to look into Nick's face.

The man was massive—well over six feet, broad-shouldered, and heavily muscled. Like Rook, the blend of his features included full lips and high cheekbones. Also like Rook, he wore his hair to his shoulders, though Nick's looked coarser and wavier than his brother's. The autumn sun picked out sienna undertones in his warm, brown skin. He smelled faintly of sweat and honey, underlain with musk.

It was all Jamie could do not to lick his lips.

Once upon a time, the reaction would have been natural. But it had been so long since he'd felt anything but numb, it caught him by surprise. Like a sudden spark on a fog-shrouded night.

Guilt followed instantly on the heels of surprise. He'd seen Wyatt's body only hours ago, and here he was, lusting after another man? What the devil was wrong with him?

"What do you want, witch?" Nick asked. No—demanded. His eyes were so dark it was hard to tell where the iris ended and the pupil began.

Upstairs, Nick hadn't seemed inclined to talk to anyone, only to imperiously order they answer him. But Jamie couldn't let his one possible connection to Wyatt walk away without at least trying for more.

Jamie thrust out his hand. "Jamie MacDougal."

Nick glanced at Jamie's hand but didn't take it. "I don't learn the names of witches."

The brief flash of lust was now accompanied by growing annoyance. Did the fellow have to be so damned rude? "You cared about Wyatt, or you wouldn't have come just to ask who killed him. Did he…did he ever mention me?"

Stupid question. But he had to know.

Nick shrugged. "No. I barely knew him."

Jamie frowned. Something seemed off about Nick's answer, though he wasn't entirely sure what. "Then why are you so interested in his death?"

"Because he was a feral," Nick said, as if it were the most obvious thing in the world.

"So?"

"Someone has to look out for the ferals of this city." Nick's lip curled slightly, showing a glimpse of strong white teeth. "If the MWP won't do it, then I have to."

"Why?" Jamie asked. "No offense, but you don't seem the type for charitable works."

"Why?" Nick looked at him as though he'd lost his mind. "I just *told* you why. No one else will. Charity has nothing to do with it."

It wasn't much of an explanation, but maybe it didn't matter. "Wyatt and I were friends," Jamie said. "But the army declared him dead, after his witch was killed in Cuba. I just…I want to know what happened, after Eddie died. Why he never tried to contact me. Or any of the other Rough Riders."

Jamie braced himself for the usual reaction to his service history. Instead, Nick's glower only grew angrier. "Oh, of *course* you're a Rough Rider," Nick muttered. "Fancy yourself a horse breaker, do you?" Before Jamie could object, he barreled on. "As I said, I barely knew the man. But I can guess why he deserted easily enough."

"You can?" Jamie asked.

"Tell me, what would have happened to him if he had stayed, with his witch dead. Would they have left him unbonded?"

"I...I don't know." Jamie had never considered such things. "Probably not. The need for hexes on the battlefield was too great. The fighting was over in Cuba, but if there was a shortage of familiars in the Philippines, they might have sent him there."

"There's your answer, then." Nick let his arms drop. "He got away from one witch. Why would he have waited around to be handed over to another? He saw his chance at freedom and he took it."

Jamie gaped. Could it be true?

Nick's full lips quirked in a sort of bitter smile. "Think about it," he advised. Then he turned and walked away, leaving Jamie standing alone in the October sun.

"More potatoes, Jamie?" his sister asked.

Jamie leaned back from the table with a groan. The family dinner after Sunday Mass had been a tradition since their parents and uncle had come over from Ireland. "I can't fit another bite in my stomach, Muriel."

"You're still too thin," she fussed. The heat of the kitchen had wilted her curly hair, but she refused to crack a window, certain they'd all catch a chill and die. "You don't eat as you should."

"I eat plenty," he objected. He reached for the bucket of beer, intending to pour a bit more into his glass, only to have her snatch it up and pour for him.

"Here," she said, handing the glass to him, as though he couldn't pick it up from the table. "Is there anything else you need? A pillow for your back?"

Jamie inhaled deeply and reminded himself Muriel loved him. They'd grown up with the usual sibling squabbles. Time was, she would have told him to pour his own beer, or get his own pillow. Didn't she have enough work with two children?

But that had been before he'd come back from Cuba with part of a leg missing.

He took a sip of beer and sighed. Across the table, Uncle Hurley mistook his sigh and saluted with his own beer. "Nothing like a bit of drink to warm the blood, aye?"

"Aye," Jamie agreed. He watched as Muriel's twins played with the wooden train Hurley had bought them for their birthday. Hurley lived with Muriel and her husband, Zhu Fan. Between Hurley's most recent promotion, and the money Fan brought in from the laundry, they could afford a relatively spacious apartment, without having to take in additional boarders to pay for it.

A few years ago, when they'd all been crammed into the same tiny apartment, Jamie had loved playing with the boys. He'd romped around the room with one on his back and the other clinging to his leg, while Muriel threatened to hit him with a wooden spoon if he knocked anything over.

Everything changed when he returned from Cuba. Muriel treated him as though he was made of glass, and Fan no longer seemed to know how to talk to him at all.

One of the boys, Colin, left the train and launched himself into Jamie's lap. Jamie started, sloshing beer onto his hand and the table.

In an instant, Muriel was on her feet, her face set in a thunderous scowl. "Outside!"

"But, Ma," Colin pleaded.

"I said out! If you're going to run around like wild animals, you can do it where you won't be a bother to anyone else."

They made for the door, but Colin paused. "I just wanted to ask Uncle Jamie when he's moving back in."

Muriel glared, and he hurried after his brother, the door banging shut behind them. "Saint Mary, they're going to be the death of me," she said.

Jamie knew he shouldn't ask. He should just let it lie, at least until Muriel brought it up. Instead, he said, "Why does Colin think I'm moving back in with you?"

He'd stayed with them for a while, after returning from Cuba. Hobbled around on his crutch, or paced the halls and stairs outside, learning to walk with the prosthetic. Bit back cries of pain during the night, when he woke to waves of agony from a foot that wasn't even there anymore.

"We have the space," Muriel said. "I've talked it over with Fan, and he'd love to have you back with us."

Jamie glanced at Hurley, who had suddenly become very interested in the newspaper in front of him. "I appreciate it. I do. But I've my own place to live."

"I worry about you, all alone in your apartment," she said. "What if something happened?"

"Nothing's going to happen."

His irritation must have begun to show despite his best efforts, because Hurley said, "Leave the lad alone, Muriel." Hurley put down his newspaper and took out his pipe. "Tell us about your work, Jamie. When are they going to promote you to detective?"

The new topic was only slightly more welcome than the previous one. There'd never been any question Jamie would follow in Hurley's footsteps and become a policeman the moment he was old enough to do so. It had been his duty, both to the family and the force. Since the MWP paid a bit better and his scores on the witch potential tests had been high enough, Hurley had encouraged him to go in that direction, rather than join the regular police.

If Jamie had gone to the regular police instead, maybe he would have done his uncle proud. Begun the slow climb up the ranks, rather than remain in the same position for years.

"That ain't the way things are done in the MWP," he said. "You know that. Only bonded witch-familiar pairs get promoted above officer."

"Then bond," Hurley said, as though it were the easiest thing in the world. "The MWP has unbonded familiars. Just pick one. That's what they're for."

Jamie couldn't imagine it. Just walking up to a familiar and asking if he'd like to throw in together for the rest of their lives. "That ain't how it works."

Hurley frowned. "Ain't it? Familiars contain magic inside them, but they can only use it to turn into animals, right? They can't charge hexes or the like."

"Right," Jamie said, "But—"

"A witch like you doesn't have any access to magic without a familiar," Hurley went on. "But once you do bond with one, you can draw on their magic and use it to charge whatever hexes you want. Use it as you see fit."

"A hexman still has to draw the hexes, but yes," Jamie said. "Though I can make some of my own. But it's more than that. A bond is a commitment. You're stuck with one another after." Unless a hexbreaker got involved. But the talent was vanishingly rare; generally that wasn't an option.

"Like a marriage?" Muriel said.

"Sometimes?" Jamie tried to think how to make them understand. "People get married for all sorts of reasons, don't they? Sometimes it's love, and sometimes it's for security, and sometimes they're just good friends who figure it might as well be each other than someone else."

Muriel seemed to consider. "What about like in the dime novels? Where a familiar finds her witch? The one she's destined to be with?"

"Every familiar has one witch their magic is most compatible with. If they bond, the magic will be stronger—a *lot* stronger. But bonding with another witch just means the hexes won't be as powerful. There's nothing more to it than that. No destiny involved."

"The MWP will make you a detective, even if your hexes ain't the strongest, though," Hurley said, as though he hadn't listened to a word Jamie said. "Any familiar will do, am I right?"

"Yes."

Hurley tugged on his moustache, a sure sign of mulling something over. "Next raid, I could try to strike a deal…"

"You ain't thinking of pairing Jamie with a dangerous familiar, are you?" Muriel exclaimed. "It'd be too risky for a whole man, let alone—"

She caught herself, but it was too late. Jamie shoved his chair back and rose to his feet. "I should get home."

"Jamie, love, I didn't mean for it to sound like that," she said, holding her hand out to him.

He avoided looking directly at her as he pulled on his coat and scarf. "I know."

"Think about what I said," Hurley called after him, as he made for the door. "Or if it's that damned chief keeping you from picking out one of the familiars, let me know, and I'll go straight to the Police Board. Or to the governor."

Jamie made his way down the stairs and back onto the street. The fall air brought him the scents of burning coal and apple pies. His damaged knee ached, responding to the change in seasons. At least his apartment was near enough he could walk rather than having to manage the stairs leading to the El platform.

He thrust his hands into his pockets and tipped his head back. The sky above him was blue and contained only wisps of clouds. A bird circled high overhead, too far away to guess at its species. It might even have been an eagle.

Jamie's throat tightened with grief. God, Wyatt. He didn't know what to think, what to feel. He'd mourned Wyatt for over a year, believing him dead. Now Wyatt *was* dead, horribly so, and sometimes Jamie felt like he'd already done his grieving, and others like he was starting over again.

He still couldn't believe Wyatt had deserted. Could Nick have been right? Did Wyatt flee the army because he didn't want to bond again so soon after Eddie's death?

Nick. Jamie had found himself thinking of those flashing black eyes quite a bit over the last day. The way Nick's coat had strained over his shoulders. How the light fell over his warm skin. Then he'd remember Wyatt had just died, and grief and guilt fought with desire, until he felt sick with it.

Wyatt and Eddie hadn't been lovers, but they'd been close as brothers. Their bond had been real, and Wyatt would have grieved bitterly when Eddie died. But the need for hexes had been real, too. There had to have been some witch Wyatt wouldn't have minded bonding with. Maybe even Jamie.

They might have bonded, and Wyatt wouldn't have felt the need to desert. Things would have worked out differently. Wyatt would still be alive. Or hell, if Jamie had been with them on the special mission, maybe Eddie wouldn't have been killed in the first place.

But he hadn't been there. And when Wyatt came to New York, he chose to let Jamie believe he was dead. He surely blamed Jamie for Eddie's death. For everything.

Jamie put his head down against the wind and kept walking. Overhead, the bird wheeled higher and higher, alone in the flawless sky.

Nick wasn't entirely surprised when Rook knocked on the door to Caballus Sunday afternoon.

When the liquor laws had changed to mandate only hotels of ten rooms or more could sell alcohol on Sundays, most saloons knocked together ten tiny spaces, made an alliance with the local prostitutes, and happily continued business as usual. But the prospect of even more inspectors and coppers barging into what ought to be a haven for ferals stuck in Nick's throat, like he'd tried to swallow a too-large chunk of apple. So he let the saloon close for the day, and instead spent it going over the books, or doing needed repairs.

He unlocked the door and waved his brother in. "Left the witch at home? Or is he the church going sort who disapproves of business on Sunday?"

Rook pointed to the sign in the window. "Believe it or not, Dominic respects that you don't want witches here."

Nick went behind the rough plank that served as a bar and fished out two glasses and a bottle of rum. "Cheers."

Rook dragged up a chair and seated himself at the bar. "Cheers." He took a drink—then broke into a coughing fit. "What is this swill?"

"Rum." Nick shrugged at Rook's skeptical look. "Or so they say."

"Dad would be disappointed in you for trying to pass this off as anything other than paint thinner."

Nick laughed softly. "True enough. I'd get his 'you know better, son' face for this."

It was a long standing joke between them. Their father had raised neither hand nor voice to them as boys…but he'd certainly had a way of making his displeasure known.

Hell, Nick missed him. Rook had always been closer to their ammi, but Nick had wanted nothing more than to be just like Dad.

"You didn't come here to relive old times," Nick said.

To his surprise, Rook's expressive face lapsed into sorrow. "No, but…I thought we could spend a little while, at least. It's been a long time since we just talked."

Nick took out a rag and began to wipe down the bar, even though it didn't really need it. "Since you joined the MWP."

They'd had arguments before then, of course, just like any other siblings. But the day Rook came to him, said he was going to join the MWP as a familiar…that had been more than an argument.

The sense of betrayal still stung. "You have the MWP and a witch to look after you," Nick said. "But there are others who don't, and I have to put them first. I don't have the time for social visits."

"Do you have time for anything?" Rook asked. "Mal says you don't have friends, you don't sleep with anyone more than once, and according to him, it would take wild horses to drag you out of Caballus." Rook pretended to ponder. "Or maybe you are the wild horse, I can't recall."

Nick ignored him. "The fox needs to keep his mouth shut." Malachi was another traitor, gone off to be the pet of a rich nob. "Why are you here, Rook?"

Rook sighed, but didn't press the matter. "I wanted to ask you again about Wyatt. Did you tell the truth about barely knowing him? Because if he was mixed up in something illegal, I promise, we don't care about that. Dominic and I just want to bring his murderer to justice."

They'd care if they knew the truth. Nick had put out feelers, hoping to find Wyatt's apartment—or wherever he'd been staying—before the coppers could. He doubted Wyatt would have been so foolish as to write down anything compromising, but he didn't want to take the chance. So far, though, nothing had turned up.

"What was the blood hex for?" Nick asked, instead of answering. "Tell me that."

"We don't know." Rook swallowed more of the rum, wincing as he did so. "We brought in Tom—the hexbreaker—but he didn't sense anything other than the Great Hex."

"What does that mean?"

"It could mean just about anything. That the Great Hex overwhelms Tom's sense of a lesser hex. That the blood hex did whatever it was meant to do, and there was nothing left to sense. Or it was never even charged at all." Rook shrugged. "Maybe the killer wanted to confuse us by making the murder look like something it wasn't. Or maybe they're a lunatic who doesn't really understand you need a witch and familiar to make hexes actually work. But, given the trouble we had with blood hexes a couple of years ago, we're taking it seriously."

Not as helpful as Nick had wished. "Thanks. As for Wyatt…I didn't know him well. I swear," he added, as Rook gave him a look he recognized from their mother's face. "I didn't even know he'd been in the war."

At least, not until the witch had mentioned it. The witch with the brown splotch in one green eye, and the pretty mouth made for sin. The way he'd looked at Nick, the tip of his tongue just touching his lower lip, like his thoughts trended in the same direction…

Fur and feathers. It was a good thing Nick had a policy against fucking witches, because the man was surely a temptation.

Rook sat back. "All right. I believe you don't know anything more. So what were you doing in the park that night?"

Time to start lying, and not just by omission. "I went out for a run. Sometimes I feel confined. I can't exactly turn into a horse here in the bar."

"You could if you were a reasonably sized horse," Rook countered with a grin. "But no, you have to do everything as extravagantly as possible. Giant man, giant horse."

"Ammi said I took after our grandfather," Nick protested. Their mother's mother had been Indian, but her father had been a sea turtle familiar from Samoa. He'd guided ships of every sort across the ocean, to ports from New York to the Caribbean and beyond. A big man, by all accounts, just like Nick.

"Yeah, yeah." Rook waved a dismissive hand. "So the fact you knew the victim was just a coincidence?"

"You said yourself I know half the ferals in the city." Nick shrugged. "It's true."

"All right, then." Rook finished his drink. "It was good seeing you, brother. Really."

Nick bit his lip. He shouldn't ask. There was no *reason* to ask. He already knew he'd never bond; time now to forget the man even existed. "That witch at your desk yesterday. The one who came running after me."

Rook eyed him warily. "You mean Jamie MacDougal?"

"Tell me about him."

"*You* want to know about a witch?" Rook stared at Nick as if he'd lost his mind.

Which he apparently had, to ask at all. "If you don't want to tell me, don't." Nick flung the rag onto the bar.

"No, no." Rook continued to eye him uncertainly. "He's not bonded, but his witch potential scores were high enough to earn him a place in the MWP. He drives the wagon—picks up bodies, transports suspects. That sort of thing." Rook paused. "His uncle is with the regular police. Inspector Hurley O'Malley."

Cold water dashed any lingering desire. "The head of the Dangerous Familiars Squad?"

"The very one."

It was stupid to be disappointed. "So he hates familiars."

"Jamie? Don't be ridiculous." Rook frowned. "He can't help being related to O'Malley. I can't say I know him well, but he obviously cared about Wyatt."

The fact he'd bothered to chase after Nick despite having a limp seemed proof enough of that. Not that it mattered. Nick would never see him again.

"So why are you asking about him?" Rook watched Nick carefully. "About a witch?" Then his eyes widened. "He isn't *your* witch, is he?"

"Of course not!" But Rook didn't look as though he bought the lie. Time to make Rook leave, before he could stick his beak into things that weren't any of his business. "I just like to know the enemy. Speaking of which, you'd better run along to your owner. Dominic might start wondering what's taking his pet so long."

It worked. Rook's nostrils flared. "Fuck you, Nick. Dominic isn't the enemy."

"He's a witch."

Rook shook his head, like he thought Nick was the one being unreasonable. "Not every witch is out to get you—"

"A witch shot Dad dead!" Nick slammed his hand flat on the bar. "Then another took Ammi away and got her killed. If you had any respect for our parents, you never would have joined the MWP, let alone bonded with one of their kind."

Rook's eyes widened—then narrowed in anger. "How dare you. You talk about respect, but you won't acknowledge the fact Ammi *chose* to bond with a witch. She did the best she could for us, and her witch died right beside her in that mine collapse. She didn't hold all witches accountable for what happened to Dad."

"But your precious police don't hesitate to hold all familiars accountable for the massacre in the cathedral," Nick spat back. "Your master's no better than the rest of them. Dominic cares about you because you're useful, but he's as much a leech as all the others."

"I'm not listening to this." Rook's mouth flattened in anger, and he stalked to the door. "I miss our parents, but insulting Dominic isn't going to bring them back. So keep a civil tongue in your head about the man I love, or don't speak to me again."

CHAPTER 5

JAMIE'S SHIFT WAS almost over when the call came in to pick up another body in Central Park.

The sun rose over the city as he drove the wagon into the park. A few early risers from the riding academies on West 54th and Central Park West took advantage of the cool morning to exercise the horses and themselves. Bird watchers clustered near the Pond, peering through their binoculars. Away from the wide drives and bridle paths, park-goers rode bicycles or strolled briskly through the drifts of falling leaves. At least until they reached Bow Bridge, just west of Bethesda Fountain, where police turned them aside.

Trepidation drew Jamie's nerves tight as the wagon approached the cast iron bridge. The almost delicate span leapt across the Lake, its reflection shimmering in the water below. The design of interlocked circles and hexes that formed its railings added to the impression of grace, like the drawn bow of an archer.

The thought caused him to lift his hand to his chest. He'd taken to wearing Wyatt's necklace, hidden beneath his clothing. It was just a coincidence, of course; the name of the bridge had nothing to do with Diana. But it left him uneasy nonetheless.

Jamie climbed down from the cart and approached the scene slowly. As the smell of blood grew stronger, he had to force his legs to keep moving. The awfulness of Wyatt's corpse came back, thickening his blood and making it hard to breathe.

Jamie pushed himself forward. If he lost his ability to view murder scenes, he'd have no choice but to leave the MWP. Being a copper had structured his entire adult life, save for his brief stint as a solider. He couldn't imagine doing anything else.

He looked at the face first, even though he didn't want to. Relief rushed over him: the woman wasn't anyone he knew.

Shame followed hard on the heels of the thought. Whoever she'd been, she had people who loved her, who would grieve her death.

As with Wyatt, her body was surrounded by a hex drawn in her own blood. She wore clothes that looked to have been washed a thousand times, sleeves thin at the elbow, skirts ragged at the hem. Her half-open eyes showed irises of ruddy amber, like a fox's.

Another familiar, then. Just like Wyatt.

Dominic and Rook stood off to one side, along with the liaison, Quigley. Detective Tom Halloran crouched beside the hex. His familiar, Cicero, observed closely as Tom laid his hand carefully on the bloody marks.

After a long moment, Tom shook his head. "I can't sense anything but the Great Hex." He rose to his feet, and Cicero handed him a handkerchief to wipe any traces of blood from his hand.

Dominic sighed. "Thank you, Tom. So. It looks as though we have some maniac killing familiars." He glanced at Quigley. "Will the regular police help us with the investigation?"

Quigley looked grim. "I wish I could say, 'Aye, of course!' I'll push for it—you know I will. But right from the start, they've said the hexes make it the MWP's problem."

"They probably don't want to investigate because the first victim was just a feral," Cicero said. "Judging by the state of her clothes, this one likely was, too."

"Do you think so?" Jamie asked. "I mean, that they don't care because Wyatt was a feral?"

Cicero cast him a pitying look. Despite the early hour, his yellow-green eyes were perfectly outlined with kohl. "It's how the world works, James."

"Not to mention, Wyatt was violating the Pemberton Act," Tom added. "They ain't likely to spend much time worrying about a dead criminal."

Jamie hadn't even thought of the Pemberton Act in relation to Wyatt, though of course eagles were on the list. At least if Uncle Hurley had caught him, he'd still be alive.

Though not for long, given he would likely have ended up shot for desertion.

Jamie's throat tightened. Damn it. None of this should have happened.

"It's a cursed shame." Quigley looked sadly down at the woman's body. "I hope you can at least find out who she was."

"I'm sure Rook knows someone who could identify her," Cicero drawled.

Rook's full lips tightened. "Unfortunately." He turned to Jamie. "It's our unlucky day, MacDougal. We're going to have to stop by my brother's saloon."

"Are you sure you don't want a hand with that?" asked the man delivering the beer. He squinted at Nick from under a thatch of dirty blond hair, as though even the light of early morning was too much for his eyes.

Nick bit back his irritation. The same brewery had supplied Caballus for years, and the old man who had driven the keg-filled cart before understood the rules. But he'd retired, and this new one couldn't seem to get it through his head that Nick didn't let just anyone into Caballus, no matter their business.

Instead, he heaved one keg easily onto his shoulder and tucked another beneath his arm. "Just wait here."

"It would be faster if you…" The man's voice faded as Nick walked away.

He hauled the kegs into the front room; he'd transfer them to the cellar once he had them all unloaded. Kyle arrived halfway through, and Nick put him to work making space in the cellar while he continued to haul kegs. As he pulled the final one off the cart and waved at the driver to continue on, another wagon pulled up.

This one had the MWP's shield blazoned on the side, and was driven by the witch with the particolored eyes. His witch.

Those eyes traveled over Nick's chest to his arm—which, yes, was probably bulging impressively under the weight of the keg he balanced on his shoulder. Nick had taken off his coat and rolled up his sleeves, and he knew from experience his muscles showed to good effect. Jamie wasn't the first to look, and probably wouldn't be the last.

But the tiny swipe of a tongue-tip over Jamie's lower lip sent a shock of heat straight to Nick's groin.

Fur and feathers, no. Bad enough his magic was stupid over the man; his body didn't need to join the act.

He tore his gaze from Jamie and focused on Rook, who crowded between Jamie and Dominic on the narrow driver's seat. "I didn't think I'd see you around again so soon. What do you want?"

Rook jumped down from the wagon seat. "We need you to look at a body."

Oh hell. "A feral?"

"A familiar, anyway." Rook swung open the back of the wagon.

Nick put down the keg. He glanced at the saloon, saw Kyle watching through the window with a worried frown. Nick shook his head—no sense exposing Kyle to the coppers without need.

Nick's legs felt like lead, reluctant to move. He forced them to anyway, and joined Rook at the rear of the wagon. Rook flipped back the edge of a blood-soaked sheet.

Nick's heart sank. "Pia," he said, careful to keep his voice steady. "She rents—rented—a room in the tenement upstairs."

"When did you last see her?" Rook asked.

Nick rubbed at his face. "A couple of days ago. She was behind on rent, so I stopped by her apartment. What happened?"

"The same thing as happened to Wyatt," Jamie said. "She was killed in Central Park."

Nick stilled. He'd worried the killer had murdered Wyatt because of his work with the fugitive ferals. But Pia had nothing to do with that. She'd just been an ordinary woman, laboring as a seamstress in a sweatshop on Second Avenue. Trying to get by, and yes, she was late coming up with the money to pay him, but the same could be said for plenty of the ferals he rented to.

She'd moved here to be safe, after one too many close calls. She'd been under his protection.

And now she was dead. Murdered.

"I don't think we should give out too many details to the public," Rook said, before Jamie could offer anything more.

A light blush pinked Jamie's cheeks. Nick couldn't help but wonder how far it spread over the skin hidden by the uniform. Then cursed himself for doing it.

"Sorry, sir," Jamie said, ducking his head. Sir? To a familiar?

"So now I'm a member of the public?" Nick asked, to distract himself.

"That's exactly what you are." Rook put his hands on his hips and stared up at Nick. "Now if you were part of the MWP, that would be a horse of a different color."

"Rook," Nick said threateningly. Dominic sighed from the driver's seat.

Rook failed to look abashed. "Any idea who might have seen Pia last?"

"She has two roommates. I could ask—"

"No, you can't," Rook interrupted. "This is a police investigation, Nick. Stay out of it. We'll ask the questions."

Dominic pulled out his pocket watch. "Not today, though. Owen is expecting us to help sort through the latest batch of seized hexes."

The devil? "So now contraband hexes are more important than murdered ferals?"

"Of course not." But Rook didn't meet his eyes as he said it. "But you read the papers, don't you? The reformers have the Police Board in an uproar over the illegal hex trade."

"The Heirs of Adam." The words scalded Nick's mouth. "Bunch of tight-assed, limp-pricked moralizers. They hate any magic, but they've got you jumping to their tune?"

None of the coppers looked happy about it, which cheered Nick slightly. Rook scowled at him. "The Police Board hasn't been pleased with us since that idiot Cavanaugh tried to poison Roosevelt."

"It's *your* fault for catching him," Nick said.

"It is not!" Rook squawked, flapping his arms indignantly. "The man murdered a bunch of people, and tried to have us killed, too!"

"One of our own trying to kill New York's richest last November only made things worse," Dominic said. "If the Police Board tells Ferguson to throw all his resources into finding illegal hexes, he has no choice but to follow orders. There's already been talk of replacing him with a non-witch. We're doing everything we can, but we can't risk ending up with someone like Reverend Ingram running the MWP."

"True enough," Nick said, though he hated to find himself in agreement with a witch.

"I'll talk to Ferguson," Dominic added. "As soon as we return to the Coven. I'll ask him to argue the case with the Police Board."

Nick stamped a foot. "Will that do any good?"

Dominic looked mildly surprised that Nick had addressed him directly. Well, he shouldn't get used to it, that was for sure. "I'm...not hopeful," he admitted. "People die all the time in this city. If not for the blood hex drawn around the bodies, it wouldn't even be remarkable."

Of course not. If ferals could expect justice, they wouldn't need a place like Caballus. Like the colony Nick ran in the tenement above.

"It ain't right," Jamie said. Nick glanced at him in surprise, but his attention was focused on Dominic. "If some maniac is killing familiars, it ought to be top priority. Not an afterthought, to get around to as we can."

"I'm not disagreeing," Dominic said. "But unless you can conjure up another witch-familiar pair for Ferguson to assign the case to, it's the way things are."

Nick's heart kicked against his ribs, and his mouth went dry. Because of course, he could provide exactly that.

No. The very thought was absurd. Witches had killed his parents, stolen his dreams, and seduced his brother.

Rook gently laid the sheet back over Pia's face and shut the back of the wagon. His gaze went to Nick, but he flashed into crow form without saying anything. Dominic held out an arm, and Rook landed on his wrist. Dominic stroked Rook's beak tenderly with his free hand, and the crow leaned into the touch, seeking comfort.

Wyatt had been doing his best to help ferals targeted by the Pemberton Act. And Pia…

She'd just been trying to survive. Nick was supposed to have kept her safe. That was his duty and his promise to every feral in his colony. But somewhere along the line, he'd failed her.

He knew witches. He also knew that, when it came to Jamie, nothing would ever make Nick consider a permanent bond. He was safe, or at least as safe as any familiar could be. Surely he owed it to Pia, to Wyatt, to make use of the situation.

Jamie lifted the reins. Before he could think too hard about it, Nick said, "MacDougal."

Jamie paused. Nick took a deep breath.

"Come back to Caballus this afternoon. Three o'clock. That'll give us time before the evening rush."

"Time for what?" Jamie asked blankly.

"Nothing I want to talk about in front of other ears," he said. And headed back inside, before he could change his mind.

Nick poured another shot and asked himself what the hell he was thinking.

He'd spent the entire day on edge, going back and forth as to what course of action he should take.

Yes, Jamie MacDougal didn't seem like a bad sort—for a witch. But

Nick didn't really know anything about the fellow, despite the conversation with Rook. They'd exchanged a few words, nothing more.

The fact Jamie was his witch meant nothing. Just look at what had happened to Cicero's friend Isaac. His witch had turned out to be an utter asshole who couldn't stand the thought of a fey Jewish familiar, and responded to Isaac's declaration with his fists. For once the MWP had done the right thing and thrown the bastard out, but that didn't mend Isaac's broken bones, nor his trust. If he'd just come to Nick…but no, Isaac left the MWP, determined to stand on his own two feet, and ended up force bonded to a madman who only wanted to strip him for power.

At least Nick didn't have to worry about Jamie delivering a beating. Not that Jamie couldn't probably hold his own against most men, but even in human form Nick had a good seven inches and sixty pounds on him.

Nick didn't want any part of the MWP. Didn't want to put even the smallest amount of trust in a witch. If he went through with this, it would mean trusting multiple witches not to stab him in the back. Jamie, the hexbreaker, hell, maybe even Kopecky.

But the hard truth was, ferals were dying. Even if no more murders occurred, he owed it to the living ferals to try and solve the first two. But what if it turned out to be like the ax murders in Texas, and the killings continued? An entire police force determined to stop the Midnight Assassin had failed. No one was going to put in that level of effort for a few ferals in New York.

No one but him.

"It ain't fair," Jamie had said. And he'd wanted to know about Wyatt, that day in front of the Coven. Yes, like any witch, he'd probably viewed Wyatt more like a pet than a person. But at least he cared a little.

Nick snorted and shook his head. A damned low bar to set, and chances were Jamie still wouldn't clear it.

But this wasn't about Jamie MacDougal. It definitely wasn't about Nick's stupid magic, which seemed to think bonding with Jamie a fine idea. It was about Nick looking in the mirror every morning to shave. He didn't want to be ashamed of the man looking back.

The bell over the door chimed, just as the clock struck three. He looked up, past the few drinkers who had gathered in the saloon at this hour, and saw Jamie standing nervously in the doorway.

No uniform…and dressed nicely, like a man who hoped to make an impression. Neat coat, trousers, even his shoes shined to a gloss.

Of course, he'd look better with nothing on at all.

Nick shoved the thought aside. He didn't fuck witches, and he wasn't about to start now. No matter how appealing the thought might be.

"I need to step out a bit, Kyle," Nick said. Kyle nodded, and Nick made for the door.

The tenement entrance was only a few feet down. "Follow me," Nick told Jamie, and led the way up the stairs and inside. Nick's apartment was on the first floor—one of the few luxuries he granted himself, along with no roommates to share the space. The apartment doubled as his office, and a desk took up much of the front room, its surface piled with ledgers. Bookshelves held older ledgers, crowded against the novels Nick enjoyed in his spare time.

"Have a seat," he said, pointing at one of the chairs near the desk. "Would you like a drink?"

"Nay, thank you though." Jamie sat down. He rubbed his hands over his thighs, and Nick found himself following the movement. "So… you asked me here, because…?"

There it was. Time to make a decision.

Nick drew a deep breath. Before he could think on it too long, he said, "I want you to bond with me."

Chapter 6

Stupidly, Jamie's first reaction was disappointment.

When Nick had asked him to return, for a reason he didn't want to say aloud in front of anyone else…well. Jamie had been looking at Nick…and Nick had been looking back, he was certain of it. The raw attraction hadn't been just on his side after all. He'd felt the spark of desire catch flame. A little candle, burning away the numb, gray fog that had enveloped him body and soul for far too long.

Guilt had accompanied the desire, of course. Wyatt's body was still in the morgue, for God's sake. Even if it hadn't been, Jamie hadn't touched another man since Wyatt. How could he even think about falling into bed with a grumpy arsehole like Nick, especially now?

But it had been so long, not feeling anything. He told himself it wouldn't really count, if he tumbled Nick. Nick obviously wasn't looking for anything serious, not with a witch. Maybe Jamie should have had more self-respect than to sleep with someone who clearly didn't like him, but the memory of those bulging muscles, of Nick handling the beer kegs like they weighed nothing…

He'd taken the time to dress as well as he could. Even put a vial of oil in the pocket of his overcoat, just in case. Walked the whole way from the El half-sick and half-hard.

But it turned out sex wasn't what Nick was offering. At all.

Jamie wondered if he should have accepted the drink. "You…want to bond…with me?"

Nick ran a hand back through his long black hair. He'd been working the bar, and either shed his coat or not bothered to put one on since this morning. The white shirt was rolled up to show off his brown forearms. The fabric pulled taut across his shoulders every time he moved.

"It would only be temporary." Nick's flashing eyes met his defiantly. "I know about the hexbreaker. I'm not looking for a new career with the MWP, and I'm certainly not looking for a witch."

Jamie felt off-kilter, the way he had when he'd first been learning to use his prosthetic leg. Back when any misstep sent him tumbling to the ground. "Are you saying…that is…am I your witch?"

Nick reared back, eyes going wide. "No."

Thank heavens. Jamie pitied any poor witch saddled with a curmudgeon like Nick. "But you want to bond with me. Temporarily."

"You heard what my brother and his witch said this morning." The chair creaked as Nick restlessly shifted his weight. "The Police Board has the MWP in a bad position. But if Ferguson had a pair not already assigned to this illegal hex nonsense, they might be able to do something without the Police Board even realizing."

"Oh." Jamie's mind reeled. It might work.

Except he didn't even know this Nick. Other than he was Rook's brother, and gorgeous. And only interested in Jamie as a way into the MWP.

Not to mention, Nick's proposition felt deceitful, bending the rules every which way. The sort of thing Jamie had never been comfortable with.

"We solve the murders, keep any other ferals from being killed, and then have the hexbreaker destroy the bond," Nick went on. "After that, we'll part ways and never see each other again."

"What happens if we don't find who killed them?" Jamie hated to even contemplate the idea there would be no justice for Wyatt, but he had to consider it. "Crimes don't always get solved. Just look at the Whitechapel murders. Or the Midnight Assassin down in Texas."

Nick didn't look happy at the reminder. "One month, then. If we haven't made progress in thirty days' time, we break the bond."

Jamie gripped his knees. The left ached where surgeons had pulled out a chunk of shrapnel. He didn't like Nick's scheme, not at all. But the idea of just turning him down and hoping Rook and Dominic had time to look into the killings between their other duties didn't sit right with him, either. "I'll think about it."

"What's there to think about?" Nick demanded. "You're a witch. You'll have access to my magic for a month. Why wouldn't you want that?"

"Because it ain't that easy!" Jamie lurched to his feet. "If I bond with you, *if* Ferguson agrees to this idea of yours, I become a detective and try to find the murderer with you—then you leave a month later, and what? I get demoted, which won't look good on my record no matter the cause."

"Of course," Nick said, folding his arms over his chest. "I should have known you'd put your career over the lives of ferals."

"I ain't saying that!" God, Nick was lucky someone hadn't murdered *him,* out of sheer frustration. Had he actually considered putting aside his grief for Wyatt to sleep with this man? "I ain't saying I want to work with an arse like you, neither. I surely don't want to bond with you, even temporarily, if you ain't so much as willing to let me think it over."

He started for the door. "Wait," Nick called.

"You ain't given me a reason to," Jamie said, and slammed the door behind him.

A few hours later, Jamie sat in the driver's seat of the wagon, waiting for the other MWP police officers to return with suspects in handcuffs. Supposedly a gang was making illegal hexes out of the basement of a ramshackle building on Hamilton. There was a feral colony nearby; probably the gang had been here for years, selling to the ferals and the other poor members of the neighborhood. There hadn't been any unexpected deaths or other complaints registered against them, so their hexmen must have some idea what they were doing.

But the Police Board wanted all unregulated, unregistered—and untaxed—hexes gone. So the MWP came in force. Or at least, sent in the biggest men, or the familiars who turned into the biggest, most fearsome, animals. Nick would have fit right in.

Nick.

The feral's plan was insane. Ferguson would never go along with it. Jamie should have forgotten about it the minute he stepped out the door.

"Really, James, your face could curdle milk," Cicero informed him. "Which would be a dreadful waste of both the milk and a pretty face."

The small man perched on the driver's seat beside Jamie, one leg crossed over the other, hands neatly folded on his knee. As usual, he dressed outrageously—a scarlet coat in a feminine cut with a green carnation in the buttonhole, his eyes lined with kohl.

Jamie felt heat rise to his cheeks at the compliment. "You—you shouldn't say things like that," he stammered. "Ain't you with Tom?"

Tom Halloran had come along not only for his ability to deal with any hexes thrown at them, but for his imposing physique. He wasn't as big as Nick, but more than large enough for Jamie to be anxious to avoid any misunderstandings concerning his lover.

"Of course we're bonded. Is that what you mean?" Cicero blinked at him innocently—then laughed at Jamie's expression. "Yes, darling, I'm quite attached to my Thomas. But I'm not dead, and there's no harm in looking." He picked a piece of lint from his pressed trousers. "Besides, this waiting is dreadfully boring."

"Then why are you out here instead of in there?" Jamie asked. Tom hadn't seemed at all surprised when Cicero remained behind.

"Do I look like I go around subduing hardened criminals?" Cicero sniffed delicately. "Thomas doesn't enjoy it, but he's quite good at it. Anyway, this raid isn't even after the interesting sort of hex. We raided a brothel last week—the madam was offering free hexes to encourage flagging gentlemen to go for another round."

Jamie felt his face go scarlet. Such hexes were legally available only at pharmacies—not exactly difficult to get, but expensive and indiscreet enough to encourage a thriving underground trade.

Cicero laughed again. "You blush like a virgin, darling. Now see, this was worth waiting out here rather than risking having my tail stepped on inside." His yellow-green gaze returned to Jamie. "So why the long face?"

Jamie hesitated…but Cicero and Tom weren't assigned to the murders, despite Tom's assistance with the hexes. It might be easier to talk about it with him. "I can't stop thinking about Wyatt. The first feral killed in the park."

Cicero frowned slightly. "I heard you knew him before. In the army."

Jamie should have guessed. Rook and Cicero were the two biggest gossips in the MWP—and that was saying something. "We were close."

"Well, of course. Who can resist a man in uniform?"

"I was in uniform, too," he reminded the cat.

"Even better." Cicero lounged back bonelessly. "I imagine seeing him again was a shock, since he was supposed to have died over a year ago."

"Aye." The horse nickered softly, and Jamie realized he'd been clutching the reins too tightly. He forced his hands to relax. "I can't help but ask myself why he never contacted me. Maybe he was afraid I'd turn him in, or...I don't know."

"This can't be easy," Cicero said. "I *am* sorry, James. Truly. Rook and Dominic will do everything they can to find who killed him and the other one."

"Pia," Jamie said automatically.

Everything they could...which was much less than usual. Any illegal hexes brought from this raid would add to the pile already on Dominic's desk.

His stomach twisted. "What if I could do something?" he asked.

"Like what?"

Jamie hesitated. "What do you think of Rook's brother? Nick?"

"I think Nicholas is a bloody fool," Cicero said without hesitation. "But he can afford to be one, since he transforms into a rather large horse." At Jamie's questioning look, he shrugged. "It's much harder to capture and force bond something like a horse than it is a cat, or a crow, or a dog. Not impossible, obviously, but more difficult, especially in a city. The problem with Nicholas is he thinks everyone should be like him—living in so-called freedom, away from any sort of protection against unscrupulous witches."

Cicero's delicate shiver told Jamie he wasn't just speaking hypothetically. "You had a bad experience?" Jamie asked.

Cicero paused before answering, eyeing Jamie up as if judging whether or not he was worthy of the story. "Every familiar has a version of the same tale, darling. We're walking down the street, minding our own business, and suddenly feel a little sting. A hex to check if we're bonded or not. Sometimes we've no idea where it came from. Sometimes, it's all too obvious. After I joined the MWP, I could flash my familiar's badge, and they'd slink away. Before, though...it's not fun, running for your life, hoping you aren't bolting right into an ambush."

"I don't suppose it would be." Had that happened to Wyatt, after Eddie died? At least he could fly away.

"But Nicholas views it as throwing away our freedom. To be fair, he does his best to protect the ferals living under his care. But he can't be with them all the time." Cicero watched Jamie out of the side of his eye. "If you want to know more, talk to Malachi. He lived in Nicholas's colony for a while."

"Malachi was a thief," Jamie said. Not much of an endorsement for the sort of company Nick kept, even if the fox had gone on to join the MWP.

Cicero shrugged. "I doubt Nicholas cared one way or the other. He has very specific concerns: hating witches and protecting familiars."

"Why does he hate witches?"

"Well, I'm sure *I* don't know." Cicero sighed dramatically. "Honestly, why are we talking about Nicholas? He's so dreadfully boring compared to me. Why on earth are you asking about him?"

Jamie licked lips that had gone dry. "No reason."

"Fine. Don't tell me. Ruin my night." Cicero laced his hands around his knee. "But let me ask you one thing. If you have a chance to do something about the murders, as you said, what's keeping you from it?"

Fear. Fear was the answer that popped into Jamie's head, and as much as he wanted to deny it, he couldn't.

He'd let Wyatt down once before, by not being there with him when Eddie died. Failed so bad, Wyatt hadn't even tried to contact him once the familiar reached New York.

Now Wyatt was dead, and there wasn't much Jamie could do to make up for his past failures. But it wasn't nothing.

Nick might know a lot of ferals, but he wasn't an MWP officer. Jamie was an officer, but he just drove the damned wagon. Could they even hope to solve the murders? True, if Ferguson approved their plan, Rook and Dominic would help, but would it be enough? Or would Jamie just fail Wyatt one more time?

If he didn't try, he couldn't fail.

Or maybe he just failed in a whole new way.

He took a deep breath and let it out slowly. "You're right," he said. "Thanks, Cicero."

Cicero winked at him. "My pleasure, darling."

"Another death?" Conrad asked. The other ferals in the hidden cellar stared at Nick fearfully. One of the young whimpered; he wasn't certain which.

He'd delayed telling them in the hopes he could reassure them he was doing something about the situation. That clearly wasn't going to happen, though.

Probably for the best, really. What would the other ferals, here and in the saloon above, think if he worked openly with the police? It would ruin his reputation. If Jamie had taken him up on the offer, he would have had to lie about the situation; otherwise, everyone would assume Nick had sold them out.

"Yes," Nick said, holding up his hands in a pacifying gesture. "But, terrible as it is, it's good news for you. Pia wasn't involved in smuggling ferals. So Wyatt's death likely didn't have anything to do with it, either. Which means I can risk contacting someone else without leading a killer to them."

"What does that mean for us?" asked the bear, Rachel, crossing her arms.

"With any luck you'll be out of this basement in a day or two." Relieved smiles greeted his words. Nick would be almost as glad to have them gone. He could feed them for a while, but costs added up fast, and it wasn't as if any of them were paying customers.

Not to mention the longer they were here, the more chances something might go wrong. Say, for his witch's uncle to arrest him.

What had he been thinking, offering to bond with O'Malley's nephew? What was he going to do for a follow up, offer to suck Ingram's cock?

The stupid thing was, he'd been disappointed when Jamie turned him down. It didn't make sense. What sort of witch refused power when it was handed to him?

His disappointment hadn't had anything to do with the witch, of course. Only that finding out who had killed Wyatt and Pia would be a hell of a lot harder, without the information the coppers withheld. Nothing more.

Nick left the hidden ferals, picked up a crate of bad whiskey to serve as his excuse for going into the basement, and trudged up the stairs to the saloon's main room. The mismatched tables were crowded tonight, and customers lined up along the wooden plank of the bar. But rather than the raucous gathering one might expect, the mood was subdued. Anxious.

No one had come here tonight to have a good time. Not after word of the second murder spread through the feral community. Rather, they'd come to huddle together, where they might be safe from the outside world for a little while.

Kyle worked the bar—no fancy cocktails here, just five-cent beer and ten-cent whiskey. Caballus was in the upper tier of dive bars, but it was still a dive bar. No one with money to spare drank here, but it was still far better than the places that served the drippings from kegs and half-drunk glasses, all mixed together.

Ammi would have been appalled. She'd hoped for better for both her sons.

Well, then, she shouldn't have put her trust in a witch, should she?

The bell above the door jingled, and the saloon fell silent. Nick turned, ready for trouble.

Not ready for the kind of trouble that actually greeted him, though. Jamie MacDougal hovered on the doorstep, as if unsure whether to come inside.

"Mind the place for me," Nick told Kyle, because he didn't know how long this might take. Then he strode across the room and grasped Jamie by the shoulder. "Come on."

He led the way to his apartment and shut the door, to give them privacy. "What do you want?" he asked without preamble.

Jamie leaned his right shoulder against the wall just inside the door. "I've been thinking about your offer."

Nick leaned against the wall as well. So close, he could make out the startling spot of brown amidst the green of Jamie's eyes. The faint scent of sandalwood cologne drifted up from his skin.

Nick caught himself licking his lips. Curse it. "I thought you'd made up your mind already."

"I had." Jamie wavered, then shrugged. "But once I had the chance to think, as I'd requested, I decided that getting justice for Wyatt is worth putting up with a grumpy bastard like you."

Startled, Nick laughed. "Not many people would say that to my face." He considered Jamie carefully. "One month."

"Aye. One month." Jamie held out his hand.

Uncertain if he was making the biggest mistake of his life, Nick shook it. Jamie's hand was warm, strong, lightly callused. A mix of fear and desire curled through Nick's blood at the touch. Fear, because he was agreeing to the one thing he'd sworn never to do.

Desire, because a man couldn't help but wonder what those lips would look like kissed. Or wrapped around his cock.

No. He didn't fuck witches. And of all the witches he didn't fuck, this one was at the very top of the list. The most unfuckable.

He blinked and realized he was still holding Jamie's hand, like an idiot. Letting go, he stepped back and put space between them. A sliver of fear worked its way down his spine, but he set it aside. "All right. Let's do this."

"Now?" Jamie asked, eyebrows lifting.

As though he hadn't had to screw his courage to the sticking point to even get this far. Nick folded his arms over his chest. "Any reason not to?"

"Only that we should probably talk to the others—Rook and Dominic, if not Chief Ferguson—and make sure they'll even let us work the case if we do this?"

Nick glowered…but the witch was right, curse him. "Fine," he said. "I'll meet you at the Coven first thing in the morning." He shook his head. "Rook is never going to let me hear the end of this."

CHAPTER 7

"WHAT?" ROOK SQUAWKED. *"You* want to bond with a *witch?"*

Jamie had gathered everyone Nick requested in the interrogation room on the Coven's lowest level, as it was the only place large enough. Rook and Dominic were there, along with Tom and Cicero, and of course Jamie and Nick.

He didn't tell them why, only that Nick needed to talk to them somewhere private. But the whole time, his belly had been tying itself in knots. He'd lain awake half the night, wondering if he was doing the right thing, agreeing to Nick's mad plan. What Wyatt would think about it all.

He reminded himself he was doing this for Wyatt. The last thing he *could* do, and it shouldn't have felt like a betrayal. If anything, Wyatt was surely the one who had betrayed Jamie, by letting Jamie think he was dead.

If he hadn't wanted Nick, it might have felt different. Simpler.

Nick stamped his foot against the stone floor. "Temporarily," he clarified. "Only long enough to catch the murderer. But yes."

Rook turned to Dominic. "Am I dreaming? Hallucinating? That must be it. I accidentally activated one of the illegal hexes, and it's done something to my mind. That's the only explanation."

"Perhaps we both did," suggested Dominic, who stared at Nick as though he'd never seen him before. Tom Halloran only looked confused, but Cicero had started to smirk. Jamie remembered their earlier conversation; apparently, he'd given more away to the cat than he'd realized. Heat crept up his face, and he prayed no one else noticed.

"Now if only we could find a witch willing to put up with a horse's arse," Cicero drawled. "And the rest of him, too, I suppose."

"One moment." Dominic held up his hands. "MacDougal, is that why you're involved in this? Nick thinks you're going to bond with *him?*"

"Absolutely not!" Rook exclaimed in horror.

Jamie stiffened. Did Rook not think he was good enough for Nick, even temporarily? "We don't need your permission," he snapped, at the same moment Nick said, "You damned hypocrite."

Rook focused on Jamie. "I know my brother, so let me guess how this went. Nick came up with this crackpot idea, and now he's charging ahead and dragging you along behind him. Just like he does with everyone."

Nick's nostrils flared, and he drew himself up. "That isn't true."

"Of course it's true!" Rook turned on his brother, lips pulled taut against his teeth. "You've done it your whole life."

"Rook," Dominic said. "Perhaps you aren't thinking clearly about this. The unfortunate truth is, we could use the help."

Rook shot Dominic a glare. "I'm thinking clearly, all right. Jamie, this is a terrible decision. I know you're desperate to do something. But you don't know my brother."

"Nick wants to get justice for Wyatt," Jamie said. "As well as for the other dead ferals. What else do I have to know?"

"Nick isn't looking for a partnership," Rook said. "He wants to use you to get a foot in the door at the MWP. The moment he has access to our case notes, and a badge to wave at suspects, he'll gallop off and leave you in the dust."

Jamie wavered. Rook did know his brother best. But if he didn't take Nick's offer, Wyatt's killer might get away.

"Did you ask yourself why Nick chose you, out of all the potential witches?" Rook turned his gaze pointedly to Jamie's left leg. "Do you think it might be because he assumed you'd be grateful for the opportunity?"

All the air left Jamie's lungs, as if he'd been slapped. "Rook!" Dominic exclaimed in shock. Cicero's eyes widened, and Tom looked horrified.

They saw him the same way Muriel did. As an invalid. Someone not up to the job.

Which meant Ferguson probably did too. Even if Jamie found a permanent familiar, once Nick was gone, he'd end up on a desk somewhere, shuffling papers.

He turned to Nick, half-afraid he'd see pity etched there. But Nick's thick brows had drawn low into a scowl. "What the hell are you talking about?"

"You don't know?" Jamie asked.

"What, that you're some kind of fucking war hero? A *Rough Rider?*" His lip curled on the last words. "I imagine you've got your pick of familiars. There are always fools searching for a bit of reflected glory, but Rook ought to damn well know I'm not one of them."

Instead of replying with words, Jamie jerked his left pant leg up, over the shoe and sock meant to make the foot look normal, exposing the smooth wood of his calf.

Nick's dark eyes took in the sight—then he snorted. "If you're looking for pity, look elsewhere, *witch.* At least you volunteered for it."

"I ain't looking for pity," Jamie snapped, stung. He let the pant leg fall.

"It seems you underestimated Nicholas, Rook," Cicero said. "If he didn't know about James's injury, he couldn't have been planning to take some sort of advantage of him."

Before, maybe. But now that he knew, would he view Jamie as not up to the task?

Rook folded his arms over his chest. "It's still a terrible idea."

Tom's brow was furrowed. "Jamie ain't your witch, right, Nick?"

Nick's mouth thinned. He shifted his weight and looked away. "No."

"Don't you see?" Jamie asked. "If Nick was looking to use me, as you say, surely he'd lie about it and say I was." He levered himself to his feet. "Besides, I can make my own decisions. So are you going to let us help with the investigation, or not?"

"You do need the extra hands," Cicero pointed out.

"No one asked you," Rook snapped.

Dominic put a soothing hand to Rook's arm. "Cicero isn't wrong. If Jamie is sure…"

"Aye," Jamie said firmly. "I'm sure."

Nick turned his glare on Tom and Cicero. "You *swear* to break the bond in one month, no matter what."

"Unless both of you ask us not to," Cicero replied.

"Aye," Tom said, holding out his hand to shake on it. "I promise."

Nick ignored the hand. "Fine. I can't believe I'm doing this. Come on, Jamie."

"Where are we going?" Jamie asked.

"Outside. I need the room."

Jamie led Nick toward the interior courtyard, his gut a jumble of emotions. "Shouldn't we ask Ferguson first? Make sure he'll agree to this?"

"It'll be harder for him to refuse if we've already bonded," Nick replied. Jamie wasn't entirely certain of that, but he didn't say anything until they reached the yard.

A wagon clattered past and into the street, the morning shift driver hastening out on a job. Otherwise, the area was quiet, save for the horses stirring in the stable.

Nick took in the courtyard, then nodded at the stable. "In there, to start. In case someone else comes into the yard."

The remaining horses lifted their heads and watched them curiously. "I spend most of my shift here," Jamie said, pointing at the nook with a chair and stove, unlit for now. "Or I did. I suppose I won't be back for a while. Until next month."

"Or less," Nick said. "If we're lucky."

"Aye." Jamie turned to face him. "Now what?"

Nick looked as though he nerved himself to do something. He stepped closer, right into Jamie's space.

Jamie swallowed hard. His prick twitched at the nearness; he fancied he could almost feel the heat of Nick's body through the chilly fall air.

He forced himself to crane his head back and look up at Nick, to focus on his face alone. Not that it helped. Nick was a real stunner, with those generous lips and broad nose. And his eyes, so dark that the dim light hid the boundary between iris and pupil. Jamie sucked in a lungful of air, smelled hay and horses, the comforting scents of the stable. But something else, too. A trace of sweat and musk that went right to his groin.

Wyatt had smelled of feathers, like dust and sand. Some people had found his pale yellow eyes unnerving, but Jamie had loved them, from the first second he saw them.

Nick stared back at Jamie, lips parted. Then he pressed them together, swallowed. "Close your eyes."

Jamie obeyed. He sensed Nick looming over him, closer and closer. Hot breath feathered over his face, coffee and mint. Strong fingers cupped his jaw, and the shock of it went through him, stoking the embers of desire into a flame. An involuntary moan escaped him, and

Nick's breath caught audibly.

Warm lips brushed against one eyelid, then the other. "Let me in, Jamie," Nick whispered.

The taste of blood filled Jamie's mouth. The wild thought came to him that he could tilt his head back just a little farther, catch Nick's mouth with his own.

He sensed Nick step back, cool air rushing into the gap between them. He opened his eyes; Nick's cheeks had flushed darker, his lips parted again. For a moment, he thought Nick would shove him down into the nearest pile of hay and fuck him senseless.

Maybe he shouldn't want that, but Saint Mary help him, he did.

Then Nick tossed his head, hair flying, as though shaking something off. "Come on," he said gruffly, and stomped out to the tiny yard.

Jamie welcomed the cold even more than usual, because it at least took the edge off the erection tightening his trousers. He followed Nick, until Nick stopped abruptly and turned to Jamie.

"A few things, before I let you look through my eyes," he said. "You might fancy yourself a rough rider, but don't even *think* about breaking me."

Jamie's eyes widened. "I ain't—I wouldn't!"

"Also, use my magic without my permission, and you'll get a fist to the face. Understand?"

Whatever had been between them in the stable had evaporated. Jamie should have been relieved. "I promise."

"And another thing—don't think you'll be riding anywhere on my back. Ever."

Jamie held up his hands. "I won't. I swear it."

Nick's brows drew down. "I'll hold you to that."

Then he was gone, replaced by one of the biggest horses Jamie had ever seen, at least seventeen hands of solid muscle.

Jamie stepped back, realized his mouth was hanging open, and shut it. But Saint Mary, Nick was just as gorgeous in his horse form as he was in his human. Though big and solid, Nick was no draft horse. This was a warhorse, nimble despite his size. His coat was black, not a single white hair anywhere on him. The mane and tail streaming in the autumn wind had a slight waviness to them, much like Nick's human hair. Thick hair—feathers, though that had always struck Jamie as an odd word to use in conjunction with horses—concealed most of his hooves.

Nick swung his head around and stared at him. *"Close your eyes."*

Jamie blinked at the voice in his head, then obeyed. The view that bloomed behind his eyelids was disorienting, to say the least. He could see most of the yard—far more of it than he was used to seeing at once. The colors seemed oddly dull. The sight of his own face, eyes closed, was even stranger.

Then Nick reared, stretching up and up, as if to emphasize just how much smaller Jamie was than him. Enormous hooves churned the air—then came down again on the bricks with a decisive *crack*.

"Message received," Jamie muttered, and opened his eyes.

Nick transformed back into his human shape. "Good," he said. He looked away, staring at the open gate, as though he considered bolting through it. "Finish it, then."

Jamie took out his notebook and flipped to an unlocking hex he'd drawn. For practice, he thought, but it was good enough to serve as the real thing. His hand hovered over it, but he paused. "May I use your magic to charge this unlocking hex, Nick?"

Nick's head snapped around, as if he thought Jamie mocked him. Then his scowl relaxed. "Yes. You may."

Jamie wasn't entirely sure how to go about it. He laid his fingers on the hex, concentrated on Nick, and felt heat bloom behind his heart. An odd sort of flow, from the warm spot to his fingers, and into the hex.

He shut the notebook. "It's done," he said.

Nick rubbed at his chest. So he felt something too. "Let's go tell Chief Ferguson. The sooner we get started with this, the sooner we'll be done."

"No." Chief Ferguson said. "Absolutely not."

Nick's nostrils flared, and he sucked in a deep breath. He knew he'd been stupid to put his trust in witches, but he hadn't expected it to come back on him quite so soon.

At his side, Jamie stiffened. "Sir—"

"I'm not done, MacDougal." Ferguson rose to his feet, glaring at them both. His owl familiar clacked her beak and puffed up her feathers angrily on her perch. "You don't come to me beforehand. You don't ask for permission. Instead, you stroll in here and *tell* me about this plan of yours, after you've already bonded? Have you forgotten who's in charge here?"

"No, sir," Jamie said, but his lower lip stuck out mulishly.

There had been a moment—more than a moment—in the stable, when Nick had wanted to bite that tempting lip. Jamie had shut his eyes and tipped his head back, exposing his long throat, and the sight had gone right to Nick's cock. He'd wanted to put Jamie over the little desk in the corner and hear him moan again and again.

He took a deep breath and focused on Ferguson's reddened face. That ought to be enough to kill any desire, surely.

"Is it you in charge, MacDougal?" Ferguson demanded. "Is it your uncle?"

"No, sir," Jamie repeated.

Well, he wasn't about to let Jamie take the full brunt of abuse alone. Nick put his shoulders back. "We're trying to *help* you, witch," he said to Ferguson.

"Maybe I don't want your help." Ferguson didn't look the least intimidated. "I've heard things about you, Nick. Things that don't incline me to let you join the MWP, no matter who you've bonded with." He sat back in his chair. "This isn't your saloon. You can't just stroll into my office like you own the place. Working here means you have to take orders. From me. A witch."

Nick had been a fool to imagine the MWP would cooperate. "I should've known you don't give a damn about dead ferals."

"Don't try that with me, horse. You can't manipulate me that easily." Ferguson glanced at Jamie, then back at Nick. "If you think I'm going to let you take advantage of MacDougal here, you're wrong."

Not this again. Before Nick could protest, Jamie said, "The shell hit my leg, not my brain. Sir."

At least Ferguson had the grace to look guilty. "I didn't mean... You're right, MacDougal. That came out wrong. I understand you're eager to make detective. But this isn't the way to go about it. We have some unbonded familiars in the MWP whose time to choose a witch is almost up. Go find Halloran, have him break this bond. Talk to the unbonded. Get to know them. Find out if any of them are interested. You'll have a desk up here in no time."

"With all due respect, this ain't about my career." Jamie's spine was ramrod straight, his jaw hard. "Nick and I will work together. He didn't ask me to do this with him just for show."

"Damned right I didn't," Nick said. He shouldn't care one way or the other what Jamie thought of him, but the idea rankled. In theory, he'd use a witch if it suited him—witches certainly never hesitated to use familiars, after all. But given the man had turned down his offer at first, Jamie didn't strike him as the type to let himself be used.

"I know the feral community, better than any of your tame familiars," Nick went on. "I can get answers no one else can."

Ferguson's jaw firmed. "No. That's my final—"

There came a frantic knock on the door. "What?" Ferguson barked.

A pale young witch stuck her head in cautiously. "Sorry to interrupt, sir, but I thought you should know. There's a woman here who says she might have some information on the feral killings."

"I was riding my bicycle through Central Park," the woman said. She clutched a hot cup of coffee without drinking it, as if drawing strength from its warmth. "The best time for bird watching is early morning, you see."

Nick leaned against the doorway to the interrogation room, arms crossed over his chest. Ferguson and Athene had collected Rook and Dominic on the way down to interview her. Nick followed without asking for permission, and Jamie did the same. Ferguson hadn't yet remarked on their presence, though Nick didn't doubt he was aware of it.

"What did you see, Miss Clayton?" Athene asked. She'd taken human form, and sat across from the woman.

"The weather was fair, so I went up to the Blockhouse. I thought it would be a lovely view, with all the turning leaves painting the park in orange and red and yellow. But as I approached the ruin, I saw a smear of blood on the stones of the doorway, and another on the steps." She swallowed. "I remembered reading something in the papers about a murder. Well, my first thought was the killer might have been lurking about, waiting for a new victim, so I snatched up my bicycle and left as quickly as possible."

"Did you touch anything?" Athene asked. "Take anything away?"

"No." Miss Clayton shook her head. "I know better than to disturb a crime scene." She lowered her voice. "I read the Howl and Roger dime novels, you see."

Nick barely restrained himself from rolling his eyes.

"Thank you, Miss Clayton," Athene said. "We'll look into it as soon as we can."

Once the woman had left, Jamie said, "How soon will that be?"

"We could put off looking at illegal hexes and go now," Rook suggested hopefully.

Ferguson rubbed at his face. "No. The reformers have got the papers in a frenzy, which means the Police Board is pressuring me in return. We need arrests, but we also need convictions."

Jamie's eyes flashed like green fire. "This can't wait! I know the Police Board are threatening to replace you with a non-witch, but in the meantime we have a killer on the loose."

"This might not have had anything to do with the murders," Athene pointed out. "The blood could have come from anything."

"Or there could be another body inside," Dominic said unhappily. "We can't just let this go, Ferguson."

"Jamie and I could look into it for you," Nick pointed out.

"Aye," Jamie said. "Don't look a gift horse in the mouth, chief."

Rook let out a cawing laugh. Ferguson sighed, as though asking himself why he put up with any of them. "Fine. I'll let MacDougal and Nick take a look at the Blockhouse. On one condition." His gaze shifted to Nick and turned into a scowl. "You take any order you're given. From me, from Kopecky, from your brother—it doesn't matter. Rook and Kopecky are still the ones officially in charge of the investigation, so they'll tell you what to do. And you'll do it. The first time you disobey, you're gone."

Nick ground his teeth. He wanted to argue. To say he wasn't going to let a damned witch boss him around.

But maybe it was already too late for that. He could feel warmth burning behind his heart, the spot where the bond with Jamie lived. He wanted it gone.

He'd always told himself he'd do whatever it took to protect ferals. To keep them safe, so they didn't have to bow and scrape to witches just to get by. So instead here he was, doing the bowing and scraping for them.

Fur and feathers. They needed to catch the killer so he could put all this behind him.

"All right," he said. "I'll do it."

Ferguson nodded and made for the door. Athene took on owl form and followed him out.

"Why am I having trouble believing you'll do what anyone tells you?" Rook asked, once Ferguson was gone. "Jamie, I know it's asking a lot, but please rein him in."

Nick snorted. "Just don't try to do it literally." He let his arms fall. "Can we go, witch?" he asked Dominic.

"Yes." Dominic glanced at Jamie and grimaced. "Good luck."

CHAPTER 8

FRUSTRATION TIGHTENED JAMIE'S chest, and he made for the Third Avenue El as quickly as he could. Despite the cool air, he was soon sweating with exertion, his breath coming hard as if he had run the distance. Which maybe he could do, if he could afford a fancy prosthetic with hexes and the like, instead of just making do with his government issued one.

But he didn't *need* to run to be a good detective, so it shouldn't matter. Except it obviously did to Ferguson and everyone else.

For all the talk about his service to the country, for being a Rough Rider, people still only saw the wooden leg.

Before the war, he'd been, if not the most popular fellow, at least someone invited out for drinks with his friends. But his friends had drifted away, and his fellow MWP policemen didn't think he was good for anything more than paperwork, and the man he'd been in love with was dead without even trying to speak to him again, and now he was alone with a grumpy familiar who would be leaving anyway in a month's time, and—

Consumed by his thoughts, he didn't pay enough attention to walking. His wooden foot came down wrong as he descended the platform on 110th Street. The prosthetic leg went out from under him, and he let out a startled cry of pain, stump and knee twisting. But before he could fall, a large hand wrapped around his arm.

Nick hauled him upright easily. Jamie's face flushed with

embarrassment. "I don't need your help," he muttered, pulling his arm free.

Nick arched a brow. "Who said I was helping you? If you fell on the stairs, you might knock someone else over on your way down."

Hell. Jamie sighed. "Sorry," he said, as they descended to the sidewalk. "I should have been paying more attention."

"You seemed lost in thought." Nick cocked his head. "But then you're a witch, so I'm guessing it was unfamiliar territory."

The casual insult, delivered without rancor, drew a startled laugh from Jamie. "Did I seem surprised when you shifted into an entire horse earlier? Because I was just expecting the back end of one."

Nick grinned, which somehow made him look even handsomer. Not fair, not fair at all.

"Thanks for not letting me fall," Jamie added.

"I thought about it," Nick said, "but Dominic and Ferguson would have assumed I pushed you."

"Aye. Probably." Jamie sighed. "They mean well, I suppose. I'm grateful Ferguson gave me my old job back, when I returned from the war. Though if it had involved anything more than driving the wagon, I'm starting to wonder if he would have."

The crowds on the sidewalk parted for them. Some of the women clutched their bags tighter at the sight of Nick, and the men shot him unfriendly looks. Nick didn't seem to notice, though Jamie doubted he was as oblivious as he appeared.

"He would have found something." Nick glanced at Jamie out of the corner of his eye. "You're a war hero, after all."

Jamie looked away. "Right."

"It doesn't seem to give you much pleasure. You could be drinking out on it every night. Stabbing your wooden leg for the entertainment of onlookers."

Jamie shrugged uncomfortably. Up until now, it seemed Nick had seen him as a man like any other. He didn't want that to change. "Then ask them to buy me a new one when it splinters apart?"

"A good point." Nick nodded at the low wall in front of them. "We're here."

Warriors' Gate read a block set in the stone wall bordering the park. There was no actual gate, of course, just a gap opening onto the trees of the North Woods beyond. Gray stone heaved up just on the other side of the carriage drive, building to the rise on which the Blockhouse stood.

Falling leaves streamed on the wind as they made their way along the winding paths through the trees. The North Woods were deserted except for the two of them, and the sounds of the city seemed to die away even as the foliage rose around them. A squirrel chittered angrily. Birds scratched amidst the dry leaves on the ground. They might have been strolling through some rural paradise, rather than hunting a killer in the heart of the city.

"Hard to believe this used to be a fort in the countryside," Nick said, looking up at the ruin.

"Was it?" Jamie asked. The building was now nothing more than four stone walls with no roof and empty inside. The hexes carved into the stones, to strengthen them against cannon fire, probably hadn't been charged in a century. "Do you think the killer is in there?"

"No idea. So we should probably be careful about approaching. I'm not looking to get shot or carved up."

A shiver passed through Jamie. He touched his chest with one hand, where Wyatt's necklace hung beneath his clothing. "Aye."

They made their way cautiously along the worn earth of the path, until it ended atop gray rock. The doorway into the small ruin lay to the left, and they exchanged a glance. "I've got the uniform," Jamie said. He took his single-action Colt revolver out and checked it. "I'll go first."

Nick nodded. Jamie's breath was tight in his lungs as he stepped around the side of the building, to the base of the steep, high stairs. "Police!" he barked with all the authority he could. "Hands up, and get out here!"

Nothing. Silence except for the sigh of the wind through the trees, the scuttle of dry, dead leaves across the rock.

As Miss Clayton had said, a bloody smear clung to the rock of the empty doorway. The rectangular opening revealed worn earth and nothing else. No movement, though it was entirely possible someone hid just to the side, out of sight.

"Keep an eye out," Nick said, and charged up the stairs and through the doorway. Jamie tensed—but a moment later, Nick stepped back out. "No one's here now. But someone definitely has been."

The stairs were oddly high—to discourage attackers?—and had no railing. Nick didn't say anything, only held out his hand. Jamie grabbed it, let Nick provide some of the leverage and balance for him to make it into the fort. "Thanks."

"Not a bad place to sit and watch the park," Nick said. "You can see people coming and going through Warriors' Gate and Strangers' Gate. Not to mention anyone wandering the North Woods."

"Aye." Jamie stepped into the Blockhouse and looked around.

Someone had definitely been here, all right.

Words written in dried blood scrawled along the stone walls, the letters spiky, jagged, frantic. Jamie read them aloud: "It is the blood that maketh an atonement for the soul." He frowned, searching his memory. "That's from Leviticus, ain't it?"

"Oh, good," Nick muttered. "Not just a maniac, but a religious maniac."

Nick slowly circled the old fort's tiny space, every sense on alert. The writing on the walls sent a new wave of unease through him every time he looked at it. Anyone who went to the trouble of scrawling a Biblical verse in blood had to be completely unhinged.

"As if there weren't enough religious lunatics making trouble," he said.

"Maybe Reverend Ingram did it," Jamie suggested. "Danced up here naked in the moonlight…"

"Not a mental image I wanted, thanks."

"Look." Jamie bent carefully and picked something up from the ground. Nick joined him. A length of bone lay in the palm of Jamie's hand. Someone had carved lines and symbols into it that Nick didn't recognize. The bone had cracked down the center, disrupting the patterns.

"Bird bone. From a large species." Nick took the bone in his hands and turned it over. "Looks to be the right humerus. Are those hexes scratched into it?"

"I ain't sure." Jamie tucked it carefully into an inner pocket. "Once we're back at the Coven, we'll ask our forensic hexman about it. Dr. Owen Yates."

Nick scowled. "I met Yates last year. Pompous, self-serving nob. One of my former tenants bonded with him. It was his wedding that led to the fucking Pemberton Act. And he ended up leaving his bride at the altar on top of it all."

A frown crossed Jamie's handsome features, and his particolored eyes darkened. "The Pemberton Act is meant to keep people safe."

How naïve could even a witch be? "It's meant to demonize familiars and give Pemberton a political boost."

"That ain't true!" Jamie looked up at him earnestly. "My uncle heads up the Dangerous Familiars Squad, so I think I know a little more about it than you do."

Damn it. Nick had let himself forget Jamie's connection with O'Malley.

Which was dangerous. Not just to him, but to the ferals in his cellar.

He ought to let the matter drop. Safer that way. But Jamie's defense of his uncle, of the squad, spurred Nick on. "Know more about it, do you? Then tell me this, witch. Do you know he gets a bonus for every familiar he drags in?"

"Of course," Jamie said. "It's dangerous work, ain't it? No reason he shouldn't be compensated."

Nick's stomach fell, and he cursed himself for it. It wasn't that he'd thought Jamie would prove different from any other witch. But having the truth right in front of him was disappointing, somehow.

"If it's dangerous, it's because they're making it so, by hauling off those who just want to live their lives in peace." Nick shook his head. "What if the law was aimed at Irishmen? What if you hadn't done anything wrong, but the police said you had to be watched over by an Englishman all the time, or else go to jail. What would you do?"

He expected Jamie to reply with the usual, flippant "Obey the law." It was an answer people trotted out when they knew there was no chance of having such a law actually aimed at them. But to his surprise, Jamie hesitated.

"It ain't the same," he said at last. "The ferals killed a lot of people at the cathedral."

"A good thing Irishmen never kill anyone, then." Nick turned away. "Come on, let's…what is that?"

Something long and white lay on the ground, half lost in the grass. Nick bent to pick it up. Jamie's eyes went wide, and he reached for it.

"An eagle feather," he whispered, cradling it in his hands. "Wyatt's feather."

Jamie stood in the corner of Dr. Yates's lab, watching while the forensic hexman drew up hexes to prove what Jamie already knew in his gut.

The feather had belonged to Wyatt. Which meant he'd been in the park in eagle shape at some point.

Had the killer held him captive first? But there was no sign of a cage in the Blockhouse, or even somewhere for an eagle to be tied down. Could it mean Wyatt had known his murderer?

Jamie's head ached. He felt dizzy and sick, grief and vague guilt swirling together in his belly.

Dr. Yates's fox familiar, Malachi, perched on the edge of the worktable. "So how's Daniel?" he asked Nick. "He still chasing balls at all hours of the day or night?"

Nick. Jamie should probably have guessed he'd be opposed to the Pemberton Act. He didn't understand, though, that was all. He didn't know Uncle Hurley.

Hurley was a good man, who had taken in his sister's children without hesitation and raised them as his own. Who'd worked long hours to provide for them, so they'd never know the kind of want that afflicted so many other orphans in the city. Who went to church every Sunday and never hesitated to help out a neighbor. He wouldn't be involved with the Dangerous Familiars Squad if they had done anything wrong.

"Daniel is a dog," Nick said. "So yes, he's chasing balls. At least he's not licking a pair belonging to a witch."

Mal's eyebrows rose—then he let out a barking laugh. "Same old Nick, eh? And here I thought you'd joined us." He tapped the silver badge pinned to his vest.

"Like hell you did." Nick's usual glower settled over his face. "Stop trying to act like we're friends, Mal. The Pemberton Act is your fault."

Mal's mouth fell open. "How the devil is it *my* fault?"

"You worked right beside the ringleader." Nick glanced contemptuously around the room. "It's amazing you lot can find your asses with both hands and a map, let alone solve any crimes."

"I wrote to Senator Pemberton arguing against the Act," Yates said coolly. Jamie had always found him a bit cold, with his pale hair, silvery eyes, and formal demeanor. "The senator wasn't at the wedding—he had to decline the invitation at the last moment, due to ill health. He didn't hear what was said that day, so I tried to enlighten him as to the wrongs done Bertie and the others. Not to excuse their actions, but to explain. Unfortunately, Pemberton wasn't interested in my opinion. The Yates fortunes are not what they once were, after all." He held up one of the hexes he'd drawn. "The feather doesn't match."

Jamie blinked. "What?" He'd been so certain.

"The feather doesn't match the blood or hair taken from Wyatt's body." Yates indicated the hex. "If it belonged to Wyatt, the hex would have turned black. Green tells us it came from someone else."

"The devil?" Nick said. "What does that mean?"

"That another eagle familiar was in the park?" Yates shrugged.

Jamie shook his head slowly. He'd been so sure.

Nick stepped up beside Jamie. The heat of his body seemed to reach

Jamie's skin, even though inches of air separated them. "What about the bone? It's big enough to be eagle. Does it match the feather?"

Yates's pale brows drew together, and he pulled out two more hexes. After a moment, he nodded. "Yes. The bone and the feather came from the same bird."

"Same person," Nick corrected.

Jamie swallowed bile. But Yates only looked annoyed. "There's no reason to think they came from a familiar. Cultures the world over have used the parts of ordinary animals in all sorts of ceremonies."

"So what do the markings mean?" Jamie asked. "I know a few hexes, but the lines don't look like anything I've seen."

Yates leaned back in his chair. "That's why I've sent for—never mind, here they are."

The door opened, and Dominic and Rook entered. "You found something?" Dominic asked. "We're in the middle of sorting through the latest batch of illegal hexes, so we don't have much time."

"Yes." Yates handed the bone to Dominic. "What do you think of this?"

Dominic frowned. "It looks a bit like one of the partial hexes from the device you reconstructed last year. Is it?"

"Not quite." Yates took back the bone and stared at it. "I'm not sure, but it might be a very primitive hex. Like the ones found scratched into ancient stones, relying on the native power of the object."

Mal let out a whistle through his teeth. "I remember you talking about that. You said sometimes they used bone, didn't you?"

"Yes." Yates put the bone down carefully. "Hexes this old, though…we don't really know what they do, generally speaking. The knowledge was lost to time or the Inquisition."

The fine hairs on the back of Jamie's neck stood up. "An old hex? The blood hexes drawn around the bodies…those could be old, too."

"So?" Nick asked, obviously confused. "What does it matter?"

"Old magic has cropped up twice in the last two years." Rook put a hand on Dominic's shoulder, but he kept his gaze on Nick. "The information wasn't released to the general public, but it was bad. Really bad."

"And connected with the theriarchists," Mal added.

Nick didn't look happy. "Murdering ferals for no good reason doesn't sound like something theriarchists would do."

Rook's mouth flattened. "Ask Isaac what they would do."

"If Isaac had come to me, he wouldn't have gotten hurt in the first place," Nick shot back. He glanced at the clock. "It's almost five. I'm going to the saloon."

"We should question Pia's roommates," Jamie said, before Nick could turn away. "I'll come by in the morning and help."

Nick hesitated, and Jamie's stomach clenched. "I can talk to them myself, tonight," Nick said.

"We're in this together," Jamie reminded him. "Working together. I want to be there."

For a moment, he thought Nick would dismiss his request out of hand. Nick's nostrils flared slightly...and he nodded. "You're right. Come by first thing in the morning, witch."

The door shut behind him. Rook stared at it, then shook his head. "I love my brother," he said. "But I don't trust him."

"What do you mean?" Jamie asked.

"I mean he'll tell the truth as far as it suits him and lie about the rest." Rook shook his head. "As far as he's concerned, right now, we—the MWP—are the lesser of two evils. But you're still a witch, Jamie, and Mal and I are traitors to his cause. If it suits him, he'll lie to us, and not feel an instant of guilt because of it."

It wasn't what Jamie wanted to hear. "He's passionate, I'll give you that," he said, recalling their argument over the Dangerous Familiars Squad. "But he seems like a good man."

"He is," Mal said. "If you're a feral, he'd go to any length to help you." The redhead's mouth curved into a rueful smile. "But if you ain't, you're on your own."

Rook and Mal knew Nick better than Jamie did, true. But at the same time, they obviously had personal quarrels with him. Rook especially. "I ain't seen nothing yet to make me think ill of the man. He's a giant arse, but that don't mean he ain't trustworthy."

Rook pinched the bridge of his nose. "Maybe you're right. I *hope* you're right. But just...be careful. For both your sakes."

Chapter 9

The sun had just broken the horizon when someone knocked on the door to Nick's apartment. He'd barely slept last night, even after he'd crawled into bed well after the bar had closed. In the dark of the bedroom, with nothing else left to distract him, he'd been all too aware of the little coal of heat tucked into his chest.

The bond with his witch.

With Jamie, of the green eyes interrupted by a splash of brown. Of the supple lips and handsome face. Heat swept over him, and Nick almost put a hand to his prick, before remembering he didn't fuck coppers, and he *definitely* didn't fuck witches. Not even in his own imagination, where no one else would ever know.

He'd know, and that was enough. He couldn't start thinking of the witch as someone he wouldn't mind taking up against a wall, because the situation was complicated enough as it was.

So he'd closed his eyes and tried to picture someone else while he stroked his prick. But his mind kept returning to Jamie, and his eventual orgasm left him feeling oddly disappointed.

The knock came again. Nick sighed and turned away from the mirror where he'd been in the midst of shaving. "All right, all right."

He swung open the door and found the man who'd occupied his thoughts in the flesh.

Jamie wore plain clothes today instead of the uniform. A wool overcoat, not new but not too worn, held off the chill of a frosty

October morning. The suit beneath was newer; a slight bulge above and around his left knee interrupted the fit of the trousers. A trace of sandalwood cologne teased Nick's senses, made him draw in a deeper breath.

Jamie arched a brow, and Nick realized he was standing in the door like an idiot, half his jaw still covered in shaving soap, the razor in his hand. "Good morning to you," Jamie said, and held up a paper sack. "I brought doughnuts."

"Why?" Nick asked suspiciously, because when did witches ever do anything just for the sake of it?

"Because I'm hungry." Jamie lowered the sack and cocked his head. A sly smile played on his lips. "Ain't you?" As if he knew what Nick was really hungry for.

Nick's stomach chose that moment to growl loudly. Jamie laughed. "Well, that answers that."

Nick stepped back and ushered him into the apartment. "There's coffee on the stove—help yourself."

While Nick finished shaving, Jamie poured them both coffee. "You look done in. You ain't running the saloon and working for the MWP both, are you?"

"What sort of fool question is that? Of course I am." Nick wiped the last traces of soap from his face. In truth, he needed to hire another bartender, in addition to Kyle.

But the ferals hiding in the cellar complicated things. He couldn't just hire anyone—they needed to be absolutely trustworthy. And trust was hard to come by these days, even between ferals.

He hated thinking a feral would betray other ferals. But he knew from experience that some would. Instead of working together to raise up all familiars, they'd tear each other apart. Fight over scraps on the floor, while the witches feasted at the table.

"Did you get any sleep at all?" Jamie asked around a mouthful of fried dough.

"I'll sleep when I'm dead," Nick snapped. "Keep your concern, witch. I don't need it."

Jamie looked doubtful, but shrugged. "Have it your way. Oh, before I forget, I have something for you."

He took a silver badge from his coat pocket and held it out. Nick stared at the stylized cat in the center, the symbol of the MWP familiars.

Agreeing to work with them was one thing. But this made it seem more real, somehow. He was a copper, at least temporarily, and the badge made it impossible to deny.

Like it or not, the day might come when he needed its authority. He took it gingerly, and pinned it to the inside of his coat, where it wouldn't be visible.

His appetite had deserted him, but he choked down the fried dough anyway. No sense letting Jamie see his unease. "Let's go, then," Nick said, once he'd washed the doughnut down with coffee. "Doreen and Estelle have jobs they need to get to, and I don't want to delay them."

Jamie nodded. "That's one of the reasons I came early."

The witch's words caught Nick off guard. Bringing breakfast, taking into mind Pia's roommates had other things to do than just wait around…it was considerate. Which he hadn't expected from a witch.

Jamie wanted something. That was the only explanation. Thanks to the fucking bond, he already had Nick's magic. Did he think he was going to trick Nick into making it permanent?

If so, he'd soon find Nick wasn't such an easy mark, to be bribed by doughnuts and achieving a bare minimum of decency.

"Come on," Nick grunted. "Just let me do all the talking."

"I don't usually let witches come here," Nick said as he led the way up to the second floor. "Now it's twice in a year." He shook his head, as though it were somehow a personal failing.

Jamie followed him up, taking the stairs carefully since he didn't want a repeat of yesterday. Still, it was hard to concentrate on where he was going rather than gawk at his surroundings. It wasn't like any other tenement he'd ever seen, but instead altered to accommodate the fact those living here weren't restricted to human form. Perches jutted out from the wall, and the windows off the landing had platforms outside where avian familiars could land and shift shape. Many of the doors had smaller flaps cut into them; a fox darted out one, followed by a tabby cat, and vanished past them in a streak of fur. The air smelled musky, the scent of animals living in close quarters to one another.

Unwelcoming gazes fixed on Jamie: from open doorways, from ferals on the landings, or birds on their perches. Did Nick's tenants know his identity, or were they just wary because he wasn't a familiar?

Nick stopped in front of a doorway just off the landing and knocked. A woman opened it; she'd been in the process of dressing, and her shirtwaist was only partially buttoned over her chemise. Heat rose to Jamie's face and he transferred his gaze hastily to Nick.

"Doreen," Nick said. He didn't seem perturbed by her partial undress. Or very interested in it at all, as he didn't give so much as the slightest downward glance. "I have some questions about Pia for you and Estelle, if you've the time."

Doreen finished buttoning her shirt and peered around Nick's solid bulk. "Who's that with you?"

"Jamie MacDougal," Jamie said, giving her a quick bob of the head. "I'm with the—"

"He's helping me find out who killed Pia," Nick interrupted. Had he not told anyone he was working with the MWP? That he'd bonded, even temporarily, with Jamie?

It shouldn't have made any difference. If Jamie had thought about it, he wouldn't have expected different. Still, he felt as though he were Nick's dirty little secret.

Doreen stepped back. "Come in."

The apartment was tiny, nearly every square inch packed with belongings, though it lacked human beds. A perch stuck out from one wall. A pile of pillows and a thick blanket, both covered in animal hair, lay near the small stove where another woman was brewing coffee.

"Nice view," Jamie said, nodding at the window. In the distance, the thirty-two stories of Madison Square Garden towered over the surrounding buildings. The gilded statue of Diana atop the tower flashed in the rising sun.

"What is it you want to know about Pia?" the other woman, presumably Estelle, asked.

"If anything had changed for her recently." Nick's large frame made the room seem even smaller. Jamie lingered in the doorway so as not to crowd anyone. "Was she still working at the sweater's on Second?"

Doreen nodded. "Miserable prick, that one. Always trying to put his hand down her shirt or up her skirt."

"She was late with her part of the rent," Nick said. "Any particular reason why?"

The two women exchanged looks. Then Estelle shrugged. "She wasn't doing too well. Drinking more than she should have, taking some of them illegal hexes, the sort that make you feel good for an hour or two, no matter what else is happening."

"Recently, she'd started going to church," Doreen added. "I don't know which one, but she seemed more depressed when she came back from services, not less. A few days ago, she said she might have some way to get money, to pay the rent."

"So what was she doing?" Nick asked.

"I don't know." Doreen held up her hands. "That's the Lord's honest truth, Nick."

"Speaking of money," Estelle said. "We'd best be getting on, or else we'll be locked out before our shift starts."

"One last question," Jamie said. "Did she know an eagle feral? Name of Wyatt?"

Doreen frowned in concentration, then shook her head. "Not so far as I know. Estelle?"

"If she did, she never mentioned him to us," Estelle agreed. "Now we really do have to leave." She hesitated and glanced at Nick. "I know the rent on the room is short, but we didn't expect to have to make up for Pia's share. We'll get it to you, Nick, but we need a little time."

Nick shrugged. "You've already paid your agreed-upon share for the month. No need for more until November. Just let me know when you find a new roommate. Or if you'd like me to find one for you, I can do that."

Estelle's face softened, and Doreen looked on the verge of tears. "Thanks, Nick," Estelle said.

They all trooped out of the apartment, and the two women hurried off down the hall. Though noises still came from the floors above them, it seemed everyone in the neighboring apartments had either left for work or still slept. "That was kind of you," Jamie said into the silence. "Most landlords wouldn't be so understanding."

Nick tossed his hair back out of his eyes. "What other landlords do isn't my problem."

"Still." Jamie stopped walking. Nick paused as well, turning to face him. Light filtered in from the stairwell, outlining Nick's warm, brown skin with cool silver.

Jamie's breath caught in his throat. He'd thought a lot about Nick last night, and not because of the case. Remembered the way Nick's big hands had cradled his jaw, the softness of his lips on Jamie's eyelids.

Maybe he'd just spent too much time alone in bed, with only his hand for company. During the months of recovery from his injury, wrung out by pain and grief, he'd had neither the opportunity nor the inclination to find a lover, even for one night. And at first, a little voice of doubt had shadowed his thoughts, making him question whether anyone would even want him again. He'd moved past that—his leg wasn't going to grow back, and if anyone had a problem with it they weren't someone he wanted to sleep with anyway. But he'd felt so distant from everyone else, it didn't seem worth the effort to bridge the gap.

Maybe it was just the bond, but he didn't feel distant from Nick. Except in the most literal sense, in that there was still unfortunately clothing and space between them.

He had to focus on the case, not on Nick. "I know Rook and Dominic had unbonded familiars looking into it, when they could," he said, "but I realized I'd never asked you. Do you know where Wyatt lived? Did he have an apartment, roommates we might talk to?" He swallowed, not wanting to ask. "Potential lovers?"

Nick cocked his head. "You were more than just friends who served together, I take it."

Jamie felt heat creep into his face. "Aye."

"What did his witch think about that?"

It seemed an odd question. "Eddie? He kept look out for us more than once. He and Wyatt loved each other, but more like…like brothers. Besides, Eddie liked women, anyway." Jamie shook his head. "None of that matters. Just answer my question."

"No." Nick folded his arms over his chest. "As in, 'no, I don't know.' I put out word among the feral community, trying to find out if he had an apartment. Roommates, as you suggested. But no one seems to know anything. It's like he was a ghost."

"So you had the same thought—that there might be something in his apartment, or wherever he laid his head," Jamie said. Rook's warning about Nick came back to him. "Why didn't you say anything?"

Nick shrugged. "I hadn't found anything out. There didn't seem to be any reason to bring it up."

"You're part of the MWP now, Nick." Jamie tried to keep the irritation out of his voice and failed.

Nick seemed about to protest, but caught himself. "Fine. I won't do it again. I'm not used to working with other people, that's all. I'll let you know if I learn anything. In the meantime, though, there's something else I'd like us to do."

Jamie could think of any number of things he'd like to do, but from Nick's grim expression, he had the feeling none of them were about to be suggested. "What's that?"

Nick lowered his head, and the fall of his hair cut off the light from his face. "I didn't want to do this, but we've no choice. It's time to talk to the ferals of Central Park."

The brisk fall air felt good against Nick's skin, after the close confines of the tenement. Gray skies stretched overhead, and the scent of threatening rain rode the wind. He matched his stride to Jamie's as they made their way through the bustle of the streets. Neither spoke, but the silence was strangely companionable.

No. He couldn't get too comfortable with the witch. Certainly not until he figured out exactly what Jamie wanted from him. If he really was trying to convince Nick to make their situation permanent, or if he had some other scheme in mind.

They went up Fifth Avenue, past the Italianate mansions and fancy churches. He kept his eyes fixed on the street, bands tightening around his chest. Rumor had it the massacre at the church had started because the Vandersee family sold off one of their own to a witch, to hide the fact they had familiar blood. As if being a familiar was something to be ashamed of.

Plenty thought it was. He lifted his head again, tossed his hair. To hell with anyone who believed he ought to feel bad for being himself.

He became aware of Jamie's eyes on him. He looked down, saw a little grin on Jamie's face. "What?"

"Nothing," Jamie said. "Just admiring the view."

"Lots to see, if you're into architecture," Nick said, deliberately misunderstanding.

"I'm more of a natural studies man, myself."

He shouldn't feel pleased, over some witch's compliments. Not when he'd just told himself to keep his distance, that Jamie must have some ulterior motive. But he did, anyway.

When they reached the Plaza at Fifth and 59th, traffic slowed to a crawl. Some group stood right at the entrance to the park, facing outward. The sound of a shouting voice echoed over the chatter of those who had stopped to gawk.

"What's this, then?" Jamie asked, brow furrowing. "Temperance league? Votes for familiars?"

Nick's height gave him the advantage. But when he spotted the man at the heart of the gathering, he would as soon not have looked. "Ingram."

The preacher stood there in his severe black coat and hat, like an unusually puritanical crow. Members of his flock formed a dark-clad mass behind him, while others moved through the crowd with offering baskets held out.

"He's the Heirs of Adam looney, ain't he?" Jamie asked.

Nick grinned, despite himself. "Not an admirer?"

"Considering he calls us devil-worshippers for following the teachings of the Belfast Pope, and for acknowledging Mary Magdalene as the Holy Familiar?" Jamie cast Nick a sardonic look. "I can't say as I've considered inviting him over for a cup of tea, no."

The crowd forced them to slow, which meant having to listen to Ingram spew his bile. It was much like his attempt at preaching in front of Caballus: a lot of nonsense about Eve and the Serpent, but with the added bonus of raving about the Whore of Babylon. So Ingram had problems with women as well as familiars; not much of a surprise. That type always did.

"How long have we campaigned for laws against the vile practice of sodomy?" Ingram ranted on, hands clenched fervently in front of him. "A practice spread among us by familiars, to weaken true men? But no—our politicians refuse, turn aside from the path of righteousness, so they might suckle at the teat of magic."

"I ain't certain whether the fellow needs a good tumble, or should be banned from ever touching another person," Jamie said sotto voce.

Nick chuckled. He turned his attention from Ingram, let his eye rove over the crowd. One of the parishioners behind Ingram caught his attention. Like the rest, he was dressed all in black, his hair cut severely short. He held his hands clasped before him, lips moving frantically, eyes squeezed shut as if his entire body poured effort into his prayers.

"Society must turn its back on the dangerous practice of using magic." Ingram flung his arm out as if to indicate the park, or maybe all of New York. "We've allowed Satan to corrupt us with the promise of easy solutions to our problems, rather than setting our hands to the hard work God intended. How has he done that, friends?"

Jamie rolled his eyes. "I was just as happy not to do the hard work of dying from infection, after the surgeon took my leg, thanks."

"By sending demons to mislead our children. They let Satan in, and he teaches them to take on the forms of animals. Who then tempt others from the righteous path." Ingram pointed dramatically at Nick. "There! One of the devil's minions walks among us even now, spreading evil and corrupting the hearts of men."

Nick tensed. But the crowd didn't seem particularly interested in him, beyond a couple of glances.

The frantically praying man behind Ingram opened his eyes, though. A shock went through Nick at the sight of pale golden irises.

The man was a familiar.

But why the hell would any familiar throw his lot in with Ingram? Was he deranged? Certainly, he didn't look as though he was there against his will. Quite the opposite, given the venomous glare he gave Nick.

Maybe he just needed some encouragement. "Hey, you," Nick called. "If you get tired of listening to this horse shit, come see me. There will always be a place for you at Caballus. You don't have to be ashamed of who you are."

The familiar paled, closed his eyes, and began to pray even more frantically, if possible.

"Come on," Jamie said, touching Nick's elbow. "You can't save everyone."

Nick gladly followed him. Once they were away, Jamie said, "Ingram is crazy if he thinks people are going to stop using magic. Especially the rich. No society lady is going to give up the witch in the laundry, using hexes to make her whites brighter, let alone the rest of it."

"Unfortunately," Nick agreed.

Jamie's brows rose. "You ain't telling me you *agree* with him?"

"That I'm a minion of Satan?" Nick snorted. "Hardly. But the more hexes we use, the less value familiars have as anything other than a source of magic."

He still remembered the stuffy room, lined with medical texts, a human skeleton displayed in one corner. The way the man behind the desk had laughed at Nick, while explaining that of course it was impossible to admit a familiar to the college. Not when a familiar would just quit the moment he found his witch.

"But you run a saloon and a tenement," Jamie pointed out.

Nick ground his teeth together. "Not my first choice, witch."

"Oh." Jamie was quiet for a moment. Then he said, "Ingram was right about one thing, though."

"What's that?"

"You are a temptation." Jamie winked.

Heat flushed through Nick's body. "Somehow I don't think that's the sort of tempting he had in mind," he said, before he could think better of it.

"I don't know. He was pretty focused on the whole sodomy thing."

It was just harmless flirting. Flirting, and doughnuts, and that little moan when Jamie had tipped back his head in surrender.

It didn't mean a thing.

Chapter 10

As they entered the park, the wind picked up, and a damp gust flung leaves at them. Jamie hunched his shoulders and shoved his hands deeper into the pockets of his overcoat. His fingers encountered a glass bottle; he'd forgotten to take out the oil from the other day.

He'd been wrong about what Nick wanted from him that day in specific. But not in general. At least, he didn't think so, considering the looks Nick had given him since.

He'd been alone for a year, mourning. But Wyatt had only been dead for days. A part of him cringed when he flirted, and another part yearned, and still a third part clung to sorrow, until he didn't know what he wanted any more. Or ought to want; or was permitted to want.

"You *cannot* tell anyone about this," Nick said.

"What is it I ain't telling, exactly?" Jamie asked.

"There are a handful of ferals living wild in the park." Nick's reluctance was clear in every line of his body. "Since that's illegal, they stay away from non-ferals most of the time."

"But you still know them," Jamie said. He shook his head in admiration. "Rook was right. You really do know every feral in the city."

Nick's brown cheeks flushed darker. "They know they can trust me. Which is why you can't tell anyone. Thank God you didn't wear your uniform today, or we'd never even get near them."

Jamie glanced up at him. "Is that why you haven't told anyone you're working with the MWP?"

He'd hoped he was wrong, but Nick's expression told him otherwise. "The MWP doesn't care about ferals," Nick said after a long moment. "At least, not until after they're dead, and then only if magic or hexes were involved. The regular police are even worse. We're on our own. So it's up to us to look out for each other."

"I see," Jamie said. He wanted to argue, but wasn't sure he could. If Nick was wrong, then why had only the two newest, most inexperienced MWP detectives been assigned the feral murders? When the millionaire Jacobs had been bashed over the head, no amount of effort to solve the case had been too great.

"Some of the ferals we meet might be…a little odd," Nick said. The troubled note in his voice caught Jamie's attention. "Most of them make sure to take human form on a regular schedule, at least for a few hours, but it's not always enough."

"Enough for what?"

"To remember they're familiars." Nick's breath turned to steam in the cold air. "We aren't meant to stay in one shape for too long at a stretch. If a familiar remains in animal shape for an excessive amount of time, they start to forget their human side. Become more and more an animal, until in the end, no memory of their human self is left."

"Oh." Jamie shivered. "And if they stay human overlong?"

Nick's eyes widened. "Well. Not a question most non-familiars would think to ask. It's just as bad. We forget our animal selves. Become more and more human, until we can't remember being anything else." Nick shuddered, like a horse flicking flies from its hide.

Jamie took the time to think through his words before responding. The image of Nick strolling up Fifth Avenue returned to him forcefully. The way he'd tossed his head, nostrils slightly flared. An arch to his neck just as proud and strong as the horse he could become. Like he didn't give a damn about all the wealth and power surrounding them.

Like he'd spit in the devil's eye, if he had half the chance.

"It's just as bad, because you're losing *you* either way, right?" Jamie asked.

Nick's gait stuttered. "I…yes. I'm not a horse, or a human. I'm a familiar. Whichever shape I happen to be in at the moment doesn't change that."

Jamie nodded. "Seems like this is the sort of thing they ought to teach…I was going to say when we join the MWP, but by then it's too late."

Nick shrugged. "I'm not disagreeing, witch. But right now, we've got more pressing matters."

Nick led the way to the trees near the old reservoir, not far from Cleopatra's Needle. "Bess likes to hunt this part of the park," he said, scanning the branches over their heads. "So she spends a lot of time perching near—there."

A Red-tailed Hawk sat on a low-hanging limb, one foot drawn up and her feathers slightly fluffed. But though her pose was casual, Jamie felt certain she watched them closely.

Nick glanced around, as if making sure no one else was nearby. Then he called up: "Bess! I need to talk to you. It's important."

She put her other foot down and sleeked her feathers, but made no move to join them.

"He's with me," Nick said, with a nod at Jamie. Jamie noted he didn't add anything along the lines of *"You can trust him."*

Apparently Nick's presence served as enough reassurance, because the hawk glided down. Before her talons touched the ground, she transformed into a middle-aged woman wearing a simple dress and nothing more.

When she spoke, her voice was rusty. The words came slow, as though she struggled a bit to remember them. Was she one of those who had spent too much time in her animal form, and started to forget her familiar self?

"What do you want?" She directed the question at Nick, but never took her eyes off Jamie. They were a deep, dark brown like her hawk form's, and watched him with the same intensity.

"We're looking into the feral murders here in the park," Nick said. "Do you know anything about them?"

A shiver ran through Bess, and she folded her arms over her chest. "They happened at night. I was asleep. I didn't see anything."

"That ain't what Nick asked," Jamie pointed out. She knew something, he was sure of it.

As she spoke and moved, Bess seemed to grow more comfortable in her skin. As though using the human half of herself was like stretching a stiff muscle, easier to move the more it was worked.

"I don't pay attention to humans," she said scornfully. "I hunt, sleep, and live as a hawk. What do I care about some wraith?" It sounded as though she was trying to convince herself as much as them.

"Wraith?" Nick asked.

She sighed. "Go ask the owl north of here. He likes to sleep in a hole in a tree in the Ramble, not far past Bow Bridge."

"Where the second body was found," Jamie said.

Bess looked at him as though he were an idiot. "Yes. Now leave me alone. Some of us still haven't eaten today."

Bess shifted into hawk form and took off, quickly disappearing from view. "Friendly sort," Jamie said dryly. "Do many ferals live in the park, then?"

"Not many." Nick started off. "And don't ask for details, because you aren't getting them." There were too many ways this could go wrong. "And don't tell any other witches, or your friends at the MWP. If I find out witches are hunting the park for familiars..." He let the implied threat linger in the air.

Jamie's dark brows drew together. How the man still managed to look handsome with a scowl on his face, Nick didn't know. "I ain't going to tell anyone. Far as I can see, they ain't hurting anything if they want to live here in animal form."

"Some would say it's a waste of magic," Nick challenged. Jamie had taken him by surprise earlier, when he'd instantly understood Nick's point about familiars being neither human nor animal. "They could be making money for some witch. Instead they're just moochers living off the bounty of the park."

Jamie's scowl eased into a troubled frown. "I suppose. I mean, I can see how people might say that."

Of course he did. Just like any witch.

"But it ain't doing any harm," Jamie went on. "So why shouldn't they stay?"

Did Jamie believe that, or was he just saying it to keep Nick happy? He didn't seem like the deceptive sort. Nick had already trusted him too much by letting him know ferals lived in the park to begin with. Today, Jamie's uncle was rounding up so-called dangerous familiars. Tomorrow, it might be any unbonded familiars at all.

Golden leaves tumbled from the trees as they strolled in silence. The clouds thickened as they walked, and the scent of rain touched the air. They crossed Bow Bridge, entering the Ramble. The little woodland seemed to cut them off from the rest of the park, even more than the North Woods had done. Hills rose and dived more sharply, interspersed by stretches of gray bedrock.

A short distance north of the bridge, they came across the owl's tree. Rather than a rich red or blazing yellow, its leaves had turned brown, mottled with spots of black. Many had already fallen to create an ugly carpet around its roots, and the limbs seemed to be slowly breaking and crumbling away. The bark hung off in sheets, revealing rot beneath.

Anywhere else, it wouldn't have been odd. Trees got sick and died, just like everything else. But here…

"Huh," Jamie said, coming to a halt. Rain began to patter down around them, and he pulled up the collar of his coat. "I thought the Great Hex was supposed to keep everything in the park, you know, healthy. Or healthful. Both."

"It's probably just an old tree," Nick said, as if he knew a damn thing about horticulture. "Nothing a hex can do about that."

"Maybe," Jamie said dubiously. "Do you think this is the right tree, then?"

Nick cupped his hands around his mouth and called. "Owl! Bess sent me to you. I'm Nick."

Several moments of silence followed, his call echoing weirdly through the Ramble. Then a piece of bark seemed to peel off a nearby oak. Nick registered the fragment as a Screech Owl only an instant before it landed and shifted into a thin, brown skinned man.

Unlike Bess, his clothing was in tatters, and far too short in both leg and arm for him. He held his yellow eyes nearly closed, and remained almost motionless once he landed, as if he still had feathers to camouflage him.

Scared, then. Of them, or something else?

"Nick." His voice was hoarse, more like an owl's angry hiss than anything human. "I've heard your name. From the other ferals."

A chill ran down Nick's spine. He never wanted to become like this—barely clinging to the memory of being a familiar. Still, he forced his face to remain neutral as he nodded. "I need your help. Do you know about the murders in the park?"

The owl went even stiller, if that were possible. His eyes closed altogether. Not quite playing dead, but almost. "There. On the bridge."

"That was one of them. Another feral was murdered before her." Nick paused. "Did you see the killer?"

For a moment, Nick didn't think the owl would answer. He stood absolutely motionless, and fear seemed to roll off him in waves. "Nothing human," the owl answered at last. "Nothing alive."

Nick exchanged a baffled glance with Jamie. "What do you mean, nothing alive?" Nick asked. "Ghosts don't use knives."

Memories of his familiar nature must have been rising in the owl, because he shook his head. A human gesture. "It was made from black mist, streaming around it in the wind. There were horns. Bones. *Teeth.* When it looked up—there was nothing beneath the hood. The woman had a gun. She shot it, but it kept coming. Like it couldn't be killed, because it wasn't alive to start with." His eyes snapped open, wide and bulging. "It was a wraith. And we're all cursed now."

Then he changed into owl form and was gone.

The rain chose that moment to turn into a downpour. Within seconds, every inch of Jamie's exposed skin was soaked. Water streamed from the brim of his hat.

"Is there somewhere we can take shelter?" he asked over the rush.

"The Cave isn't far from here," Nick said, and started off, forcing Jamie to follow.

The Cave was well hidden, accessible from the Lake by boat, and down a flight of stone steps by foot. Foliage and artfully placed boulders hid the entrance until they were practically on it.

Nick ducked inside first. "Empty," he grunted. "Good."

The Cave was both narrow and shallow—but it was dry, which was what mattered. Jamie took his hat off and shook the water onto the floor. "Do people take shelter in here often, then?"

"You could say that." Nick leaned against the wall, his long black hair dripping water. "It's easily accessible if you know it's here. Hidden from prying eyes…let's just say more than a few men and women have found it a convenient spot for either work or pleasure."

"Oh." Jamie's face flamed at the thought they might have interrupted a couple in the midst of…things. "That's good. That it was empty, I mean."

Nick didn't bother to reply, only stared at the rain, as though it had done him a personal slight.

Jamie groped for something to fill the silence between them. "What do you think?"

"About what?"

"The Wraith." The brief soaking had been just enough to set a chill in Jamie's bones, and he wrapped his arms around himself to still his shivers. "Do you think…I mean, the owl said it wasn't human."

Nick pulled off his scarf and wrung the moisture from it. "I think his imagination ran away with him. There aren't any such things as wraiths, or ghosts, or specters." He glanced at Jamie. "You don't believe in that nonsense, do you?"

"I…" Jamie trailed off, uncertain how to answer. Of course he believed in ghosts—who didn't? Everyone he knew had a story, if not of their own encounters, then those of a friend. Or a friend of a friend.

"Never mind." Nick's mouth thinned with displeasure. "No ghost killed Pia. Or your Wyatt."

Of that, Jamie felt more sure. "Nay. And he wasn't my Wyatt." Not anymore, anyway. If he ever had been. The thought hurt.

"Eddie's Wyatt, then."

"Why do you have to be such an arse?" Jamie snapped. He was wet, and cold, and trapped in a cave with a man who seemed determined to push him away at every turn. "I ain't your enemy."

"What do you want from me, witch?" Nick shoved himself off the stone wall and stalked across the Cave to where Jamie stood. In the dimness, it was hard to make out his expression. "Stop playing games and just tell me."

Jamie's throat constricted. He could think of all sorts of things he wanted from Nick. Nick's scent, of sweat and sweetness, seemed to go straight from his brain to his prick. He took a step back, fetched up against the rough rock wall. "What do you mean?" he managed to ask.

Nick crowded even closer, forcing Jamie to crane his head back to look up at him. Trapped between the much larger man and the cave wall, his mouth went dry with lust.

"Witches always want something." Nick's voice was low, an intimate growl. "Usually it's obvious. Magic. Money. Power. But you…I can't figure you out. You haven't used my magic without asking. You brought me breakfast. You defer to my judgment. You flirt. I'm not falling for your tricks. Just tell me what the hell it is you want from me."

Grief and desire warred in Jamie's blood. "I want to find out who killed Wyatt," he said. "That's it. If you feel like you got to be a fucking bastard about it, fine. But don't you go accusing me of trying to trick you somehow. I don't know why you're so damned angry all the time, but I ain't done anything but try to be nice to you."

Nick's lip curled. "I don't want you to be nice to me."

"Then let's turn the question around. What do *you* want?"

Nick's eyes widened slightly. He looked like a man struggling to come up with an answer…or struggling against the answer that had sprung to mind.

Then Nick's mouth was on Jamie's—hard, almost angry, but desperate too. Jamie could feel Nick's teeth through the press of their lips, and he returned the kiss with desperation of his own. He thrust his fingers into Nick's hair, clutching at the soft strands as if to keep him from pulling away. Nick's hand slid around the back of Jamie's neck, gripping the exposed skin between collar and hair. Jamie found himself pressed between the hard stone of the wall, and the hard muscle of the man. And oh God, the sensation did things to him, dragged a moan up from the depths of body or soul, or both.

Nick broke off the kiss to stare at Jamie. His eyes were wild, lips parted, breath rasping as if he'd been put through a race. "I don't fuck witches."

Well, that was damned unconvincing. "But do you let witches fuck you?" Jamie asked. "Because I have oil in my pocket right now." He shrugged at Nick's incredulous look. "When you ordered me to meet you the other afternoon, I thought you had something different in mind." He'd tried not to think too hard about why he hadn't bothered to take the oil out of his pocket. "So what do you say?"

"Go to hell," Nick growled, before slamming his mouth down on Jamie's again.

They wrestled Jamie's overcoat off—or maybe they wrestled each other, or both. A tangle and shove of limbs, and Jamie barely had time to rescue the oil from the pocket before the coat fell on the cave floor. Nick grabbed him roughly, tried to spin him to face the wall, and nearly sent him to the ground.

"Watch it—the leg—"

Nick steadied him, then pushed Jamie's shoulders forward, so his arms braced against the wall, hips canted back. There was something delicious about the surety of Nick's big hands on him, pushing his suit coat up, unbuttoning bracers, then gliding around to start on the buttons of his trousers.

The chilly air was a shock against heated skin. Nick plucked the bottle from Jamie's hand. Jamie wanted to turn around and take a look, but before he could, Nick's arm snaked around his waist. The length of Nick's cock pressed against one buttock, leaving behind the slickness of precome.

Then Nick's fingers pushed into him, and Jamie closed his eyes, struggling to relax, to breathe. He moaned something incoherent, his face resting against his arms, the rugged wall of the cave inches away. "Nick..."

Nick shifted position. The broad head of his prick pressed against Jamie's opening. "This what you want, witch?" and it was more a challenge than a question.

"Aye, damn it," Jamie said.

"Take it then."

Chapter 11

Jamie bit his lip against the stretch as Nick pushed into him. For a moment, he rode the edge of pain—but then something inside relaxed, and Nick grunted as he shoved further in, all the way to the hilt.

"Fuck," Nick swore. He withdrew, almost all the way out, but before Jamie could whimper a protest, he buried himself again, with a twist of his hips that sent Jamie's back to arching and his hands scrabbling on the damp rock for purchase. Stars of pleasure spangled his vision.

He reached for his cock, but Nick slapped away his hand. "Oh no," he growled in Jamie's ear. "You didn't think I'd take it easy on you, did you?"

Jamie made a strangled sound, certain he'd never been more aroused in his life. Nick's arm tightened around his waist—and then he started to thrust in earnest.

The rain swallowed Jamie's moans, while Nick fucked him mercilessly. Nick's arm around his waist, face nearly pushed into the wall, his body speared on Nick's cock while his own ached for relief. He tried to brace his arms, to push back, but his strength was nothing against Nick's. Somehow, that only made it more exciting.

"You like this, don't you, witch?" Nick said—no, demanded, because of course he did, this was Nick after all. His teeth grazed the exposed back of Jamie's neck.

"Bite me," Jamie gasped, before he could think better of it.

Nick's teeth closed on the back of his neck, not hard enough to break the skin, but enough to send a shock through Jamie. He groaned, and the sound or the act seemed to push Nick further to the edge. Nick's big hand closed on Jamie's prick, even as his hips drove harder. Jamie gave himself over to all of it: the grip tugging hard on his cock, the strong arm holding him up, the teeth in his neck and the prick in his arse.

The heat of the bond, burning in his chest like he'd swallowed a star.

His spunk hit the wall with the force of his release. Nick left off biting him, pressed his face into Jamie's shoulder, and shuddered as he came.

Jamie blinked slowly. He felt bruised: his arms against the stone, the back of his neck. His arse, which would make sitting a reminder.

He wasn't going to think about Wyatt right now. Especially not the murmur of guilt starting at the hind part of his brain.

Nick released him and pulled free. He didn't say anything. Jamie hauled his drawers and trousers back up; by the time he'd buttoned his bracers, Nick had retreated to the Cave's entrance.

Everything that had been so good moments before now felt horribly awkward. Jamie cleared his throat. "Nick…"

"Are there any bat familiars working for the MWP?" Nick asked abruptly.

Jamie gaped at him. It wasn't that he expected a fuck against the wall to change anything between them, but at least Nick could look at him. "I…I don't think so," he said. "Why?"

"Because, whatever else he might be, this Wraith is flesh and blood." Nick's eyes remained fixed on the rain. It had slowed to a drizzle, drops ruffling the surface of the Lake and weighing down the orange and yellow leaves of the foliage clustered around the Cave's opening. "What we need is for someone to keep an eye on the park at night, and report anything suspicious to us the moment they see it. An owl might do, but they're slow fliers. If the MWP doesn't have someone, I do."

"Oh." Jamie tried to focus on the case. "We should let Dominic and Rook know what we're doing. What we discovered."

"You do it. I'll find Rodrigo." Nick finally glanced Jamie's way, though only for a second.

"He's the bat?" Jamie asked.

"Yes. Don't forget to make sure the MWP hands over the cash to pay him." Nick took a step toward the entry, then paused. "Remember, you swore not to tell anyone about the ferals here in the park. Come up with whatever lie you like, but don't breathe a word about Bess or the owl."

"I won't," Jamie said. Nick looked as though he was about to leave, so he added, "Wait."

Nick stopped. "What?"

God. Jamie's cheeks burned, but he wasn't going to let Nick walk out like nothing at all had happened. "It was good. You know."

Nick swallowed, the brown skin of his throat working. "It won't happen again."

He spoke the words with such finality that Jamie couldn't think how to answer. Nick ducked his dark head, hunched his shoulders, and vanished back out into the overcast fall day.

Jamie took his time getting back to the Coven. The encounter with Nick had left him off-balance and feeling as though he ought to be ashamed.

He hadn't slept with anyone for over a year, hadn't even *wanted* anyone. Too much pain, in his heart and his leg, to even think about it. And he'd chosen to break that drought with a man who wouldn't even look him in the eye afterward?

To hell with Nick. Jamie knew he should have insisted on going with him to find this bat familiar, but after the way Nick had acted, he just wanted to put as much distance as possible between them.

Which maybe was what Nick had hoped for all along. Who could tell? Nick was an arse at the best of times. If Jamie had any sense, he'd forget what they'd done. Put it all behind them and get on with the job.

He found Dominic and Rook at their desk, stacks of hexes piled around them. Dominic looked exhausted, his eyes red as he peered carefully at one hex after the other, while Rook took notes on his observations. "Running you ragged, ain't they?" Jamie asked with forced cheer.

Dominic's lips pressed together as he put down the magnifying glass. Rook had no such reticence. "Running us in circles with pointless nonsense," he said, glaring at the cheap paper hexes. "I hate this."

Jamie hooked a spare chair from a nearby desk and dragged it over. He sank down with a wince, reminded despite himself of the encounter with Nick. Heat rose to his cheeks, and he prayed no one noticed. "What's wrong?"

"The Police Board want us to be...thorough," Dominic said carefully.

"By which they mean literally inspecting each and every hex to testify they were drawn by the same hand." Rook flung up his own hands in frustration. "It's stupid. If the first twenty are, surely the last twenty will be as well."

"A random sample would be enough to issue a warrant," Dominic said. "Should the perpetrator ever be caught, anyway. There would be plenty of time to go through them all before a trial."

"So where is my dear brother?" Rook asked. "Galloped off on his own already?"

"Nay. We decided to split up." Jamie shifted uncomfortably. "Get more than one thing done at a time."

"I'll bet," Rook muttered. "Nick always—"

"Not now, Rook." Dominic put a soothing hand to Rook's arm. "I assume you came here to report, Jamie?"

"Aye. We questioned some potential witnesses." He gave them the barest outline of what he and Nick had discovered, leaving the identities of the ferals vague enough no one would guess they lived in the park in animal form.

He left out the part about fucking Rook's brother in the Cave, too.

"You just let Nick go off on his own, to bribe a civilian into becoming part of the investigation?" Rook asked when he finished.

"Ignore him," Dominic said to Jamie. "Nothing about this investigation is going to be routine. Including keeping all this to ourselves, and not sharing our information with Ferguson."

Jamie frowned. "We ain't?"

"What he doesn't know, the Police Board can't easily find out."

"Ah."

The truth was, none of this sat well with him. There was a chain of command, and Jamie had been used to following it, even before he'd joined the army. Hurley had raised him to know his duty, take orders, and bend the rules only so far. Now here he was hiding the truth about ferals living illegally in the park and deliberately failing to report to the chief.

It was as though he'd stepped through a mirror the night Wyatt died, and found himself in some twisted version of reality. "We'll keep at it, then."

"Try to rein Nick in," Rook said. "Make sure he includes you. I notice this bat familiar will be reporting to him, not you." Rook ground his teeth. "Mark my words, given half the chance he'll go galloping off alone and confront this Wraith character by himself, without any thought as to how dangerous it is. I'd prefer he not become the next victim."

Jamie's stomach twisted. However conflicted his feelings were at the moment, the thought of Nick getting hurt—sliced to pieces—made him sick.

Rook was Nick's brother. Maybe he could shed some light on the puzzle that was Nick. "But why? He knows I'd help him, so why not work with me instead of taking off on his own?"

Dominic shrugged. "He doesn't exactly trust witches."

"I don't fuck witches," Nick had said. But that had turned out to be a lie.

"Then what about Rook?" Jamie asked. "Whatever bad blood is between you, and I ain't asking you to say, surely he'd let you help."

Rook let out a cawing laugh, but it held no humor. "Me? I'm the biggest traitor of all, according to Nick. I joined the MWP, when I could have stayed with him. Worked at his dive bar and slept in his apartment —what more could I *possibly* have wanted out of life?"

Jamie winced at the bitterness in Rook's voice. Still… "That does sound like Nick. It's a shame, though. Brothers shouldn't let something like that come between them. Family's about the only thing you can count on in this world, ain't it?"

Rook took Dominic's hand firmly in his. "Dominic is my family. And Cicero, silly cat that he is. Isaac. The rest."

"What about Nick, though?" Jamie asked. "That is, does he have anyone?"

Nick seemed so…solitary. The other ferals obviously looked to him, trusted him, but Jamie hadn't gotten so much as a hint there was anyone he could look to in turn. So he wasn't surprised when Rook shrugged again. "Nick, need someone? That's a laugh. It's him against the world, don't you know."

Was that why Nick hadn't wanted to look at Jamie, after buggering him against the wall? Because for just a moment, he'd let himself be… not alone?

But that would imply the sex meant something more than just a quick tumble, whether he'd meant it to or not.

Hell. Jamie felt more twisted up than a bag of eels.

Dominic sifted through the hexes piled on his desk. "Rook, would you mind flying down to Owen's laboratory and getting a pair of those hexes he uses to test blood stains and the like?"

Rook frowned suspiciously. "Why?"

"It occurs to me we should have some on hand. Just in case." Dominic's attempt at innocence fooled no one. But Rook only shook his head, shifted into crow form, and glided away.

Dominic rubbed his forehead. "Now he's singing bawdy songs

through the bond, just to annoy me."

"I take it you wanted to talk to me alone?" Jamie asked.

"I probably should have tried to be a bit more subtle about it." Dominic rubbed his forehead a second time. "Dear lord, Rook, those aren't even the proper lyrics." He let out a sigh and sat back. "I only wanted to say that Rook and Nick might bicker, and refuse to see one another for months on end, but if something happened to Nick, it would break Rook's heart."

"You're asking me to keep an eye on him," Jamie guessed.

"He's the last of Rook's family." Dominic met his gaze frankly. "I'd take it as a personal favor."

"Aye." Jamie levered himself to his feet. "I'll see what I can do."

Jamie didn't have a desk, so he left the detective's area. Maybe he'd sit in the stables for an hour or two, clear his head and consider what he ought to do next. He didn't want Nick confronting the murderer alone, that was for certain. He wouldn't have even if Dominic hadn't felt the need to ask him.

Poor Nick. Nick, who would lose his mind if he knew Jamie felt even a flicker of pity for him. Too angry and proud to unbend even a little, who thought he could carry the weight of the world on his shoulders, with no family to rely on.

Muriel drove Jamie crazy, but if he'd had to make his way alone after he'd lost his leg, it would have been a thousand times harder. Having her to rely on, when he was still skinny and shaking, barely able to use a crutch let alone a prosthetic, had made all the difference. She'd given him a place to rest and recover, a refuge where he could try to put the war behind him and adjust to a life that wasn't quite what he'd imagined.

Nick didn't have that.

Had Wyatt?

It didn't seem likely. Not if his mother and brother had belonged to some kind of anti-familiar church like the one that looney Ingram ran. They probably weren't too keen on the fact Wyatt slept with men, either; those kind never liked anyone different from themselves. Even if Wyatt had been desperate enough to go to them, they would hardly have welcomed him with open arms.

Jamie touched the pendant hidden under his clothing. If only they could find where Wyatt had been staying, maybe they could discover some clue as to what he'd been doing. Even if it didn't lead them to his killer, it would be nice to know if he'd had someone to rely on. Someone he could trust, the way he apparently hadn't trusted Jamie.

"Jamie!"

Startled, Jamie looked up, and saw his uncle coming toward him. "Uncle Hurley? Is everything all right?"

Hurley beamed at him. "I only just heard the good news today." He wagged a finger at Jamie. "Why didn't you let me know you'd made detective?"

Jamie's heart sank. It hadn't even occurred to him to let Hurley know. If his arrangement with Nick was meant to be permanent, he would have brought Nick over to meet the family the first day.

But it was just a sham. Just an excuse for them to be able to investigate.

Uncle Hurley would be disappointed. Jamie knew he should tell him anyway, but the words stuck in his throat. So he merely shrugged. "They've been keeping us busy."

"Good, good." Hurley clapped him on the shoulder. "I've got some news of my own that calls for a bit of a celebration. Surely you've enough time to dine with your favorite uncle? "

"You're my only uncle," Jamie pointed out with a grin. "But aye, I think I have the time."

Fucking Jamie had been a mistake. Of all the stupid things he'd done in his life, this had to be at the very top of the list.

Nick shook his head as he clopped down the stairs to the cellar. When he'd left the Cave, he'd had every intention of pretending it had never happened. Forget the way Jamie's hurt expression tugged at his heart. He'd wanted to pull the witch close again, kiss away the confused disappointment darkening Jamie's particolored eyes.

Nick couldn't stop thinking about it. The way Jamie had groaned, the taste of his skin when Nick bit his neck, the tight heat of his body around Nick's prick. It made him hard all over again, which put paid to any hopes that fucking the witch once might have been enough. Instead, it seemed to have made things even worse.

Nick tried to convince himself it was just the accursed bond. But he knew better than that. Some bonded pairs fucked, and some—like his damned brother and Dominic—fell in love and made cow-eyes at each other. There were those who fell in love but didn't give a damn about sex. Some were good friends, but either had other people, or didn't care for either love or fucking.

So it wasn't the fault of the bond, but Nick's own damned stupidity. Jamie was Inspector O'Malley's nephew. Jamie might not be virulently anti-familiar, but he'd been quick enough to argue his uncle's case. If he had the slightest notion what Nick had hidden down here, Nick would probably end up hauled off to the Menagerie alongside his charges.

What had happened in the Cave had been insanity, nothing less. It couldn't—wouldn't—happen again.

Assuming Jamie would even be willing, the way Nick had acted toward him.

Nick opened the hidden door in the cellar far more forcefully than he needed to. Before his eyes could even adjust to the dim light of the lantern, hands seized him by the vest.

He swung without even thinking, heard a grunt as his fist connected with flesh. He'd been spoiling for a fight all afternoon, and there was a strange sort of relief in being able to finally have a target. He twisted to avoid a knee to the groin, grabbed a handful of clothing, and slammed his attacker into the wall.

"Stop!" Rachel shouted.

Nick blinked, his eyes adjusting. Conrad glared at him, yellow eyes bright with fury. "Let go of me, horse," he snarled, and there was a bit of the tiger's growl in the warning.

"What the hell was that all about?" Nick asked, tightening his grip.

Conrad hissed, lips drawing back from his teeth. "We're tired of sitting in this trap of yours." He wrenched himself free, and this time Nick let him go. "How much longer do you think we'll wait?"

Nick took a deep breath, tamping down on his anger. The small room had taken on the natural smells of too many people and not enough fresh air. "Not much longer."

"It's always night down here," Rachel said. She looked anxious, though, not angry like Conrad. "We haven't seen the sun in…I don't know. It's impossible to keep track of time, with nothing but the lantern."

"I want to go home," said one of the younger ferals. He kicked morosely at the floor.

"I know you're afraid," Nick began.

"We're not afraid." Conrad made a show of wiping his sleeve clean, like a cat licking itself. "We're sick of waiting for the coppers to find us."

Nick's temper reached its limit. He poked a finger into Conrad's chest. "You go running off without a plan, you're as good as caught."

"Maybe, but I don't hear you offering any plans," Conrad retorted.

"Then stop complaining and listen up." Nick glared at him. "I've managed to find one of Wyatt's contacts. The one who arranged things with the ferry boat captain."

Fur and feathers, it hadn't been easy. After he talked to Rodrigo about keeping watch on the park, he'd trudged all over Manhattan, hunting down any information. He still hadn't been able to find out anything about Wyatt, or where the eagle had been staying, but he'd made more progress than anyone else could have.

As Rook had said at the beginning of all this mess, Nick knew half the ferals in New York, if not more. Not just knew them—he had their trust. Because he'd proved himself over and over again, putting the welfare of ferals ahead of everything else in his life.

Maybe it had cost him: friends, family. Lovers. But he had to believe it was worth the sacrifice.

"I've sent a note," Nick said. "I need to coordinate with the ferry captain. But with any luck, you'll be on your way in two or three days."

"Praise God," Rachel said, closing her eyes fervently.

"We'd better be." Conrad took a step forward, back into Nick's personal space.

Damn it, he was tired. He'd spent hours tramping around the island, until his feet and legs ached. Now he faced a long night at the saloon, half-hoping, half-dreading Rodrigo showed up in the middle of it with news about the killer.

Conrad was tired too, surely, of the tiny space and its four walls. But Nick decided he didn't care at the moment.

Nick echoed the step, so they were right up in each other's faces. "You want to leave?" Nick asked. "You want to find your own food, transportation, and water? Well, go to hell. You can't."

Conrad's eyes widened, but Nick only pointed at the young ferals. "I don't give a damn if you get caught and shipped off to the Menagerie. Not with your attitude. But them? You run, and you're putting everyone at risk. You might think you wouldn't give the coppers anything, but after a few days of accommodations that make this cellar look like a palace? No food, no water? Some people might stand that sort of treatment, sure, but I won't take the risk you're one of them." He let his arm drop. "So sit down. And you grab me like that again, I promise you'll be sorry."

Conrad's yellow eyes sparked. But he took a slow step back.

"Fine," he said. Having to get in the last word. "But don't take too long."

Nick stepped to the door. "It'll take as long as it takes," he said. And shut the door before Conrad could respond.

Chapter 12

"To your promotion!" Hurley said, raising his glass. They sat at a table in a saloon not far from Jamie's apartment.

Jamie's throat tightened. "So what is this good news you have to share?" he asked, hoping to divert Hurley's attention from himself.

Hurley put down his beer and wiped the foam from his mustache. "My work on the squad has been noticed. I'm getting a medal, and word has it Senator Pemberton himself will be at the ceremony."

"That's wonderful," Jamie said. But his normal rush of pride was tempered by the memory of Nick's words yesterday, concerning the Pemberton Act. About how it punished everyone for the deeds of a few.

Uncle Hurley wouldn't be involved in anything wrong; of that much Jamie was certain. He was just doing his duty, that was all. Arguments about whether a law was just or not belonged to the politicians. It was a policeman's job to enforce, not to judge.

Wasn't it?

He had the feeling Nick wouldn't agree with that sentiment at all. Thank Mary, Jamie had let Nick go off on his own, because otherwise this dinner would be even more painfully awkward.

"I'm glad you took my advice," Hurley said. "So what sort of familiar did you get?"

"A horse." Should he go into more detail, or would that only make things worse when he and Nick parted ways at the end of the month?

Hurley didn't seem particularly interested, though. "Makes sense you'd pick a horse, Rough Rider." He grinned and held out an unlit cigar. "Quick—draw up a fire hex and show me your magic."

Jamie shook his head. "No one uses hexes to light their cigar." Well, maybe rich nobs; that sounded like something people with too much money might do.

"I ain't asking you to do it all the time. Just this once." Hurley's grin faded a bit. "Take pride in your accomplishments, lad."

Jamie's chest tightened. Hurley wanted him to rely more on his history as a soldier. To parlay being a Rough Rider into a political career, or at least use it to move up the chain within the police department. Just like Hurley had done a few years ago, when he saved then-Commissioner Roosevelt from a poisoned hex.

"I can't, Uncle," Jamie said. "I promised not to use his magic unless I asked first."

The last of Hurley's smile vanished. "You did what? Why?"

Jamie shifted uneasily. "It's his magic, ain't it?"

"Nay. It's *yours.*" Hurley shook his head. "What sort of nonsense has the MWP put in your head? You're the witch, Jamie. It's up to you to decide when and how to use your familiar's magic, and for good reason." He leaned over the table. "One thing working on the squad has taught me, it's that the world is ordered the way it is for a reason. Familiars might look human, at least some of the time, but they ain't like you and me. They're controlled by their emotions. No logic at all. That's why the Good Lord gave them witches to watch over them."

Jamie tried to imagine Nick's response to the idea he needed anyone else ordering his life. "We're a team," he said.

"I never claimed you weren't," Hurley replied. "I'm sure you'll do fine together. Just remember who's holding the reins." He laughed at his own humor. Jamie managed a weak chuckle, and nothing more. The joke rubbed him the wrong way, leaving him unsure how to respond.

Nick would know. He wouldn't just quietly roll his eyes at Hurley's attitude.

Surely it wasn't worth picking a fight with Hurley tonight, though. Not when Jamie would be back to being unbonded in less than a month.

Jamie excused himself as soon as they cleared their plates and started back to his apartment. He'd managed to find a decent enough place, on the first floor so he had only a minimum of stairs to navigate. A couple of neighbors sat on the stoop, and he paused just long enough to exchange a few words with them before continuing in.

His crutch leaned against one of the two shabby chairs in what could generously be called a parlor. He sat down, rolled up his trouser leg, and unlaced the prosthetic with a sigh. The thing fit well enough and wasn't too heavy, but it was still a relief to have it off. Especially since he'd done more walking in the last two days than he was used to. He carefully cleaned the cup the stump rested in, and set it aside to dry overnight.

What was Nick doing now? Working, most like. He'd looked so tired this morning. Worn down, as if from more than the loss of a couple of nights' sleep. As if the weight of years and not days accumulated on his shoulders.

Jamie focused on the bond. On that little patch of warmth in his chest. It told him Nick's general direction, though nothing else. If Nick had been in horse form, at least they could have talked.

This was stupid. He wasn't some youth, swooning over his first love. Nick barely even seemed to tolerate Jamie's presence, most of the time.

He'd certainly tolerated Jamie well enough when he was balls-deep in him.

Maybe that was Nick's problem. He'd sworn he didn't fuck witches, but the draw between them had been undeniable from the first, even before they'd bonded. Did he feel he'd betrayed his principles?

Nick was full of fire, like the broncos real rough riders knew how to break. Jamie didn't want to break him, though. Didn't want him to lose that fighting spirit.

Jamie sighed and rubbed at his face. Wyatt had his principles, too, just like Nick. Surely he would have felt shame over his desertion, no matter the cause. Had he stayed away from Jamie because he couldn't stand to look him in the eye? Or had it been the inevitable court-martial he'd feared?

The main fighting had been over by the time Eddie and Wyatt had been given their special assignment, or so Jamie had been told. Wyatt had left the other Rough Riders behind, flown away, let everyone think he was dead. Most would judge it the act of a coward. Wyatt had never been that.

So what was the truth? Nick believed Wyatt left to avoid bonding with another witch…and maybe he was right, but the explanation didn't sit well with Jamie.

If only Jamie had been there to know for himself.

He stared at the lower part of his trouser leg, hanging empty without the prosthetic to fill it out. It had taken a while, but he'd made his peace with the loss. He still constantly wondered what might have happened if the artillery shell had fallen short, or overshot, or even come five minutes later. Could he have saved Eddie? Would he at least know why Wyatt had chosen a path that on the surface seemed so unlike him?

Nick had sent a bat to watch for a killer who struck only after dark. When Nick got word the Wraith was back, it would be night. Jamie wouldn't be with him, just as he hadn't been with Wyatt. Of course Rook was right, Nick wouldn't waste a single moment, when hesitation might mean life or death for the Wraith's next victim.

Maybe Nick would be fine. Apprehend the killer on his own. Or maybe something terrible would happen to Nick, something Jamie could prevent, if only he was there.

One way or another, Jamie would have to keep an eye on Nick, to make sure he didn't go into danger alone.

Jamie had already lost Wyatt to the killer. He'd be damned if he lost Nick as well.

Nick sat at his desk the next day, trying to make the numbers add up. The saloon was closed, and it was supposed to be their day off at the MWP, so he hadn't bothered leaving the building. The ledgers were sadly neglected, and working through the dry columns of profit and loss had seemed a good way to distract himself from thoughts of the witch. His witch.

Not that it had worked. He'd tossed and turned all night, memories of those moments in the Cave teasing him relentlessly. Followed by unexpected flashes of remorse over Jamie's look of disappointment and hurt. As a result, the ledger blurred in front of him no matter how much coffee he drank, and the bed in the other room tempted him to collapse into its sheets and not get back up again.

Which he couldn't do. He had work. People depending on him. No time for sleep or anything else.

There came a sharp rap on the door. Nick suppressed a sigh. No doubt one of the ferals from the tenement, wanting something. More time to make the rent, or a window needed replaced, or a perch had broken and they wanted to borrow a hammer. If he was lucky, it would be a better distraction than the numbers.

When he opened the door, it was to find Jamie's pale face staring back up at him.

"What the hell are you doing here?" Nick blurted.

Jamie's dark brows arched. "You wear spectacles?"

Nick touched the pince nez perched on his nose. "When I have to do close reading. What's it to you?"

"Nothing. They look good on you." Jamie glanced casually past him. "Getting the books in order, eh? My brother-in-law owns a Chinese laundry, and I kept his ledgers when I was younger, before I joined the MWP. I've a good head for math."

The desire to have someone else break their brain on the sums seized Nick with an almost physical longing. Unfortunately, it wasn't the only sort of physical longing he was feeling at the moment. The teasing thread of Jamie's sandalwood cologne was enough to send him right back to the Cave, and his cock hardened beneath his worsted trousers.

"I'm sorry about yesterday," he said, to remind himself as well as Jamie.

"I ain't." Jamie tipped his head back to meet Nick's eyes. The brown splotch amidst the green seemed redder today, probably due to the rust-colored vest Jamie wore. "Not about the fucking, at least. Are you?"

He wasn't, which was the damned problem. "Why are you here?" he asked instead of answering. "Haven't you got anything better to do?"

Jamie shrugged. "Nay." He paused. "Or should that be...*neigh?*"

He put enough of a whinny into the word to make the pun clear. "Hilarious," Nick said. "You and Rook should have your own Vaudeville act." He stepped back. Jamie's hip brushed his thigh as he passed, sending a shock of lust right to his groin. He cleared his throat before continuing. "Fine. You can help. Just stay out of my way. No wandering around on your own. You don't set foot outside my apartment without me, and you definitely don't go anywhere near the saloon."

"Aye," Jamie agreed. He stripped off his overcoat, then his suit coat. "Where do you want me to work?"

Nick dragged a second chair up to the desk, then turned the ledger to a page he'd already completed. Covering the running total and results with spare sheets of paper, he said, "Do this correctly, and you can stay."

It was an obvious test, but Jamie didn't seem put out. Instead, he only said, "Do you mind if I take off my leg?"

On the one hand, Nick wasn't sure letting Jamie make himself any more comfortable was a good idea. On the other, he didn't want to give Jamie the impression the prosthetic bothered him.

Not that he cared what Jamie thought, of course. "Go ahead."

He settled in on the other side of the desk, intending to focus on his work. But the prosthetic Jamie propped against the desk caught his eye. Was the foot wooden, beneath the sock and shoe, or one of the newer ones with a rubber covering to make steps less jarring? The calf was wooden, the frame metal, supporting a leather inner socket. The leather sheath with lacing would go around Jamie's thigh, just above the knee.

When he looked away, it was to find Jamie watching him, a little frown line between his brows. "That's not a Palmer," Nick said without thinking.

The frown eased into a laugh. "I'd hope not. Those were popular in the War Between the States. Mine is a little bit newer than that."

"Right," Nick said, feeling foolish. The handful of soldiers his father had treated had all been older, and that had been nearly twenty years ago as it was.

"You know something about prosthetics, then?" Jamie asked.

"No." Which was more or less true. "Had some acquaintances, older men, who had bits shot off by the Confederates." Nick didn't share his history with anyone, so he added, "Do you know anything about numbers? Because I didn't let you stay so you could talk my ear off."

Jamie only laughed and bent his head over the page. In an astonishingly short amount of time, he pushed the ledger in Nick's direction. Nick uncovered his calculations and shook his head. "Wrong answer."

"Let me see." Jamie studied it again, then tapped the page. "You made a mistake on line fifteen."

Nick snatched the ledger back, then cursed aloud. "Don't look so damned smug."

Jamie leaned forward, propped his elbows on the desk, and smirked. "So, can I stay and help?"

"Fine. But I'm not paying you." Nick stood up. "I'll make some more coffee."

Chapter 13

Though Nick didn't want to admit it, Jamie's presence helped the work go faster. Not just because he could do sums at a pace that made Nick's head spin. After a tense beginning, there was something oddly relaxing about having him there.

Having company, Nick corrected himself. It could have been anyone, really.

Except Nick had trouble sometimes, keeping his eyes on his work. He found himself sneaking glances at Jamie's profile. At the way Jamie bit his lip in concentration, just the slightest indentation of white teeth against pale pink. The way he ran his hand absently through his hair, until it stuck up every which way.

The sun went down, and Nick lit the lamps, then ducked out to the little restaurant two doors down. He returned with linguini and meatballs, accompanied by an inexpensive bottle of wine.

The wine might not have been the best idea. Nick had carefully not thought about his motives while buying it.

Jamie looked at the wine, then at Nick, but didn't say anything. Once they'd settled into the meal, Nick nodded at the ledger Jamie had put aside. "If you get tired of the MWP, you can always go into accounting."

Jamie speared a meatball on his fork. "Never thought about it, to be honest. Uncle Hurley always said I'd grow up to be a copper, just like him, so I didn't really consider anything else."

Another reason to dislike O'Malley, as if Nick needed one more.

"And you always do what he tells you?"

"Of course not!" Jamie focused his gaze on his linguini. "I mean, not exactly. I know my duty, that's all. You have to understand. Hurley took in my sister Muriel and me when we were just wee little things. He was like a dad to us. It ain't easy for a man to raise up two children on his own, but he did it without a word of complaint. How was I to let him down, after all that?"

Nick let out a noncommittal grunt. Jamie shrugged, and said, "I went to the MWP because I was worried he'd try to use his influence to move me up through the ranks at the regular police. I wanted to earn it, and my witch potential was high enough for them to take me. Hell, Uncle Hurley even encouraged it, since I'd make a bit more money than a regular copper would." He paused. "Then one day last year, Uncle Hurley came by with news. He'd gotten me a place in the First Volunteer Cavalry."

The devil? Nick sat forward. "Had you asked…?"

"Nay. Don't get me wrong," Jamie hastened to add. "I was glad to do my duty. I served with some fine men. But it wasn't something I chose, exactly. Uncle Hurley had a personal connection with Roosevelt, after saving him from that poisoned hex back in '95, and called in a favor to get me a place in the unit. The next thing I knew, I was on my way to San Antonio."

Nick shook his head wordlessly. Who signed up their nephew to go off and fight in a war, without even asking if it was something he wanted first? Nick noted their wine glasses were empty and refilled them. "You didn't try to talk him out of it?"

"It was already too late. And I would've sounded like a coward, wouldn't I?" Jamie's eyes hardened slightly. "It was chaos by the time we reached Tampa. Troops everywhere, and not enough ships to take them. We had to leave the horses behind—some cavalry, eh?" Jamie downed a good portion of his wine. "Without horses, once we got to Cuba we had to abandon supplies on the beach and hope for the best. Our packs were meant for mounted troops, and now suddenly we had to carry them through a jungle on our own backs, instead of strapped to a saddle. Some men just threw theirs down and left them by the trail. You'd best believe they regretted that later on, since we didn't have supply lines worth speaking of. Then we walked straight into an ambush at Las Guasimas. It was a mess."

Nick drank his wine more slowly. "Sounds like it."

"I ain't supposed to talk about it like this." Jamie's gaze fixed on his glass, as though it held some answer for him in its depths. "I'm supposed to make it sound like fun, an adventure. A glorious undertaking, free of pain or grief or stupid mistakes that could have been avoided."

"I think you should talk about it the way you want," Nick said. "You were there—what gives anyone else the right to tell you how you ought to feel about it?"

Jamie's eyes widened, and he met Nick's gaze, surprise written all over his features. "Because everyone expects me to feel differently," he said after a long pause. "The papers portrayed it as some sort of…of Boys Own Adventure. Where even the men who died did so cleanly, with dignity, instead of screaming and suffering." He swallowed convulsively. "I don't mean to say they weren't heroes all. Good men. I would have died for any of them, and them for me. Hell, maybe if I'd been there for the battle at San Juan Heights, I'd feel more…I don't know." Jamie slumped in his chair. "Like folks expect. Like a hero."

"Anyone else know you feel this way?" Nick asked, because he thought he knew the answer, and wasn't sure what to make of it.

"Of course not." Jamie seemed to ponder it for a moment. "But you don't judge me." Then he laughed. "Wait, I take that back—you judge me all the time for being a witch. Nothing else I could say would make you think any less of me, so why not be honest?"

The words shouldn't have stung. "I don't think you're a bad sort," Nick protested. "I mean, for a witch, obviously."

"Obviously." But Jamie managed a smile. "Thanks for listening."

"Thanks for helping with the books."

Silence settled between them, but this time it felt charged. The wine had brought a slight flush to Jamie's fair cheeks, and a tiny spot of sauce clung to the corner of his lips. Nick had the overwhelming urge to kiss it away.

He knew he ought to cling to whatever was left of his principles, but he didn't want to. He wanted to pretend, for a few hours at least, that Jamie was just another man. Not his witch, not O'Malley's nephew.

Jamie must have read something of his thoughts on his face. He finished off his wine, then set it aside. "I won't do this if you can't look me in the eyes after."

Nick had bruised the man's pride, not even meaning to. "I'm sorry about that. I was upset with myself, but I shouldn't have taken it out on you."

"You're right. You shouldn't have." Jamie's gaze didn't waver. "If you're going to be ashamed of yourself after, then don't put a hand on me again. Ain't nothing wrong with what we did."

"You're a witch," Nick said softly.

"And you're not Wyatt."

The words caught Nick like an unexpected blow. He'd not thought of Jamie as a grieving lover. Of course not—Jamie was a witch, and witches only cared about what they could get from a familiar.

But Wyatt already had a witch. Whatever Jamie had felt, it hadn't been about magic, or power.

If only he'd known Wyatt better. Known why he hadn't gone to Jamie when he returned to New York.

"No," Nick said at last. "I suppose I'm not. Is that a problem?"

"Aye? Maybe?" Jamie shook his head. "He died a year ago...he died just a few days ago...and I can't see how to reconcile the two."

So much for pretending they were just a couple of ordinary men. "If you don't want..."

"I do, though." Jamie's eyes burned bright as green flames. "I do want."

If the fuck in the cave had been a mistake, this was madness. Nick knew he'd regret it later. Hell, probably they both would. But right now, with the wine warm in his blood, and the bond warm in his chest, he couldn't bring himself to care. "I'll do better this time. If you still want to give it a go, that is."

Leaning heavily on the desk, Jamie made his way to Nick's side. He braced his hands on Nick's shoulders, looked deep into his eyes, and, with a bit of maneuvering, straddled his lap. "Aye," he whispered against Nick's lips.

Nick closed his hands on Jamie's hips. Jamie's mouth was hot on his, insistent. The hard line of his erection pressed against Nick's through their clothing, and Jamie rolled his hips, rubbing them together.

Nick plucked the hem of Jamie's shirt free of his trousers and slid his hands beneath. Hot skin met his touch, and he traced Jamie's flanks, feeling the curve of rib and muscle. He bit Jamie's lower lip, then sucked on it, before kissing him again.

There came a heavy pounding on the apartment door.

Jamie tensed, and Nick swore. "Nick!" called a voice from the other side. "Are you in there?"

Oh hell. "It's Rodrigo."

Jamie swung off of him, gripping the chair for balance. After the heat of his body, the air felt cold. Nick cursed again, silently this time, and went to the door.

Rodrigo stood there, his dark curls wild around his face. A grayish tinge underlay the bronze tones of his skin. "The killer," he blurted, before Nick could say anything. "I saw him. He's in the park now, and—and I think he's murdered someone else."

Jamie swore as he laced on his leg. Of all the blasted times for the killer to show up…

Maybe it was for the best. At least he'd been here when word came. Now if he could just keep Nick from rushing off without him. "We have to go, now."

"Where was he?" Nick asked Rodrigo.

"Greywacke Arch." The handsome bat familiar shuddered. "The rumors were true, Nick. It isn't human. The man it attacked wasn't small, and it lifted him off his feet like he weighed no more than a child. It had horns, like Satan himself!"

"Fur and feathers, there's no such thing," Nick said. "No ghosts, no devils, none of it but some maniac who likes to kill ferals."

Jamie stood up and took a couple of steps to make certain his stump was properly seated and the lacing wasn't too loose or too tight. "We need to hurry. Even if we're too late to save the victim, we can at least catch the bastard."

"Agreed," Nick said grimly.

As they emerged onto the sidewalk, Jamie realized what Nick's tone had meant. He grabbed Nick's sleeve. "You ain't going without me."

Nick yanked loose, nostrils flaring. "There's no time. Even if you could run, you'd only slow me down."

No. No, he wasn't letting this happen again. He wasn't going to stay behind while Nick went on. He was going to be there with him, the way he hadn't been for Wyatt. "You ain't doing this alone, damn it! You heard Rodrigo—there's something strange going on. You're just going to get yourself killed, and for what?"

Nick clutched at his hair, paced a few steps away, then back. "Fine. Have it your way. But don't even think about *ever* telling anyone about this."

He shifted into horse form in a flash of light. Jamie had forgotten how damned *big* he was: a massive destrier whose hooves could crush a man's skull. Maybe Nick would have been fine on his own after all.

"Rodrigo, go to the Coven and let the MWP know what's happening," Jamie ordered. "Tell them to get up here and help us as fast as they can."

Rodrigo nodded and shifted into bat form without argument.

Jamie used the stoop to mount, and ended up sprawled awkwardly over Nick's back, with no saddle to help him stay on. Nick's skin twitched as he righted himself, and for a horrible moment Jamie thought instinct would take over and Nick would buck him into the street. Instead, he pawed angrily at the sidewalk.

"Hold on," he advised inside Jamie's head.

Jamie obeyed, clinging as tight as he could with his knees and gripping the flowing mane in his hands. Then Nick was in motion, going faster and faster, until he cantered onto Seventh Avenue.

The October air blew in Jamie's face, cold but exhilarating. He worried he'd have trouble staying on, with no saddle or reins, but his body somehow knew what to do. He and Nick seemed to move together, as if they'd been doing this for years. Decades. The bond, surely, was behind it, but Jamie didn't care. A strange elation surged through him at the sensation of the equine power beneath him. At the smell of Nick's sweat in his nostrils, and Nick's mane flying back to tickle his face. Hooves like thunder on the streets, and people scattering out of the way.

They entered Central Park through Inventor's Gate, and Nick stretched into a gallop on the gas lit drive. The wind picked up, and leaves streamed down from the trees, each one a moving shadow. Jamie leaned low over Nick's neck, silently urging him on. If they could just get to the crime scene in time, before the killer was done, they could put an end to this nightmare once and for all.

Then they'd go their separate ways.

A streetlamp burned below the bridge, illuminating the gray stone, the delicate shape of the Spanish-style arch. Nick stayed up on the drive, slowing to a walk. Jamie started to dismount, but he said, *"Not yet. You won't be able to get back on easily."*

"If you weren't so damn big," Jamie groused.

"Most men prefer it that way."

Jamie's eyes widened. "Was that a *joke?*"

"Maybe." Nick froze, head up, nostrils flared. *"I smell blood."*

The lamp on the path below flung geometric shadows of the arch's iron railings over the pavement. A dark shape sprawled in the center of the arch. Nick approached with caution, and details gradually became clearer. Just as with the first two victims, the corpse lay on its back. A man, by the looks of it, his throat cut and body cavity opened up. The hex painted around him in blood still glistened wetly.

"I knew him," Nick said grimly.

Jamie stared at the corpse, feeling as though the ground had suddenly shifted beneath them. The only solid thing in the world was Nick. "So did I. Or, not knew him. But I saw him last week, when Uncle Hurley arrested him for violating the Pemberton Act."

Nick's ears flattened against his head, and his upper lip drew back from his teeth. Luther. Lion familiar. He'd heard the news when Luther was arrested; everyone did.

So what the hell was he doing here now?

Jamie must have been having the same thoughts, because he said, "Did he escape from the Menagerie? I mean, he must have, right? Maybe they wanted to keep it quiet."

The witch's weight on his back should have felt wrong. Nick had half expected he'd have to fight the instinct to buck him off all the way over here. But the part of him that governed his magic must have been the same part that let him be a horse, because there had been a terrible rightness in the way they'd moved together.

Which seemed utterly unfair.

"So where did he go?" Jamie asked. "The Wraith. He couldn't have been gone long." Nick felt a shudder run through Jamie's body. "Luther—the corpse—is still steaming."

"Give me a minute."

"To what?"

"Just be quiet!"

Jamie fell silent. Nick walked past the body; every hoof fall sounded unnaturally loud. The scent of blood faded somewhat, but didn't entirely disappear. Rather, it was joined by the reek of something long dead and rotting. Nick followed the trail, straining all his senses.

There was no moon, but the gaslights along the drive offered plenty of illumination. Not to mention Nick's night vision was much sharper in horse form than in human. He could make out the thin spire of Cleopatra's Needle against the sky, and the bulk of the Metropolitan Museum of Art.

Just ahead, something moved. An inhuman figure seemed to coalesce from the shadows themselves. A thing of ragged cloth and exposed bone, as though it had clawed its way out of some desolate grave to rain down vengeance on the living. The bones clicked together with every movement, a dry sound like the legs of a beetle. A pair of curving horns rose from its head, but beneath the hood was only blackness. It stank of blood and death, and it held an obsidian blade in its claw-tipped fingers.

No wonder the ferals of the park called it a wraith.

"Saint Mary," Jamie whispered. "What is it?"

"The killer," Nick told him. *"Hold on tight."*

Then Nick charged.

He felt a flash of shock through the bond, and Jamie's knees tightened on his flanks. Hoof beats echoed like thunder from the trees.

"Are you crazy?" Jamie yelped.

The Wraith stood motionless for a long moment, as if waiting for Nick to get close. As if it had all the time in the world. When the space between them had closed to a matter of yards, it lifted a taloned hand and grasped one of the bones strung amidst ragged cloth.

Then it *ran.*

Fast—faster than anything human, that was for certain. One moment it was motionless, and the next it was all but in Nick's face, tattered cloth flaring out around it like wings, bones clattering an alarm.

Nick shied away. He tried to turn, nearly going down on his haunches, Jamie's hands locked tight in his mane and his thighs gripping hard with the effort not to slip off.

The Wraith was well past them, now, vanishing down the drive in the direction of the transverse road with all the speed of a cheetah.

"What was it?" Jamie asked, voice shaking slightly. "It looked like…"

Nick broke into a gallop, eliciting a curse from Jamie. *"I don't know what it is, but it's no ghost."* Jamie's hesitation plucked at the bond, so he added, *"Trust me."*

"I do," Jamie said, and the hesitation vanished.

Jamie trusted him, on a deep level. Nick hadn't expected that, wasn't even certain what to do with it. But maybe he shouldn't have been surprised; Jamie had already shared with him things he'd told no one else.

It almost made Nick want to be worthy of that trust.

Nick veered onto the path overlooking the sunken transverse road. The dark figure appeared to move in a series of flickers along it. But it was just an illusion: its dark clothing was revealed in pools of light from the street lamps, then vanished into the shadows between them.

The Wraith made its way deeper into the park. Did it have a hiding place in mind, or was it simply trying to outrun them?

One of Jamie's hands released Nick's mane and reached into his coat to draw out his Colt. "Stop!" Jamie bellowed at the fleeing figure below them. "Police!"

"Does that ever work?"

"Sometimes." Jamie leaned low against Nick's neck, as if urging him forward. "I don't understand. If it ain't a ghost, how can it run so damned fast?"

Nick didn't have an answer to that, so he concentrated on keeping up with the fleeing figure. As they reached the tunnel bridge over the transverse road, the wraith suddenly veered off, disappearing into the darkness.

"Where did it go?" Jamie asked.

Nick's night vision was much sharper than Jamie's. He saw the figure scramble up the rocky wall—how had it made such a steep climb so easily?—and onto the path above. Behind it loomed a tower of gray stone, reaching for the night sky.

"It's making for Belvedere Castle," Nick said.

It wasn't actually a castle, of course. Just a folly, a bit of whimsy added by the park's architects to delight visitors with the view of the Croton Waterworks to the north and the Ramble to the south.

Nick galloped over the bridge across the transverse road, up the stairs, and onto the folly's terrace. Gaslights burned all around, painting the gray paving stones in orange tones. The wind sighed around the cornices and rippled the surface of the water beyond. Fallen leaves skittered across the terrace like small, frightened animals.

The Wraith stood in the light, awaiting them. The lamps outlined its form, gleaming off the black ram's horns projecting from beneath the hood, finding the paleness of bone amidst dark clothing. Revealed, too, what shadows and speed had largely hidden. A pair of black boots, scuffed and worn in places, which solidly met the ground.

Nick didn't slow. "Drop the knife!" Jamie shouted.

The Wraith didn't drop the knife. Jamie fired, the gunshot painfully loud to Nick's sensitive hearing. The Wraith jerked slightly, as if at an impact...but it didn't fall.

By then, Nick was almost on it. At the last moment, it twisted aside before Nick could run it down. One hand shot out, and Nick glimpsed the paper hex the Wraith held concealed in its palm.

"Be bound to your human form."

Chapter 14

Saint Mary, the owl had been right. Whatever this thing was, it couldn't be human.

Jamie had shot it, dead center in the chest. He was certain of it. But it hadn't fallen, had barely flinched.

Then it struck Nick with the hex. One moment, they surged forward, the great bulk of Nick's horse shape beneath him. The next, Jamie tumbled through the air.

He struck the pavement hard, revolver flying out of his grasp. Confused instincts yelled at him to roll, that he was about to be crushed by a horse collapsing onto him. But Nick sprawled to the ground in human form, which though big, took up considerably less space.

The hex. It was the same that Uncle Hurley's men had used on Luther, to keep him from taking on his lion shape.

"Fuck!" Nick shouted in surprise. He rolled to his feet, shaking visibly. The Wraith approached from behind.

"Look out!" Jamie tried to get to his feet, but between his leg and his knee he couldn't manage it without anything to lean against. Gritting his teeth, he began to drag himself toward the nearest iron lamppost.

Nick spun to face the Wraith, hands balled into fists. The October wind caught Nick's long hair, tangling it about his shoulders. The Wraith moved silently, its ragged cloak in constant, disorienting motion. Black leather gloves concealed the Wraith's hands, and Jamie now saw each finger was tipped with the claw of some large animal, perhaps a jaguar. In one hand, the Wraith clutched a knife with a haft of black wood, its obsidian blade still wet with blood.

"Come on then," Nick growled. "Just you and me. No more dirty tricks."

The Wraith swung the blade—but the blinding speed it had possessed earlier seemed to have abandoned it. Nick blocked the blow, striking the Wraith's wrist with his forearm. The knife went flying away, into the darkness, and the Wraith leapt back.

Solid. Whatever else it was, it was solid enough to be fought.

"Now we'll settle this," Nick began.

The Wraith wrapped a taloned hand around one of the bones dangling from a harness around its chest, and whispered something Jamie couldn't quite make out. The bone cracked down the center.

What had Yates said, about the eagle bone? That the markings on it were some sort of primitive hex?

Nick charged, fists raised. The Wraith stepped to meet him. It knocked aside Nick's punch with ease, then grabbed a handful of Nick's clothing, lifted him from his feet, and threw him as though he were a twenty-pound child instead of a two hundred-pound man.

Nick flew several feet, hit the ground, and rolled to a stop. As he lay there, stunned, the Wraith began to advance on him once again.

No.

Jamie's heart thudded as he lurched the last few feet and grabbed the iron lamppost. He grasped it with both hands, using it to take his weight until he could get his good leg under him.

There was no time to look for his gun, which hadn't done him a bit of good anyway. On his feet again, Jamie limped toward the Wraith as quickly as he could. "Hey! You!"

The Wraith turned to him. Jamie brought his fists up. His mouth tasted like he'd been sucking on a penny, and his pulse drummed in his throat. "You killed Wyatt," he said, his voice oddly calm and far away to his own ears. "I'm going to see you rot for that."

The Wraith made no response. Nothing showed beneath its hood but a black void—or perhaps some sort of cloth mask, though how anyone would be able to see through such a thing, Jamie didn't know. The killer moved toward him, unafraid, lifting one claw-tipped hand.

Nick yelled and buried a fist in the Wraith's kidney.

The Wraith let out a grunt of pain and staggered. Encouraged, Jamie went on the attack even as it turned on Nick. Jamie threw a punch of his own, but it glanced off the Wraith's shoulder.

Then the Wraith twisted, lashing out. Its talons shredded Jamie's coat over his arm, and he jerked back. Stinging pain announced a moment later that the claws had reached the skin beneath.

Nick let out an incoherent growl and threw himself at the Wraith—only to be knocked aside by a hard kick that caught Nick on the hip and spun him around.

Rather than face Jamie again, the Wraith darted inside the folly. Nick rushed after, Jamie on his heels. But once inside, Jamie's heart sank.

The Wraith had vanished up a tight, narrow stairway leading into the tower. Between the tall steps and sharp turns, there was no way he could follow.

"Nick, I can't—" he started. But Nick was already pounding up the steps and out of sight.

Despair welled up in Jamie. It was Cuba all over again, with him left behind, while Nick went ahead into danger. Alone.

Alone, with the monster that killed Wyatt.

Nick's skin tingled with a combination of dread and lingering magic. The tight spiral of the stairwell left him blind to anything even a few feet ahead. The Wraith could be waiting for him, and he'd never know it until he was on top of the killer.

Nothing made sense. The sheer strength of the Wraith boggled the mind. How could anyone in human form lift Nick off his feet so easily, let alone throw him? How had the Wraith run so fast—and why wasn't it using that same speed now? Jamie had shot it in the chest, but the bullet seemed to have no effect.

The hex it had used to force Nick into human form—he'd not heard of such a thing before. Hexes existed to force familiars into animal shape, to make them easier to control. But this seemed to be the opposite.

Nick had tried to shift back on the terrace, but the buzzing on his skin had intensified, as though an electric current ran across it, and nothing had happened. The magic that had been his since puberty was cut off, and it was all he could do not to let panic take him. It felt *wrong,* all the way to his core, as though someone had sliced him in half. The tingling seemed to have faded, but how long would it take until he could shift again?

Nick followed the steps as high as he could go. A ladder led to the very top, and another doorway opened onto the flat roof of the lower part of the tower. Nick paused and peered outside, gasping for breath as he did so. There was no sign of the Wraith—but it had to have gone somewhere.

This was stupid. They had the Wraith cornered. They should wait for whomever the MWP sent out in response to Rodrigo's call for help. Let the coppers risk their asses instead.

But it was a long way to and from the Coven, and help might not be coming any time soon. After the displays of unnatural speed and strength, Nick wouldn't put it past the Wraith to be able to crawl down the side of the folly like a lizard.

The Wraith had already murdered three ferals. It couldn't be allowed to escape. Nick had to put an end to this tonight.

Nick straightened and stepped cautiously through the doorway.

He caught a blur of shadow out of the corner of his eye. A heavy blow impacted his side, sending him staggering toward the low parapet. He tried to get his arms up, to turn, but a flurry of punches left him reeling.

The back of one leg fetched up against the wall.

Nick rushed forward, hoping to get past the Wraith and away from the edge. But the killer seized him again, dragging him back with shocking strength. Nick fought wildly, only to have a hand wrap around his throat. The low stone parapet dug into his back, and he glimpsed the waters of the old receiving reservoir far below, restless beneath the moonless sky.

He might survive a fall into water. But directly beneath him, the base of Belvedere Castle rose up from the very bedrock underlying the city. If the Wraith succeeded in shoving him off, he'd be dashed to bits.

Nick clawed madly at the hand gripping his throat. The stench of death surrounded him, as though it impregnated the cloak itself. The Wraith leaned over him, and he had the horrible impression the killer enjoyed his struggles. Relished his fear, the knowledge he was about to die.

A gunshot rang out.

For a long moment, Jamie only stared at the stairway winding up into the tower. A mix of fury and terror beat through him. He'd spent months coming to terms with the wooden leg, the knee that didn't work quite right anymore. But the same helpless rage he'd felt while learning to walk again filled him now.

Nick had gone alone to face Wyatt's killer. If the Wraith murdered him, too…

Jamie spat out a curse and limped back onto the terrace. A metallic gleam caught his eye, and he bent to scoop up his dropped revolver. At least he had a weapon now. Not that it would do much good.

A shout sounded from above.

Nick.

Jamie backed rapidly toward the edge of the terrace, his head craned back, trying to see what was happening on the levels above. There—on the parapet. Movement.

Jamie's heart leapt into his throat. Nick staggered toward the low wall, all that separated him from a long drop onto the rocks below. The Wraith came into view, the curving horns of its headdress framed against the sky.

It seized Nick and shoved him off his feet. Jamie's blood turned to ice; Nick hung half over the wall, the Wraith's hand on his throat as it slowly, inexorably shoved him over the edge.

Helpless horror seized Jamie. He was about to watch Nick die, trapped on the terrace by his fucking leg, his gun inexplicably useless against the monster above. He lifted the revolver, wondering if he ought to try again anyway, even though he knew it would do no good.

The horns.

He didn't know exactly what instinct guided him, only that they looked somehow more vulnerable than the dark bulk of the Wraith's body. There was no time to question, only to sight as carefully as he could, and fire.

The shot seemed unnaturally loud in the quiet park. The Wraith's left horn shattered beneath the impact of the bullet.

It flinched, letting go of Nick. With a roar of anger, Nick shoved the Wraith back. The moment Nick was free, he took two steps forward—then shifted into his horse form.

If the Wraith meant to flee, it was too slow. Nick pivoted, then kicked behind him. Both rear hooves connected in a powerful blow, lifting the Wraith into the air—and over the side. There came a muffled thump as its body impacted the rocks at the edge of the Croton Waterworks.

Nick returned to human form and peered down at Jamie. "Jamie! Are you hurt?"

Relief surged through Jamie, so strong he sagged against the nearest lamppost. Nick disappeared; in under a minute, he emerged from the tower. "Witch?" he asked, brows drawing down. "Your arm—you're bleeding."

"I don't care about that, you stupid horse." Jamie grabbed Nick by the shoulders, gripping him tightly. "Don't you ever leave me behind like that again." He swallowed thickly. "You…you could've been killed. And I would have had to stand here and watch, helpless, and…"

"You saved my life," Nick said. Then he lowered his head and kissed Jamie hard.

It started off desperate and fast, Jamie's lips mashed against his teeth with the force of it. But after a moment, something between them shifted. The kiss softened. Nick sucked on Jamie's lower lip, and Jamie opened to his tongue.

Jamie let go of his death grip on Nick's shoulders in favor of burying his hands in Nick's long hair. Nick pushed him back against the lamppost, trapping him between the iron and Nick's body. Memories of being pressed against the wall of the Cave flared, and Jamie let out a moan into Nick's mouth. He rubbed his hardening cock against Nick's thigh, felt the responding erection against his belly through the layers of their clothing.

Nick drew back slightly, just enough to get a hand in between them and work at the buttons of Jamie's trousers. Saint Mary, Jamie wanted this, so bad, his entire body straining with the need to feel Nick's hand on his aching prick once again.

A dark shape glided past the lamp, cawing loudly.

Nick sprang back as if he'd been burned. His cheeks flushed dark, even as his expression lapsed into a scowl. Jamie's own face felt on fire, and he hastily rebuttoned his trousers, praying Rook hadn't noticed.

He had, of course. The crow circled, still cawing, then came in for a landing, taking on human form just inches from the pavement. "What was that I saw?" he exclaimed, eyes wide. "*My* brother, kissing a witch?"

"Shut it," Nick snapped. "This is none of your business, so keep your beak closed."

Rook's grin said he had no intention whatsoever of keeping this to himself. "My brother," he repeated again. "The mighty Nick, hater of witches, with his hand down—"

"We stopped the killer," Jamie blurted, just to make Rook shut up.

Rook blinked, glanced between them, then sobered. "What happened?"

"He fell off the tower." Glad to have an excuse to turn his scalding face to the cool darkness, Jamie made his way to the edge of the terrace and leaned over. "Right down…there?"

"What is it?" Nick strode over, jostling Rook out of the way to stand by Jamie. "What's wrong?"

Jamie only shook his head. A small splotch of blood showed on the rocks where the Wraith had fallen. But that was all. No limp cloak. No scattered bones.

No body.

"Fucking hell," Nick said. "It got away."

Chapter 15

Dominic, Owen Yates, and Mal arrived shortly after Rook. They combed the area, and Mal took to fox form in an attempt to track the Wraith by scent. The trail led into the water; if it emerged elsewhere, Mal didn't find it.

"Maybe he drowned," Mal said, with an air of what Nick considered unwarranted optimism. "That would be good, wouldn't it?"

Jamie only shook his head. "He…it…didn't drown."

"It?" Yates asked.

"It didn't seem human. It was strong, and fast, and survived a fall that would have killed a man." Jamie tugged his coat closer. The shredded sleeve showed a series of shallow scratches across his pale skin. "I shot it in the chest, and it didn't die. It was more like a devil than anything."

"It wasn't a devil," Nick said.

"On that, we agree." Yates held up a flattened bullet. "I found this on the terrace. I've heard rumors the government is looking into hexes to make cloth bulletproof, for use in war. But as far as I know, the concept has never been successfully demonstrated."

"It has now," Dominic said grimly. "Nick, you said its speed seemed to abandon it after a time. But it became freakishly strong."

"After touching one of the bones it wore." Nick thought back. "The bone cracked."

Yates and Dominic exchanged a glance. "It must be hexes," Yates murmured. "But I've never heard of anything like this."

"Discuss it tomorrow," Rook said. "After we've had a bit of rest and are thinking clearly." Nick just had enough time to be surprised at his brother's sensible suggestion, when Rook cast a sly look in his direction. "Some of us have other people—I mean, things—to do tonight."

Featherbrain.

Jamie moved stiffly. Probably his knee had taken a hit in the fall, when Nick was forced out from under him. The look of resignation on his face at the prospect of walking home made Nick feel unaccountably guilty.

Well, the man had saved his life. It was only natural to display gratitude. So he took on horse form and silently urged Jamie to mount, all the while ignoring the looks of shock from everyone except Jamie himself.

Tomorrow, Nick would make sure Rook understood that was all it had been. Gratitude. He wasn't about to start carting around some witch on the regular. Although the declaration would probably have more weight if Rook hadn't caught him trying to shove his hand down Jamie's trousers.

Shortly thereafter, Nick clopped slowly down 42nd Street, Jamie's weight on his back. "Here we are," Jamie said. "Home sweet home."

Nick halted outside the tenement Jamie indicated, then walked over to the stairs, in the hopes of making it easier for Jamie to dismount. When Jamie slid carefully from his back, Nick felt the loss of his warmth, the air against his hide much chillier than it should have been.

Once he was certain Jamie was down, Nick took on human shape again. They looked at each other uncertainly for a moment. Then Jamie cocked his head in the direction of the doors. "You can come inside. If you like. It's a long walk back to Caballus, after all."

"It is," Nick agreed, and kissed him. It was foolish—had been foolish from the start—but he couldn't bring himself to care. Jamie's mouth felt too good against his own, and their bodies fit together like they'd been made for one another. Desire flared from a stoked coal into a fire, burning away doubt and leaving behind only raw need.

They broke apart. Jamie grinned and grabbed Nick's hand. "Come on. I'd like a proper bed this time."

Nick let himself be led into the tenement. Jamie's apartment was on the first floor, no doubt because it would be easier than managing flights of stairs every day. As soon as Jamie shut the door behind them, Nick pushed him against it.

"What is it with you and shoving me into things?" Jamie asked, but his breath came raggedly. His eyes burned dark with desire, the brown splotch in the right one making the green seem even more intense.

Nick planted a hand to either side of Jamie's head, bracketing him in. "I think you like it," Nick challenged. He pressed his thigh against Jamie's erection, was rewarded with a gasp of pleasure.

"Aye," Jamie whispered. "Kiss me."

Nick did as he was asked. Fur and feathers, he could get lost in the contours of Jamie's lips, his tongue. Jamie's hands shaped his back, and the longing to have that touch on his skin stole Nick's breath.

Nick stepped back, shucked his overcoat and suit coat, and reached for the buttons on his vest. But Jamie grasped Nick's hands, stilling their movement. "Not so fast," he said. "We've got all night, don't we?"

Nick didn't know any more. Everything seemed like it was spiraling out of control, going too fast. Like he'd bolted and dragged a cart behind him, downhill and unable to stop for fear of overturning.

"Yes," he said, and licked dry lips.

Jamie unbuttoned Nick's vest slowly, then set to work on his shirt. He pressed his lips to every inch of skin as it was revealed. Nick tipped his head back helplessly, then gasped when Jamie's mouth found his nipple. His arms tightened around Jamie's slender form, one hand cupping the back of his head. Jamie's teeth sent a bright spark of pleasure straight to his balls.

"Oh hell," he whispered.

"Aye." Jamie drew back. His hand trailed down Nick's belly, then cupped him through his trousers. "As much as I'd like to kneel down right now and suck you, my knee ain't going to agree to it."

The mental image left Nick biting his lip for control. "Then get on the bed, witch."

Jamie didn't remove his hand, just kept fondling, sending delicious sensations racing along Nick's nerves. "Use my name, Nick."

It was his last line of defense, his only way to put some distance between them, and of course the blasted witch wanted to take it away. Nick took a deep, ragged breath. "Jamie. Will you get on the bed? Because I want to fuck you until you beg to come."

"That's what I like to hear." Jamie shot him a wink, then strolled in the direction of the bed, stripping off his coat and vest as he did so. The scratches on his arm looked shallow, and had already scabbed over.

Wyatt's pendant hung around Jamie's neck, just below the hollow between his collarbones. Nick hadn't realized Jamie took the necklace after Wyatt died, and it sent a little flash of guilt through him. He hadn't told everything he might have about Jamie's dead lover, and now here he was planning on fucking him a second time, knowing Jamie was grieving for the eagle.

Nick wished he'd had the chance to really get to know Wyatt. To learn the sort of man he'd been. Nick had the unsettling feeling he would have liked the dead familiar quite a lot.

"Is this all right?" he asked. "I'm still not Wyatt."

Jamie sat on the edge of the bed, his pant leg rolled up, exposing the leather sleeve that kept the prosthetic firmly attached. "I'm not the person I was a year ago, either," he said after a pause. "I don't know what that Jamie would have done. The one with two legs, who never imagined Wyatt would desert, or leave him alone to mourn." He closed his eyes, then opened them again. "But I want this, more than I can say. I'm sick of grief." He glanced at Nick, heat in his eyes now. "I want joy."

Nick swallowed. "Figure I can offer an hour or two of that."

Jamie unlaced the prosthetic. His leg ended a few inches below the knee, and seemed smooth and well healed to Nick's eye.

"Do I need to be careful of the stump?" Nick asked. "Is it tender, or sensitive, or…?"

Jamie shook his head. "Not anymore."

"Good." Nick pushed Jamie back, and he went, sprawled on the bed with only his unbuttoned shirt and trousers on. He looked up at Nick with a wicked grin, spreading his arms out as if to suggest he was Nick's for the taking.

Nick crawled into bed over him, lowering himself to give Jamie a deep, thorough kiss, before sitting back. Jamie let out a soft whimper of desire, hips bucking under Nick's.

"You're the one who wanted it slow," Nick teased.

"Aye, well, I say a lot of stupid things," Jamie said with a half-laugh. The skin of his chest was pale, dusted with fine hair. His pink nipples drew up tight, and Nick gave one a pinch. Jamie moaned and arched his back, clutching at the sheets. "Saint Mary, I want you. I thought the last time, it was because I hadn't slept with anyone since Cuba, but if you don't get off my cock I'm going to come like this."

Nick swung his hips away. "Surely someone with a face like yours could have his pick of partners. Especially working somewhere like the MWP, where the odds are in your favor." For whatever reason, most familiars and a good percentage of witches preferred to sleep with their own gender. Nick's father had owned Krafft-Ebing's book; the German doctor had devoted an entire chapter to the question of witch-familiar sexuality.

"A face like mine?" Jamie asked with an arched brow. "Are you trying to give me a compliment, Nick?"

"You're handsome, and you damned well know it."

"Such a sweet talker."

"Shut it." Nick reached for the buttons of Jamie's trousers. Jamie's cock jerked beneath the cloth as his fingers skated over the bulge.

He pulled Jamie's trousers and drawers off all at a go, and tossed them blindly onto the floor. Jamie's cock lay against his belly, flushed red, a glistening strand of precome on the tip. Nick slid off the bed and stripped off the rest of his clothes, desire urging him to do a dozen different things at once. Rub his cock against Jamie's, or take Jamie's prick into his mouth, or ask Jamie to suck him.

Jamie peeled off his unbuttoned shirt, but his eyes traveled up and down Nick's form appreciatively. "I always did like a man with muscles," he said, and licked his lips. "Come here. I want to taste you."

"Since when have you started giving all the orders, wi—Jamie?" Nick corrected.

Jamie arched a brow. "Are you saying you don't want your prick sucked, then?"

"I didn't say that." Nick climbed onto the bed and straddled Jamie's chest. Bracing one hand against the headboard, he leaned forward enough that Jamie could take his cock if he wanted.

Jamie didn't hesitate, grabbing Nick's hips and urging him closer, only to wrap his lips around the head. Then down, deeper, his mouth and throat hot and wet. He looked every bit as sinful as Nick had imagined he would: reddened lips, cheeks hollowed, his particolored eyes flashing up to watch Nick's face.

Fur and feathers, it felt good, better than he had any right to expect. They moved together like they were made for each other. The bond burned behind his heart, the sensation almost lost beneath the heat of arousal.

He pulled back with a growl. Jamie's fingers tightened on his hips, then relaxed. "You taste so good," Jamie panted. "Fuck. I want you to come in my mouth sometime."

"Not yet." Nick had already spotted the oil on the crowded shelf above the bed, and now he reached for it. "Tonight I'm going to fuck you again. Roll over."

"Nay." Jamie grabbed a pillow and stuffed it under his hips. "I want to see your face this time."

Nick had the sneaking suspicion that Jamie wasn't precisely lying... but what he really wanted was for Nick to see him. So Nick couldn't deny exactly whom it was he was with.

His witch.

Well, he'd asked for it, with his poor behavior the last time. He owed it to Jamie to look him in the face. Still, he wasn't going to let Jamie know that. "Any other requests, Your Majesty?"

"Horse's arse," Jamie shot back, but with a grin. "A man's got to fight for every step, just to meet you halfway."

Nick settled between Jamie's thighs. He bent down, traced a path from scarred knee to groin along the inside of Jamie's leg. Jamie let out a sound of pleasure. "Your hair feels good on my skin."

Nick obliged by dipping his head so the locks dragged across Jamie's cock and balls, too. And while he was down there, no sense in wasting the proximity. He gave Jamie's prick a long, slow lick from base to tip, catching bitter fluid on his tongue.

He paused just long enough to unstopper the oil and pour it over Jamie's balls and ass, before slicking his fingers. Setting the bottle aside so it wouldn't accidentally spill, he turned his attention back to Jamie's prick. Not taking it in his mouth, but licking and nibbling along the length, the hood. While he did so, he let his slick fingers slide down, find Jamie's passage, and push in.

Jamie gasped a little. "Good?" Nick asked. "Or too much?"

"Good," Jamie breathed. "Damn good. More, please."

Nick gave his cock a final, thorough lick. Tremors ran through Jamie's thighs, and his prick stirred in time to his heartbeat. He was close, so Nick sat back. Desire flushed Jamie's chest and face pink, his lips parted and his black hair wild. The look he gave Nick was one of scorching lust, so heated it felt like a hand on his skin.

Nick grabbed Jamie's knees, hooking them over his shoulders as he bent down. Need throbbed in his veins, and he pressed the head of his cock to Jamie's ass. Then he pushed in. Jamie's back arched, and he made a strangled sound that went straight to Nick's balls. Nick cradled his hips, working in slowly but inexorably, until every barrier relaxed and he slid in deep.

So like and unlike the time in the Cave. This was the same: bodies moving against each other, breathing ragged, the slick heat surrounding his cock. But that had been fast, desperate, a distance of clothes and denial between them. Now Jamie sprawled out luxuriously under him, thighs tight around Nick, lone heel digging in. Lips parted, hand stroking his cock in time to Nick's movements.

"It's good, ain't it?" Jamie asked. He released his cock to grip Nick's shoulders with both hands, dragging him closer. "Fuck, Nick, tell me it's good."

It was better than good. Maybe because of the stupid bond; maybe because of some other, unknowable reason. They moved together in perfect sync, bodies and breath. It was nothing Nick had wanted. He'd never thought he'd fuck a witch, certainly not *his* witch, and it was all too much, every nerve exposed and raw, as if Jamie had stripped away even his skin.

He didn't want to look down at Jamie's face and feel *this,* whatever this even was. Tenderness, and need, and something that might have been more than friendship. Tonight had been a setback, but soon enough they'd catch the killer. The hexbreaker would sever their bond, and Nick would never see Jamie again.

There was no other option. Jamie's uncle was the head of the Dangerous Familiars Squad, for God's sake. The sooner they parted ways, the better.

At first the thought of freedom had felt like the breath a man took before diving into deep waters. But now it felt like drowning.

"Yes," he said, even though he knew it would be easier for both of them if he lied. "It's amazing, Jamie."

Jamie threw his head back, long neck exposed, his chest heaving with his breaths. "Please…"

"Please what?"

Jamie shook his head, reaching again for his cock. Nick got there first, wrapping his fingers around Jamie's prick and tugging. Jamie's eyes opened wide, and he gripped the bedclothes, as if trying to keep himself from flying straight off the bed.

The time for slow and steady was over; Nick thrust harder, trying to keep the stroke of his hand in rhythm but failing. Jamie didn't seem to mind, though; he gasped and begged wildly, incoherently. "Aye, Nick, don't stop, please, harder, more…"

Sweat slicked Nick's skin, and he bowed his spine, lips finding Jamie's mouth, then his throat. "Nick," Jamie said, the sound a plea or a prayer. Then hot spunk filled the space between them, Jamie's whole body shuddering, thighs and ass clenching alike. Nick let go of Jamie's cock in favor of gripping his hips, and drove in once, twice, thrice, before cresting.

The silence was broken only by their breathing, and the faint sound of a fiddle playing in an apartment somewhere above. They remained still, locked together, but Nick had the strangest sensation of falling.

"Mmm." Jamie let go of Nick's shoulder, his hand trailing up Nick's neck to his jaw. "That was…thank you."

Nick pulled carefully free. He made sure to meet Jamie's gaze this time, turning his head only a little to press a kiss against Jamie's palm.

Jamie stretched out languidly, slender and lithe and unselfconscious. "Rest for a bit?"

Nick should refuse. Should grab his clothes and go, before things became even more complicated. But weariness seized him. He'd cantered from Caballus to Central Park, fought the Wraith, and then fucked Jamie into the bed. The idea of trudging all the way home, when he could just put his head down for a few minutes, felt impossible.

"A bit," he agreed. He stretched out beside Jamie, and tried to ignore the way his heart ached sweetly when Jamie curled into him. "Just for a little while."

CHAPTER 16

PAIN BROUGHT JAMIE abruptly out of a deep sleep. His left foot felt as though someone had it in a vise and was slowly twisting it off. He bit his lip against the agony, and tried to force his breathing from short, shallow gasps into a deeper rhythm.

The body beside his stirred, perhaps sensing the sudden tension in his muscles. Nick lifted his head from the pillow, looked around as if confused, then focused on Jamie. "What's wrong?"

Damn it. Why did this have to happen tonight, of all nights? "Foot hurts," Jamie grated out as another wave of agony swept over him.

Nick shoved his long hair out of his face. "Which one?"

The question caught Jamie off guard. "The one that ain't there."

"Phantom pain," Nick said with a nod. "Right. Does anything help? Pain hexes? Massage? Soaking the stump in warm water?"

For a moment, Jamie's mind blanked. Usually people acted like he was crazy; he didn't know what to do with calm acceptance. "Pain hexes," he said at last. "They're in the drawer over there, if you don't mind getting one. Massage, too."

The mattress rose when Nick got up, then dipped again beneath his weight. "Here." He handed the hex to Jamie.

Jamie pressed the scrap of paper to his leg. "Dr. Payne's Pain-Away, Takes the Pain Away," he said, reciting the activation phrase by heart. The sensation of having his non-existent foot crushed and twisted eased, enough for him to be able to breathe again. He started to massage the stump, but Nick said, "Lie back and let me."

A bit uncertain, Jamie did as ordered. Nick sat crosswise on the bed, his back propped against the wall and Jamie's legs in his lap. His big hands cradled the truncated end of the left one, strong and certain. "Tell me if I'm not doing it right."

Jamie closed his eyes, his gut instinctively tensing at the fear of renewed pain. But Nick's touch was gentle, firm, and after a moment he relaxed. "That's good."

Nick didn't say anything. As the pain continued to ease, Jamie opened his eyes again. Nick was nothing but a dark shadow against the pale wall. "You said earlier that you knew someone who lost his leg," Jamie recalled. "Is that how you know about this? Phantom pain?"

Nick was silent for so long Jamie didn't think he'd answer. Then he sighed. "In a way. My father was a doctor. Some of his patients were missing limbs."

"A doctor, eh?" Jamie asked, impressed. "He must've been smart, then."

"He was." Nick sounded oddly wistful. "Dad was black and Seminole. He came north and earned his degree, then settled in Brooklyn, treating anyone who would come to a black doctor. I wanted to be just like him."

Grief underlay Nick's words, like the faint scent of gangrene from an unhealed wound. "What happened?" Jamie asked quietly.

Nick tilted his head back, though his hands continued their work. "Ammi—our mother—was a familiar. Got it from her father, who was a sea turtle. He sailed the world, but settled in New York after meeting Nanni. He led ships in and out of the harbor, that sort of thing. Dead long before I was born, but Ammi always said I took after him. Said he was a big man with a big heart." Nick snorted. "I inherited the first one of those, anyway."

"Was your dad your mom's witch?" Jamie asked.

Nick lowered his head, no doubt to shoot Jamie a sharp look, going by his tone. "No. She was a feral. I don't know if she ever met her witch —she never said—but she wasn't interested in bonding. It would have taken her away from us, and she didn't want that."

"Sorry," Jamie said.

A sigh gusted across Jamie's bare skin. "It's not you I'm angry with. One of the people Dad treated was a familiar, who came to him in secret. Her witch beat her, bad. She was terrified of him, but what could she do? No one realized hexbreakers could break a bond, and it isn't as if there are many of them around to begin with. Her only hope was to go to Europe or somewhere her witch couldn't afford to follow. But she didn't have any money of her own. In the end, things got so bad Dad thought her witch might kill her. So he lent her the money and arranged for her to get away."

Jamie propped himself up on his elbows. "What happened?"

"The witch murdered Dad."

Oh hell. "Saint Mary, have grace on his soul," Jamie said. "I hope the bastard who killed him got what he deserved."

"Dad was popular. A jury might not have convicted a white witch for killing a black doctor, but let's just say it never made it to trial. They found the witch dead in a field, and not a witness to be found. No one much cared for the drunken bastard, so the police didn't go out of their way to investigate."

It was justice of a sort, Jamie supposed. "I'm sorry, Nick."

"It was hard, after that." Nick's voice lowered, though in the dimness it was impossible to make out his expression. "But Ammi was determined to do the best for us. She wanted me to be able to go to medical school more than ever. Without Dad's income, that wasn't going to happen, so…she answered a newspaper ad. A witch was looking for a familiar to bond with, to go out west and work for one of the mining companies. The pay was good, so she took it." He bowed his head. "She did the one thing she swore she'd never do, just to make sure we were taken care of. Then six months later, she was dead, too. Killed alongside the witch in a mine collapse."

"Ah, Nick." Jamie didn't know what to say. He'd been so young when his own parents had died, he barely remembered either of them. "That's awful, that is."

"When I was old enough, a few years later, I applied for medical school. They rejected me." Bitterness laced the words. "They felt there was no point in educating a familiar. After all, they said, I'd just meet my witch and quit doctoring. A witch gunned down my father, and then another got my mother killed, and then a third one I'd never even met cost me the only dream I'd ever had. So I took the money, sold off all of Dad's medical books to raise more cash, and used it to start Caballus. To give familiars one damned place where they could be themselves, without some fucking witch interfering."

Jamie's chest ached. If only there was something, anything, he could do to fix what had happened. But there wasn't. "I'm sorry, Nick. I know it don't mean anything, it's just words, but…I'm sorry." He sighed. "No wonder you hate us."

"I..." Nick's voice caught. "Some of you are better than others. How's the pain?"

"Almost gone." Jamie put a hand on Nick's arm. "Here. Lie down."

"I should go back to Caballus," Nick said, though not like he really wanted to. More like an unpleasant duty; something he felt he should for the principle of the thing. "I didn't mean to stay this long."

"It's got to be three or four in the morning. No sense walking all that way in the cold just so you can close your eyes for an hour before you have to get up again."

"True." Nick stretched out beside him, his hand resting on Jamie's belly, fingers just brushing his cock. "There might be other advantages to staying."

"There might indeed," Jamie agreed, and pulled him in for a kiss.

Nick hunched his shoulders as they walked up the marble stairs to the Coven the next morning. Fog had set in overnight, shrouding the streets in gray and enveloping the tallest buildings in low cloud. Jamie walked beside him, a friendly greeting on his lips for everyone they passed. Nick made up for it by shoving his hands in his pockets and glowering.

He shouldn't have stayed the night. Certainly he shouldn't have told Jamie everything about himself. But in the dark and the warmth, it had seemed easy. Jamie made it easy.

Fur and feathers, he was definitely not developing feelings for a witch. It was just...the sex, that was it. Had to be. His brain was a little addled, nothing more.

Any familiar with a sharp nose, who happened to be in animal form, would know he'd come straight from Jamie's bed. Rook might be a crow, and so not able to smell much in either shape, but he'd also been the one to see Nick with his hand down Jamie's trousers.

Cicero and Mal loitered about just inside the door, without either of their witches. On seeing them, Mal gave Nick a sly grin and elbowed Cicero.

"James, darling," Cicero said, draping an arm around Jamie. "How are you this morning?"

Jamie looked confused. "Er...I'm fine, thanks. You?"

"Just lovely," Cicero purred. "I slept like a kitten. How did you sleep?"

Of course Rook hadn't been able to keep his beak shut for even a few hours. "Cicero," Nick warned.

Cicero batted thick eyelashes at him innocently. "What is it, Nicholas? You really shouldn't glare so much. You'll get wrinkles."

"Get, you." Nick glared at Mal. "Both of you, scram."

Mal caught Cicero's arm. "Come on, Cicero. The mighty stallion is in a mood."

"Get!" Nick watched them scatter off down the hall, both laughing like a pair of fools.

"Nick?" Jamie said. His voice was a little uncertain. Startled, Nick looked down, but Jamie's eyes had fixed on Mal's retreating back. "You ain't ashamed of what we did, are you?"

Hell. He should have grabbed Cicero and Mal by the scruff and banged their idiot heads together. "Of course not," he said. "I just wish this lot was more respectful of other people's privacy. Rook's the worst, but Cicero isn't much better. And now they've taught Mal bad habits."

"Aye," Jamie agreed wryly. He looked up and offered Nick a rueful grin. "Why do you think I spent all my time in the stable? At least those horses don't talk."

They made their way up the stairs to the detectives' area. Nick went in front, parting the crowd so no one would run into Jamie. Rook, Dominic, and Isaac were all at Rook and Dominic's desk, heads close together in conference.

Rook glanced up as they approached, and a gleam Nick knew all too well entered his eye. "Rook…" he warned.

"Who are you?" Rook asked. "You look like my brother, and sound like my brother, but you can't possibly be him."

"Rook, please," Dominic said. He sat back and rubbed at his eyes. "Leave Nick alone. This is serious business."

"I'll say." Nick folded his arms over his chest. "Let's start with how the Wraith was somehow stronger and faster than any human ought to be. Not to mention survived a fall that should have killed it."

"It had something to do with the bones," Jamie said. "He—it—whatever—touched them a couple of times. I know I saw at least one crack. Got to be hexes."

"I'm not disagreeing with you," Dominic said. "I've never heard of hexes that could do anything like it, but I can't think of any other explanations."

"Then what good are you?" Nick blew out a hard breath. "You don't know the purpose behind the blood hexes, or the ones inscribed on bone, or how the Wraith is able to do things no ordinary mortal should.

Is there anything you *do* know?"

"Don't talk to Dominic like that," Rook said, putting himself bodily in between them. Like he thought Nick would do something to his precious witch.

"Rook, stop," Dominic said.

Both ignored him. "I'll talk to him as I please," Nick said. "I agreed to work with the MWP because I thought you'd be useful. So far, Jamie's the only one who's been any help at all."

"Do you even hear yourself?" Rook waved his arms. "We aren't *useful* enough for you. You're all but admitting you never actually meant to work with the MWP. Just use us for whatever you could get and go."

Didn't Rook remember what it was like, when it had been just the two of them on their own? Having to worry about being taken and force bonded by a witch, with only each other for protection once Ammi was gone?

Or it had been like that, until Rook betrayed him. "As if you didn't join the MWP because they were more *useful* to you than I was," Nick growled. "Or do people think you actually wanted to be an officer of the law?"

"Enough!" Isaac pushed between them. He glared first at Rook, then at Nick. "Fight on your own time."

"Fine." Nick took a step back. He could feel Jamie's eyes on him, worried, but deliberately didn't look at his witch. "I suppose none of you know about the hex the Wraith used to force me into human form, either."

"Of course we do," Jamie said.

That certainly got Nick's attention. They'd had better things to do last night than discuss hexes, and this morning it hadn't even occurred to him to ask.

Dominic sat forward. "What?"

"The hex to force a familiar into human form." Jamie's expression turned uneasy. "I'd never heard of it before I saw the Dangerous Familiars Squad use it, but I ain't a real hexman like Dominic here."

Nick snorted at that. Rook shot him a sharp look, but Dominic quelled him with a touch of fingers on his wrist. "What do you mean, Jamie?" Dominic asked.

"The Dangerous Familiars Squad has it. I saw them use it on Luther with my own eyes. It's exactly the same, down to the activation phrase."

A small bubble of silence fell over the group. "Interesting," Dominic said at last.

"That's one way of putting it," Isaac agreed softly. He'd retreated to the corner of Dominic's desk. Isaac had been through some hard times; Nick wished he'd come to Caballus for help, instead of trying to make it on his own. But Isaac was proud, and angry, and thought he'd found a way to support himself without being dependent on anyone.

He might have, if he hadn't been betrayed and force bonded. He was free again, but the experience had sent him right back into the arms of the MWP.

"I'd say ominous, as they haven't seen fit to share it with the MWP," Rook said, folding his arms over his chest. "Dominic…"

"I know." Dominic looked up. "I'll talk to Ferguson. But don't spread this around to anyone else. We've had too much trouble with betrayal from within to risk it again."

Nick shifted uneasily. He was missing something, which would probably be obvious to anyone used to MWP politics. "I don't understand."

"Later," Rook said, flapping a dismissive hand at him. "Isaac, tell them about your excursion this morning."

"I went to the Menagerie this morning, on the first ferry over," Isaac said. "Bill—that is, Officer Quigley—went with me. The warden told us Luther was still in captivity, there had been no escape, and Jamie was simply mistaken in his identification."

"I wasn't!" Jamie exclaimed.

"Did you ask to see him?" Nick said. "Take a photograph with you for comparison?"

"We asked, but were denied. I didn't think we'd need a photograph, so no, I didn't have one. I'll go over to the Dangerous Familiars Squad and ask for them to turn it over, so we can compare it with the body."

"I'll go instead," Jamie said. "Inspector O'Malley is my uncle. I'll have a better chance of getting their cooperation."

"Good idea." Dominic glanced at Nick. "Are you taking Nick with you?"

Nick rubbed the back of his neck. Come face-to-face with the man responsible for arresting dangerous familiars, while he had a pack of them hiding in his cellar? Anything that brought him to O'Malley's attention was surely something to be avoided. "I think Jamie would do better on his own."

To his surprise, Jamie looked almost relieved. He arched a brow, and Jamie shrugged. "You've got a bit of a temper, Nick. And Uncle Hurley…he's a good man, but…he don't see things the same way we do."

Nick wanted to ask what Jamie meant by that, but it wasn't a conversation to be had in the middle of the Coven. "I'll ask around the feral community, see if anyone saw or heard anything about Luther, then."

"One thing, before you go." Dominic sat back in his chair, his expression grim. "The report came from the morgue this morning. Luther was killed like the other two victims. But before he died… someone pulled out every one of his teeth."

CHAPTER 17

JAMIE ENTERED THE Dangerous Familiars Squad's station, glad that Nick had agreed to let him go alone so readily. It wasn't that he didn't want Nick to meet any of his family. But the truth was, after the things Uncle Hurley had said over dinner about familiars, Jamie worried any meeting would end up in a shouting match at best, and the information they'd come for be lost amidst the quarrel.

Not to mention, Nick might find out Jamie hadn't told Hurley their arrangement was only temporary. Knowing Nick, he'd take it the wrong way, believe Jamie meant to refuse to sever the bond.

Jamie rubbed his chest absently. Christ, he'd miss Nick when all this was over. Maybe Nick would agree to keep seeing him as lovers, even if they couldn't be witch and familiar. His body still ached this morning from being speared on Nick's cock, and fuck if he didn't want to repeat the experience as soon as possible. He thought Nick felt the same, but he wasn't certain.

Maybe someday, Jamie would meet another familiar he could bond with. The thought of bonding with someone else left him feeling oddly hollow, but surely time would change that.

The way time had changed the way he felt about Wyatt? Jamie took a deep breath. It didn't seem fair that he still loved Wyatt, and…cared for…Nick simultaneously. Could he miss his bond with Nick and still find a suitable arrangement with another familiar at the same time?

Not bonding would mean leaving the MWP eventually, though. If

Uncle Hurley would be disappointed when Jamie confessed to him the truth, that his promotion was only temporary, he'd be crushed if Jamie left police work behind altogether. It wasn't like Jamie had anything else he particularly wanted to do with his life. He needed to stop thinking with his heart and start thinking with his head, surely.

The officer at the desk greeted Jamie warmly. "You're Inspector O'Malley's nephew, ain't you? The war hero?"

Jamie flushed. That was one of the things he liked about Nick. Nick might not be able to understand his experiences on the battlefield—but he didn't pretend to, either. He didn't have any expectations of how Jamie ought to feel about the war, his missing leg, or any of it. He just let Jamie be who he was.

"Something like that," he muttered. "I'm here to talk to Uncle Hurley, actually. Is he in?"

"Aye, but you'll have to wait. Senator Pemberton is in there, talking to him as we speak." The man leaned eagerly over the desk. "So, what was it like to serve under Roosevelt? I bet you have some stories to tell."

Thankfully, Jamie was saved from having to entertain the fellow. The door to Hurley's office swung open. A handsome dark-haired man emerged first, dressed in a fine suit. "Just keep up the good work," he said to Hurley, who followed him out.

As they crossed to the door, Jamie rose to his feet. An expression of surprise crossed Hurley's face. The other man, who must be Pemberton, noticed. "Who is this, Inspector?"

For some reason, Hurley hesitated a moment before answering. "Senator Pemberton, this is my nephew, Detective Jamie MacDougal."

"He served in the Rough Riders," the man behind the desk piped up.

"Well, then it's doubly a pleasure to meet you." Pemberton shook Jamie's hand firmly. Up close, he smelled of expensive cologne. "Detective, eh? I suppose you mean to follow in your uncle's footsteps?"

Jamie couldn't exactly deny it with his uncle standing right there. "I'm with the MWP, sir," he said instead.

Some of the effusive warmth faded from Pemberton's demeanor, though his smile remained in place. "Are you? And served in Cuba?" He stepped toward the door. "I'd best be going—I have a lunch appointment with the mayor. Remember what we talked about, O'Malley."

"Aye, sir," Hurley said.

As soon as Pemberton was gone, Jamie asked, "Is everything all right?"

"Fine, fine," Hurley replied distractedly. Then he shook himself and turned back to Jamie. "So what are you doing here, lad?"

Jamie glanced at the desk officer, who was avidly listening in. "Can we talk in your office?"

They settled in. The office smelled of Hurley's cigars. A framed photograph of Muriel, Fan, and their boys sat on his desk. Hurley lit a cigar and leaned back in his chair, the smoke twining lazily around his head. "You look worried, Jamie. What's happened?"

Jamie rubbed his palms on his thighs. "There was another ritual murder in Central Park last night. I'm here because the victim was the familiar I saw you arrest. The lion, Luther."

"So?" Hurley asked, puzzled. "I assume he was released to a witch?"

Jamie shook his head. "Nay. One of the MWP familiars went to talk to the warden at the Menagerie this morning, and was told it ain't him. That I'd made a mistake."

"So you were confused."

"I ain't confused!" Jamie's right hand curled on his knee. "It was the same man, and somebody pulled all of his teeth before he was murdered in the park. We went after the murderer, and almost got killed ourselves for our trouble."

To his surprise, Hurley paled. "You shouldn't have done that Jamie. Chasing after some lunatic—it ain't safe."

Did Hurley think he couldn't perform his duties as detective because of his leg? "Why not? I'm a copper, ain't I? That's what we do."

His uncle stubbed out his cigar in the standing ashtray beside his desk, as if buying time to organize his thoughts. "You are, of course. I worry about you, though. That's natural, and I won't apologize for it."

Maybe Jamie's brush with death in Cuba had frightened his uncle. Made the man realize Jamie was as mortal as anyone else. "I understand. But that's beside the point. I'm sure the dead man is Luther, but the warden at the Menagerie is denying it. I don't know if he's trying to cover up an escape that would make him look bad, or what, but I need your help."

Hurley shook his head slowly. "I ain't sure what I can do. My job is to round up dangerous familiars and put them where they can't hurt anyone else. What happens after that is out of my hands."

"All I need is Luther's photograph from the rogues gallery," Jamie said. "That will prove me right. Then we can force the warden to cooperate, and have a chance at finding out what Luther was doing in the park before he was killed."

"You have some maniac randomly killing ferals," Hurley said. "I don't see that knowing anything about this Luther's movements beforehand will help. But I understand you want to prove yourself right about the identification, so I'll have my aide get the photograph for you. Wait here a moment."

Hurley stepped outside, and Jamie caught the low murmur of voices. "It'll be just a minute," Hurley said, returning and settling back into his chair. "How have things been going otherwise? Settling into your new duties?"

"Aye, well enough," Jamie said, and felt a flash of guilt at the lie. "I had a question, though. The hex you used on Luther that day, to make him take human form. Where did it come from?"

"No idea," Hurley said with a shrug. "It was distributed to us when the squad formed."

"Can I have one? I think the MWP could use them, and—"

But Hurley was already shaking his head. "Sorry, Jamie. They're police property. I'm sure if the higher ups want the MWP to have them, they'll hand them out in good time."

There came a soft knock on the door. A moment later, the aide stuck his head in. "Sorry, Inspector O'Malley, but I have bad news. Since the lion familiar wasn't cooperative, they sent him straight on to the Menagerie. No one wanted to risk him becoming violent again, so they kept the process as short as possible." He shrugged. "No photograph."

Hurley sighed in annoyance. "Blast it. Sorry, Jamie lad, but luck just ain't with you today."

Jamie did his best to hide his disappointment. "Oh well. There's nothing for it." He would have to find another way.

"I'll see you on Sunday, then," Hurley said. As Jamie turned to the door, he added, "A bit of advice for you, before you leave. You're still young, but the decades go past faster than you can imagine. Now is the time to think of your future. You don't want to wake up some morning fifteen or twenty years from now and find you're still just a detective."

Jamie frowned. "I don't understand."

"This case you're working on now…it seems exciting, I'm sure. But it won't take you anywhere. All the politicians—the Police Board, the mayor, the senators—have their eyes on the illegal hex work the MWP is doing. Make your mark in that area, and you're bound to get noticed by all the right folk."

Jamie's gut twisted. "People are dying, Uncle Hurley. I can't just walk away and pretend that ain't happening."

A world-weary look passed over Hurley's face. "People are always dying, lad. Trust me when I say, no one cares about a bunch of criminals and deserters getting murdered. No one is going to pin a medal on you for working yourself to the bone over some dead ferals. In the meantime, Ingram and his Heirs of Adam have the full support of some very powerful men. Not to mention the reform newspapers. If you want to advance, you need to concentrate on their concerns."

Anger boiled in Jamie's stomach, but he kept it from his face. "Ingram hates witches."

Hurley waved a hand, as though it didn't matter. "That's why you make yourself useful. Say the right words, and they won't care if you're a witch. You were smart, taking my advice and picking a familiar instead of whatever that nonsense is about familiars recognizing 'their' witch. Going for a nice, dependable animal like a horse was brilliant. People see regular horses on the street all day long. No one's scared of a horse."

Jamie half wanted to laugh, but it would have been bitter. "And the murders?"

"Will go away on their own. They always do, don't they? The Midnight Assassin, the Whitechapel killer, both got their fill of death and disappeared. Whoever did this will get tired of it and go his own way eventually." Hurley nodded. "Mark my words, Jamie. Put as much distance between yourself and this case as you can, and do the work that gets rewarded. I'll have the Police Board talk to Chief Ferguson, if need be."

"Nay." Jamie forced himself to smile. "That won't be necessary."

He left the station as quickly as he could. Once outside, though, his steps slowed.

Jamie had spent his life looking up to his uncle. Seen him as a man of honor, doing his best to protect the folk of New York. Sure, Hurley took the occasional bribe, but that was ordinary practice, part of what made the whole system work. But when it came down to it, Hurley would always do the right thing.

The coldly practical advice he'd given today had shocked Jamie. Ignore murders, because of the identity of the victims, and concentrate on illegal hexes because it was what the higher ups wanted? How could Hurley even suggest such a thing?

Had being noticed by Roosevelt and his successive rise through the ranks changed Hurley? Or had he always been this way, and Jamie just chosen not to see?

Had he ever really known his uncle at all?

"He's changed," Jamie said, staring off over the water of the Little Hell Gate. Nick stood beside him at the front of a small tug they'd hired to take them to the Menagerie on Sunken Meadow Island. Nick had gone back to Caballus, to make certain things had continued to run in his absence. After checking on the increasingly restless fugitives in the cellar, he'd caught up on a small amount of work, only to be interrupted by a message from Jamie to meet him on the docks. Jamie's interview with his uncle hadn't borne fruit, so there was only one choice left.

Go to the Menagerie themselves.

The very thought filled Nick with dread.

"Your uncle?" he asked, glad to have something to take his mind off what lay before them.

"Aye." Jamie kept his gaze fixed on the water. "He raised Muriel and me, I know I told you that before. He was a good man, a hard worker. He still is," Jamie added quickly. "He worked hard to make Inspector, and to be selected for heading up the Dangerous Familiars Squad."

"Was some of that work knowing whose ass to kiss?" Nick asked.

"I didn't think so." Jamie slammed his hand down on the iron railing in front of them. "He never made it sound that way. He'd come home and tell us about his day when we were young, and…and he sounded like a hero. I wanted to be just like him when I grew up." Jamie's shoulders slumped. "But maybe I was just blind. Maybe he was like this from the start. A man who investigated some crimes and let others go unsolved, because there was no prestige or money involved. I don't know. I feel like I've gone from solid ground to…well, to the heaving deck of a ship," he said wryly.

Nick shifted closer, so their arms pressed together. "People change, when they get a little power," he pointed out. And here he was defending the damned head of the Dangerous Familiars Squad, just to make Jamie feel a little better. It was true what they said; love really did addle the brain.

Oh hell, no.

His breath caught. He wasn't in love with Jamie. That would be stupid. It was just the lingering afterglow of the night they'd shared.

He respected Jamie. He was attracted to the man. His idiot magic thought Jamie should be his witch.

But love? No. He might fuck witches now, or at least this one, but any deeper attachment was out of the question.

"Is everything all right?" Jamie asked, looking up at him. The overcast sky dimmed the brightness of his eyes, brought the green closer in hue to the rusty brown splotch in the right iris.

"Yes." Nick deliberately tore his gaze away from Jamie's and looked out over the water. "I'd just rather be going anywhere but here."

"Aye," Jamie agreed.

The walls of the Menagerie loomed over the flat marsh grass that covered most of the island. The place looked utterly bleak even from a distance: high gray walls, a gate like something from a medieval castle, and guards patrolling with wolfhounds and other dogs meant to hunt and kill the largest predators. More guards stood at each corner of the square structure, big game rifles in hand.

The hair on the back of Nick's neck rose up. If he was caught hiding dangerous familiars, this was where he'd end up. Locked away in this desolate place, probably for the rest of his life. They'd force him into horse form and leave him that way. In a few years, he might not even remember he'd ever been anything else.

Guards gathered on the dock, watching the tug suspiciously. "Metropolitan Witch Police," Jamie called, and held up his badge.

"We already had one of yours here today," said a guard in a decidedly unfriendly tone.

"Must've been on a different matter." Jamie lied with an aplomb that made Nick feel a foolish surge of pride. "We're here to question one of your prisoners."

The guard frowned and eyed Nick suspiciously. "That your familiar? What's he turn into?"

"Just a horse," Jamie said. "Nothing dangerous."

Nick snorted. Jamie elbowed him in the ribs.

The guard shrugged. "You'll have to get permission from the warden. Come on."

Nick trailed behind them as they approached the prison. The guard seemed impatient with Jamie's slower gait, tapping his foot as he waited for them in front of the walls. At his signal, the main portcullis ratcheted open in a rattle of chains. As he passed under the arch and into deeper shadow, Nick shivered. Surely it wasn't really that much colder in the shade, but he felt as if ice had touched his bones.

The gate clanged down behind them, the sound echoing and re-echoing off the walls. They entered a vast courtyard, surrounding the prison itself. The prison consisted of five wings around a central hub, four housing prisoners and one for the prison administration. Sounds echoed from the tiny, barred windows: roars and howls, the chittering shriek of an eagle.

Fur and feathers, he didn't want to be here. He didn't want to walk through that door into the heart of the prison. But if he balked now, other familiars would die, because despite what O'Malley had told Jamie, the Wraith wasn't going to just stop. This wasn't the work of some random lunatic; last night had proved that well enough.

Jamie slowed just a bit, his fingers brushing Nick's. "I've got you, sweetheart," he murmured, too low for their guide to hear. "It's all right. We're walking back out of here soon, you and I."

Nick had never thought a witch's comfort would be welcome. "I know." He squeezed Jamie's fingers, then let go. "But I'm glad you're here with me."

The smell hit him as soon as they stepped in through the heavy iron door. The stench of too many animals kept in too small a space, with only indifferent care shown to them. The warden's office lay in the smallest wing, on the ground floor. Word must have traveled ahead, because the guard merely ushered them inside

The warden, a thin, gray sort of man, didn't bother to rise from his chair. He steepled his fingers together and leaned his elbows on his desk. "This is the second time today we've had visitors from the MWP," he said in a precise voice like the clink of chains. "This is most inconvenient."

"Separate investigations," Jamie said with a shrug.

"Your…compatriot…came with accusations of carelessness. He claimed one of our prisoners had escaped somehow."

Jamie gave him a look of wide-eyed innocence. "What? That don't seem possible. Not with all the guards and dogs, not to mention the river."

Though Nick knew Jamie had meant his words to reassure the warden as to their intentions, he had a point. How would Luther have escaped? Even if he somehow made it past the walls and guards and dogs, could lions even swim? Luther might have secretly been a champion swimmer in his human form, but it seemed rather unlikely.

Something didn't feel right. The patch of skin between his shoulders quivered, as though a stinging fly had landed there.

"Indeed." The warden watched Jamie carefully, ignoring Nick. "Who was it you wanted to see?"

This part of the plan had been Nick's. "Velma," he said. "Wolf. Killed her pregnant sister-in-law in a drunken brawl."

The warden frowned. "Why do you want to talk to her?"

"Her name came up in conjunction with an illegal hex ring," Jamie replied. "We're hoping to get some more names out of her, if we can."

"I see." The warden's frown turned thoughtful. "Very well. You'll be escorted to an interrogation room and will wait for her there."

Chapter 18

The guard led them to a barren room with only a small window and no furniture, which made Jamie wonder just what kind of interrogations happened there. "Wait here," said the guard, and stepped out, shutting the door behind him. The sound made Nick jump.

Everything had made Nick jump since the moment they'd set foot on the island. His eyes widened, his head held slightly back, nostrils flared as if scenting the air. He stamped a foot, seemingly not even aware he'd done it.

"Here now," Jamie said soothingly. He put a hand to Nick's shoulder. "This place has you spooked, don't it?"

Nick swallowed, throat working. "Of course it does."

"I ain't blaming you." Jamie stroked Nick's arm. "Just hold on for a bit, all right? We'll be out of here soon, I promise."

"I keep telling myself that." Nick let out a long breath. "They're locking up ferals here, just because they can turn into animals that frighten them. Just because the ferals don't want to be stuck with a witch."

Jamie felt sick. If Hurley could see this, would he still think the squad's work was worth the promotions and medals that came with it? "I know. But we can't do anything about it right now. Just focus on what we've come for, all right?"

Nick nodded. "All right."

The door swung open, and two guards appeared, dragging a woman between them. She was gaunt, her hair dirty, dressed only in a tattered shift. Cuts and sores surrounded her mouth, and with a flush of horror Jamie realized she must be kept muzzled in wolf form.

She cringed violently the moment she saw them. Her lips peeled back, a low growl emanating from her throat, but Jamie thought it came more from confusion and fear than any violent impulse.

"Leave us to talk to her, will you?" he asked.

The guards looked at him as though he were insane. "She'll change into a wolf and kill you," one protested.

"Leave," Nick said, glaring at the guards.

They exchanged a look, then one shrugged. "We'll be back in fifteen minutes to clean up the mess."

The moment she was released, the woman ran to a corner, nearly on all fours, as if she'd forgotten how to stand up straight. How to be human. Or, rather, how to be a familiar.

As soon as the door shut, Nick took a step toward the woman. She growled, and he stopped immediately. "Velma?" He pitched his voice low. Soothing. "Do you remember me?"

Her golden eyes blinked, and something like recognition came into her face. "N-Nick?" The word came out half cough, her voice rusty as a gate unused for a century.

"Yeah." Nick crouched in front of her, his expression grim. "It's me, Velma."

"Velma." She said the name slowly, as if tasting it. "That's me." She lifted a thin, dirty hand and stared at it. "I'm a familiar."

Saint Mary, maybe this hadn't been such a good idea. Jamie had thought interviewing someone held inside the Menagerie might bring them answers, but what could this broken wretch possibly tell them?

"That's right," Nick said. All the anger was gone from him for once. Instead, he projected an aura of infinite patience. Of strength like a stone, which any flood would break against. "We have some questions for you. Do you think you can answer?"

After a long moment, she nodded. "Yes. I think."

"As far as the warden knows, we're here to ask you about an illegal hex ring," Nick said.

Her yellow eyes narrowed in thought. "No. I never—"

"We know. It was just an excuse." Nick held out a soothing hand. "There was a feral brought here not long ago. Last night, he was murdered in Central Park. According to the warden, the body was misidentified and he's still here. Have you heard anything about an escape?"

It seemed a lot to ask someone in her condition. She bowed her head, and Jamie wasn't certain if she was considering, or simply overwhelmed by all the words. Then she spoke, her voice a low, rasping growl. "No. Not an escape. The guards come. Take some of us. Those they take never come back."

A chill ran through Jamie. "What do you mean?"

She closed her eyes, shivering in her thin shift. "They never come back."

Jamie wished there was a chair for her to sit in. He took off his coat and held it out to her. She glanced at him, then at Nick, who nodded. Taking it, she wrapped it around her thin shoulders, her slight figure appearing even smaller. "I don't know when it began," she said. "At first, it didn't happen often. The guards would come for someone in the middle of the night and take them away."

"So not the orderly release of a prisoner," Nick said.

"Worse now." She tugged Jamie's coat even tighter. "More and more disappear. None come back. The lion was one. I noticed—we don't get many of their kind. They came for him in the dark. Haven't seen him since."

There came a sharp rap on the door. "Still alive in there?" a guard called. "Time's up."

Velma snarled and tried to press herself even farther into the corner. "Nick, tell them. I didn't mean to hurt Jenny and the baby. Gin. Anger. If only I'd been in wolf form, I wouldn't have been drinking. They'd still be alive."

The guards came inside. "Leave her to us," one ordered. He held a hex in his hand, no doubt to force her back into wolf shape.

Nick stared at him, every line of his body tense. Jamie put a hand to Nick's arm. "We have to go," he said, and squeezed muscles drawn taut as wires beneath Nick's coat.

For a moment, he wasn't certain if Nick would back down. Then Nick seemed to collapse into himself. "Yes," he said, and let Jamie lead him back out, past the guards and into the fresh air of the courtyard.

Neither of them spoke until they were on the boat and starting back across the Little Hell Gate. "You all right?" Jamie asked.

Nick stared straight ahead. His brown skin looked unusually dull, his black eyes flat. "Of course."

"Don't be that way. Not with me."

Nick tipped his head back. Clouds gathered, on the verge of rain, and mist beaded on his hair. "Velma didn't kill her sister-in-law because she can turn into a wolf. She did it because she can turn into a human. That's what none of these idiots understand. It's not our animal nature that makes us dangerous."

Silence fell between them again. But as the boat finally pulled up to the dock, Nick said, "What do you think they're doing with the prisoners? The ones who disappear? Luther was murdered in the park, but what about the rest of them?"

"Hell if I know," Jamie said. "But it ain't nothing good, I promise you that."

"I can't stop thinking about something Luther said, when he was being arrested," Jamie said as they made their way back from the docks.

Nick blinked, then seemed to shake himself out of the introspective mood that had gripped him. "What?"

Even lost in thought, Nick had matched his speed to Jamie's despite the long legs that could have outdistanced him easily. It was something Jamie had noticed from the start. Nick never seemed impatient at Jamie's slower gait, nor did he act like some sort of martyr for keeping to his pace. Even when he'd been angry at having to work with a witch, he'd always taken Jamie as he was. Not tried to assign him a role as invalid or war hero.

Jamie moved closer, so their arms brushed as they walked. "He begged them not to arrest him, because he had a wife and children back in Illinois."

Nick cursed. "They won't know he's dead. I'll try to find out who they are, so I can send word. Maybe pass around a collection plate at Caballus, so they'll have a little something to get by on for a while."

"Let me know when, and I'll add some to the pot." Jamie hesitated, feeling suddenly ashamed. "At the time, I thought he was a fool. Why didn't he just bond with a witch, instead of causing so much trouble for everyone?"

Nick kept his gaze straight ahead. "And now?"

"Now I think I was the fool." They paused to let a wagon pass by. "You said your mother didn't want to bond, because it would take her away from you. Luther surely felt the same way. He was working in New York, but he must have hoped to go back to Illinois, or bring his family here. He'd built a life of his own, and now the law said he had to give it up. What else could he do but hide and hope for the best?"

For a moment, Nick seemed to weigh his answer, though Jamie

didn't know why. Eventually, though, he only said, "Not a thing."

"I'm going to talk to Uncle Hurley about this." Jamie hunched his shoulders. "I don't know that he'll listen, but this has to stop. Not just the killings, not just whatever's happening at the Menagerie, but the entire Pemberton Act. Maybe if the two of us go to Roosevelt together, he'll listen."

Before Nick could answer, a brown and white streak dropped from above, startling a passing horse. A moment later, Bess stood in front of them on human legs, her dark eyes unhappy. "There you are! I've been looking everywhere for you, Nick."

"What's the trouble, Bess?" Nick asked.

"The park." She shifted from one foot to the other. "Meet me near the Dairy." Then she was gone, back into hawk form and away.

Jamie blinked. "Well. I suppose we ought to go see what she wants, then."

Nick gazed after her, his expression troubled. "I suppose we should at that."

They made their way to the park as quickly as possible. After so much walking, Jamie reflected he'd be glad to get home and take off the leg for a while. Bess found them just as the ornate loggia of the Dairy came into view, its cheerful yellow and red paint bright against the brown pasture surrounding it.

"So what's this about?" Nick asked, as soon as she landed.

Bess pointed at the Dairy. "Ask how the cows are."

Nick and Jamie exchanged a glance, then Nick shrugged. "All right. We'll be back in a few minutes."

"Meet me at Playmates Arch," she said, and flew away.

"A woman of few words," Jamie observed.

"Indeed." Nick shook his head. "I can't help but wonder if she was always this way, or if…" He trailed off.

"She ain't Velma," Jamie said softly. "And even if she was, it would be by her own choice."

"You're right." Nick flashed him a wan smile. "Come on. Let's see whatever it is she wants us to see."

They passed beneath the colorful loggia into the building itself. A counter inside sold sandwiches, coffee, ice cream, and of course fresh milk. A woman with three children in tow stood at the counter, while the man on the other side shook his head sadly. "Sorry, but we don't have any milk today," he said. "You'll have to go to the market."

"But it's expensive," the woman protested. She pulled a patched and worn shawl tighter around her shoulders. "And not as healthful as milk from the park, everyone knows that. My girls—"

"Are going to have to get their milk somewhere else," the man interrupted. "Or invent a hex that can make milk out of air."

The woman left. "Out of milk?" Jamie asked, once she and her children departed.

"That's what I said." The man spread his hands apart. "Damned cows have gone dry. First time I've ever seen, but there you have it. I'm sure things will be back to normal soon enough."

"I'm sure," Jamie murmured, though he wasn't.

They met Bess at Playmates Arch. Falling leaves streamed on the breeze, but it seemed to Jamie that some of the trees weren't just readying for winter. Bark peeled off in sheets, and dead branches littered the walkways.

"Do you see?" Bess asked.

"The cows have gone dry," Nick said. "And the trees are dying."

"The cows haven't just gone dry. They've sickened. The pasture has died." She gestured to the trees. "I've lived here for twenty years. I've never seen so many dead trees. It's as though a blight has settled into the soil, the water, the air."

"Remember the tree near the owl?" Jamie asked. "In the Ramble? It was dying, too."

"I remember," Nick said, and Jamie felt a little flush of heat, recalling what they'd done in the Cave after. "Something is wrong here." He nodded at Bess. "You did the right thing, letting us know."

Her grave expression cracked slightly, a hopeful smile just bending her lips. "I figured you'd know what to do, Nick."

Then she was back in bird form, her red tail bright even amidst the yellow and orange leaves. Nick stuffed his hands deep into the pockets of his coat. "I wish to God I did," he said with a heavy sigh.

Jamie stared past the shuttered carousel, to the Dairy and the Pond beyond. The first row of buildings was just visible past the Pond, a reminder that they stood in an oasis in the heart of the largest city in the United States. "This has to be connected to the murders. To the blood hexes."

"Agreed." Nick shook his head slowly. "But how? The hexbreaker said he didn't sense anything but the Great Hex."

"Could they be some kind of…I don't know…anti-hex?" Jamie made a vague gesture encompassing everything and nothing. "Like an antidote to a poison hex, such as the one Uncle Hurley used on Roosevelt to save him. Except this one is breaking down the Great Hex."

"That's a question for Dominic. Or Yates."

"It's getting late, but this can't wait." Jamie glanced at Nick. "I'll write a quick summary and send it to Dominic via courier familiar. Expensive, but the MWP can reimburse me. Then after, maybe we could get dinner, before you go to the saloon?"

"I'd like nothing better," Nick said with a regretful smile. "But I have some things to do this evening I can't put off."

"Oh." Jamie tried to hide his disappointment.

Nick bumped him with his hip. "I'll see you in the morning, at the Coven. Bright and early."

"All right." Jamie hesitated, but there was no one else around to see. So he grabbed Nick's shoulders and pulled him down, just enough to brush a kiss over his lips. "Something to think about when you're alone in bed tonight, then."

Nick's dark eyes were hot, and he laughed softly as he stepped away. "That I will, witch. You can count on it."

That night, Nick stepped out into the slot of an alley behind Caballus. Far too narrow to admit a cart, it mainly existed to give the fire escapes at the rear of the buildings somewhere to let out onto. He took a deep breath, smelled garbage and coal smoke. The misty day had turned to a cool, foggy night.

Perfect.

"No one's here," Nick said. "Come on out."

The fugitives from the cellar emerged into the night air. "Free air at last," Conrad said.

"Don't get overconfident," Rachel replied. "We're still in danger."

Nick nodded. "We go fast and quiet. The fog should help. If any coppers approach, leave them to me. If we're separated, continue straight to Bryant Park. The contact there will take you to the ferry. Understand?"

There came murmurs of assent from the three adults. "Is it…very far?" the girl asked. Fear put a tremor in her voice. "Where we're going?"

She didn't mean Bryant Park. Nick wished he could tell her it was just a short trip, and then she'd be safe forever. No more fear. No more people looking to lock her up, just because of her animal form. But he couldn't, so he only said, "I'll get you there safe. I promise."

"What if I get lost in the fog?"

Nick held out his hand. She took it; his big fingers curled around her entire hand easily. "There," he said, giving her what he hoped was a comforting smile. "You just stay with me, and it'll be all right."

"Can we get moving?" Conrad asked impatiently.

Nick shot him an unfriendly look, but led the way out of the alley. The streetlights shone softly, haloed by moisture, illuminating the air around them more than the sidewalk or street. Buildings loomed out of the mist and vanished again. Cabs appeared with unnerving suddenness, the clop of the horses' hooves muffled. Saloons and brothels seemed to be doing a rousing business, though; people wanted something to warm them against the chill outside.

"The fog's a blessing," Rachel said in a low voice. "The Lord looking out for us."

Hopefully, the fog and damp would keep the coppers either tucked away somewhere warm, or prevent them from noticing the small group. Nick led the way up 37th Street to Sixth Avenue without incident.

Finally, in less than half an hour, the fugitives would be out of his hands. Nick could stop looking over his shoulder. Stop worrying he might accidentally let something slip to Jamie.

He'd almost told Jamie today. Maybe not everything, but that there was another way. That people did try, that the dangerous ferals hadn't been abandoned to their fate by everyone.

He hadn't. Not because Nick believed Jamie would bring the matter up with his uncle, but because he feared Jamie might let something slip, if he knew. By accident of course, and if the risk had just belonged to Nick, he might have told him then and there.

Too many others were involved, though. This group was almost to safety, which meant he and Kyle would also be safer, at least until the next batch came through. Though he wasn't sure he'd be able to sleep soundly again anytime soon, not after what he'd seen today.

The Menagerie had been so much worse than even he'd expected. And Velma…

That might be him, someday. Bridled, hobbled by chains. A cruel bit in his mouth. The memory of his life as a familiar slipping away one day at a time. How long would it take to forget altogether? To not recall his human shape, human thoughts, human cares. Would he even forget Jamie, in the end?

Nick shivered. He couldn't let himself focus on what might happen. If he froze, he'd be useless to everyone. He had to keep moving forward; it was the only way to take care of the ferals who depended on him.

"What was that?" Conrad asked. The tiger brought up the rear, and turned to look behind them.

They all came to a halt. "What do you mean?" Nick asked. The girl tightened her grip on his hand, and he gave her fingers an absent squeeze.

"I thought I heard someone behind us." Conrad cocked his head, listening intently.

Nick did the same. For a long moment, he heard only the sounds of distant singing from some music hall. Maybe Conrad's imagination had gotten away from him, in the fog and the dark.

There came a faint sound, like the careless scuff of a boot on the sidewalk. A rattle accompanied it, a dry click of bone on bone that brought all Nick's senses to attention.

For the first time, he cursed the night and fog that made it impossible to see more than a few feet in any direction. He strained his ears, and the soft rattle came again.

A figure emerged from the fog. Two horns rose from beneath the black hood, one of them broken off halfway from Jamie's bullet.

The Wraith.

Chapter 19

"Run," Nick said.

Everyone else seemed frozen in place. "Mother of God, what is it?" Conrad backed up slowly from the Wraith. The figure advanced implacably, fog swirling around it, and fear crackled along Nick's nerves.

"Run!" he barked. Letting go of the girl's hand, he shoved her behind him. "Take the young ones, get to the meeting point, and get the hell out of here! Go! Go!"

Rachel didn't waste time arguing. She grabbed both the young ferals and sprinted up Sixth Avenue, vanishing into the thick fog. Conrad and the third adult, a puma, hesitated. Conrad's yellow eyes darted to Nick. "What—"

"It killed Wyatt, and Luther." Nick strode past them, toward the Wraith. He had to draw its attention, keep it away from the others until they could escape to safety. "I said run!"

They bolted, the heavy fog muffling their footfalls. Nick's heart hammered in his chest, but he planted his feet and glared at the shadowy figure. "All right, you bastard. I beat you before, and I'll do it again."

Except he'd had Jamie with him, then.

The Wraith rushed him. He tried to sidestep, but not fast enough. The Wraith's fist collided with Nick's gut with all the force of a sledgehammer. Nick flew back, slamming into the sidewalk, all the air gone from his lungs.

The Wraith strode toward him, inexorable as the oncoming tide. If the fall from Belvedere Castle had left behind any injuries, they hadn't slowed it down at all. As the Wraith advanced, it reached beneath its cloak and pulled out a knife similar to the one it had lost during the earlier fight.

Nick's lungs unfroze, and he took a deep, gasping breath. He rolled onto all fours, hand slipping on something foul on the sidewalk. He had to stay out of arm's reach, no matter what.

He'd given the fugitives time to run. But if he could draw the Wraith down 37th Avenue and away from their trail, so much the better.

He surged up in horse form, kicking blindly behind him. Then he broke into a gallop and fled.

Footsteps pounded after him, unnaturally fast. A glance back showed the Wraith practically on his tail. How long could the killer keep this up?

How long could Nick? He was built for strength and agility, not endurance or speed. He'd drawn the Wraith away from the fugitives, but now it seemed likely he'd end up gutted in their stead. Assuming he wasn't the Wraith's target from the start.

He needed help.

"Jamie!" he called through the bond.

Surprise lapped back through the bond to him. *"Nick?"*

"Who else would it be, witch? I'm in trouble. The Wraith is after me."

Shock turned to stark fear. *"Saint Mary, no. Can you make it to my apartment? Where are you?"*

"On 37th, just past Sixth Avenue."

"I've got my gun—I'll yell for the beat copper. Just keep running."

Nick had the feeling another witness, one not a feral, would be more useful than Jamie's gun. *"I'm not planning on stopping, trust me."*

He thundered across Park Avenue, nearly knocking a woman to the ground when she appeared unexpectedly out of the fog. If he could get far enough ahead of the Wraith, could he shift back to human form, duck into a building or doorway, and rely on darkness and fog to conceal him?

Unfortunately, getting enough distance between him and the Wraith wasn't going to be simple. In horse form, he could easily make out the dark figure shadowing his left flank, just a few feet shy of his tail. Its black cloak billowed around it, and the white bones gleamed beneath the streetlights.

The Second Avenue El loomed out of the fog, even as a train rattled past overhead. Nick cut close to the iron trestle, hoping to force the Wraith to slow to avoid running into it. It seemed to work; he lost sight of the Wraith, and once he was back out from under the shadow of the El, he saw no one behind him.

"I think I lost him."

Jamie's fear spilled through the bond. *"Are you sure?"*

The end of the train rushed past overhead. A dark shape dropped from it, right in front of Nick.

Nick swerved desperately, even as the Wraith leapt at him with knife extended. The blade slashed across Nick's left haunch, a stinging line of pain.

"Nick!"

Nick kicked behind him, forcing back the Wraith. He caught a glimpse of paper in the Wraith's other hand; no doubt the hex to make him take on human form.

If the Wraith succeeded in hexing him, he was as good as dead.

Nick put down his head and ran. His heart labored, and foam flew from his mouth. Sweat coated his flanks. If he could only make it two more blocks, he could reach Jamie.

Just one more block.

And there was Jamie in the streetlight, leaning on his crutch, revolver in his right hand. Dimly, Nick was aware of Jamie's yells, though he couldn't hear the words over the crash of his own hooves, the frantic pace of his heart.

Jamie fired a shot past Nick. A second later, a copper in a blue uniform charged up out of the fog, gun drawn and whistle in his mouth. Unable to go any farther, Nick stumbled to a halt.

"You there!" the copper yelled, and ran past Nick. "Stop!"

Nick's head sagged, and his legs trembled. He stood very still, breathing in great gusts of air, his heart hammering. "Nick?" Jamie asked, sounding worried. "Are you all right? Oh hell—you're bleeding."

"Lost him," said the copper who'd answered Jamie's summons. "Is the horse all right?"

Jamie's hand stroked Nick's flank gently. "Come on, Nick. I can't get you inside this way. You need to turn human, okay?"

Nick bobbed his head tiredly. The effort felt pulled from his bones, and the moment he was on two feet again, he lurched and nearly fell. Jamie seized his elbow from one side, and the copper from the other. "Help me get him inside," Jamie said. He tugged gently on Nick's arm. "Come on, sweetheart. I've got you. I ain't going to let you fall."

"I know," Nick, said, forcing his aching legs to move. "I know."

*

Nick lay on his side on the bed, naked from the waist down, while Jamie tended his injured leg. The bandage glowed white against his dark skin, making the result look worse than it really was. The slice hadn't been deep enough to need stitches, and the clean edges meant the wound had practically sealed on its own.

"There you go," Jamie said, patting him on the arse. "It ought to heal quick. Probably won't even scar much."

"Thank you." Nick lay with his eyes closed, his black hair sticking to his face from dried sweat.

"Are you going to be all right? Need walked? Some hot mash?"

Nick cracked his eyelids open just enough to shoot Jamie a glare. Jamie grinned. "Now I know you're feeling better."

"Hmph." Nick closed his eyes again, but reached out blindly. Jamie took his hand. "Thank you."

"For coming to your rescue?" Jamie suggested. "Always happy to oblige."

"For that too, yes."

Jamie swallowed against sudden emotion. "I'm just glad you were close enough. If you'd been in some other part of town…" He let the thought trail off. "Where were you going so late at night, anyway? I would've thought you'd be busy with that saloon of yours."

"Kyle's going to be worried when I don't come back," Nick said, rubbing his eyes. "Damn it."

"You're in no shape to go trotting off now," Jamie replied. Nick hadn't answered his question, but he let it go. None of his business, really, and they had more important things to worry about. "Especially since the Wraith is still out there. It can't have been a coincidence he attacked you."

Nick dropped Jamie's hand and slowly sat up, wincing as he did so. "No. As much as I hate to admit it, I must have been followed." His frown deepened. "Behind that mask, or whatever it is, the Wraith could be practically anyone."

"Aye." Jamie shivered at the thought.

"He didn't try to kill me," Nick went on. "If he'd only wanted me dead, he could have gutted me before I had the chance to run. Instead he hit me. I think…I think he meant to subdue me."

Jamie's mouth went dry and his throat tried to close up. "Saint Mary, have mercy. He was going to take you to the park, wasn't he? Kill you, just like he…just like…"

Wyatt's name felt lodged somewhere in his chest. Wyatt's death had been horror enough. If he'd lost Nick the same way…

The memory of how Wyatt had looked, carved up by that knife, his body in the center of a blood spattered hex, filled his vision. But his mind tried to superimpose Nick's face, Nick's body.

His heart couldn't take it. He'd coped with the loss of Wyatt, then struggled again when Wyatt truly died in Central park. If he lost Nick, it would crush him, beyond any ability of time to repair.

Nick linked his hand with Jamie's again. "I'm safe. Thanks in no small part to you." His full lips twisted into a wry smile. "Now there's something I never thought I'd say to a witch. You've helped save my life twice now."

"Just one of many services I offer," Jamie managed to say, though the intended smirk didn't feel quite right on his mouth. "We should stay together from now on, though. It ain't safe otherwise."

Nick tensed slightly. "I can't. I have a saloon to run, remember?"

Jamie shrugged. "I'll bunk with you, then."

Nick avoided his gaze. "I don't know. You're a witch, Jamie."

It hurt, though Jamie tried not to show it. "I won't set foot in the saloon. I know I ain't welcome there. But I've already been in your apartment, twice."

Nick let out a gusty breath. "The Wraith isn't going to come bursting into Caballus to kidnap me."

"What if he's already there?" Jamie shot back.

Silence hung between them. Nick's expression grew troubled…then he shook his head. "Even so." He began to unbutton his shirt, revealing his muscular chest. "But we're together tonight, so let me properly demonstrate my gratitude for the rescue."

Nick returned to Caballus as soon as the sun was up. As he'd expected, Kyle waited for him despite his shift having ended some hours ago.

"You're alive," Kyle greeted him. "Thank God. What about Conrad and the puma?"

Nick's heart sank. "They didn't make it to Bryant Park?"

"A seagull familiar brought a note from the ferry captain." Kyle ran his hand back through tousled hair. "They wanted to let me know something had happened to you. It's worded vaguely, of course, but Rachel and the youngsters arrived at Bryant Park. They'd gotten separated from the other two in the fog. They waited, but the contact didn't dare delay too long." He let his hand fall to his side. "What *did* happen, Nick?"

"The Wraith."

"Oh God." Kyle paled sharply. "It's attacking people on the streets now?"

"I don't think so." Nick had plenty of time to ponder on the walk back to Caballus this morning. "I think it followed us."

Kyle's brows drew together. "But you said the killings didn't have anything to do with the fugitives."

"They still might not." Nick pulled out a chair and sat down, stretching his aching legs in front of him. Every muscle hurt from his run last night; likely he'd be sore for days. "The Wraith saw my face, and probably heard my name at the park the other night. Even if it—he—she—didn't, just asking around for the familiar who can turn into a big, solid black horse would lead them here sooner rather than later."

"So it might be watching the saloon," Kyle said unhappily. "Obviously it failed to kill you. What about the missing fugitives?"

Nick shook his head. If Conrad and the puma had escaped but missed the meeting, would they have returned to Caballus? Or would they try to leave the city on their own, just to avoid winding up in the basement again?

If the Wraith had caught them, killed them, Rook would have sent word about more bodies being discovered by now. But if they'd been caught by the coppers instead...

Nick didn't think they'd talk willingly. But sooner or later, one of them would break, and tell the coppers exactly where they'd been hiding. The Dangerous Familiars Squad would raid Caballus, and Nick would be lucky not to find himself locked away in the Menagerie.

"Nothing we can do about them now," Nick said at last. "Go home and get some sleep." He rose to his feet tiredly. "I'm going to scrub down the hidden room in the cellar. If the coppers raid us, I don't want there to be so much as a hair they can use as evidence."

Nick looked even more out of sorts than usual, when he met Jamie outside the Coven. "Is your wound hurting you?" Jamie asked. He knew he should have insisted on walking back to Caballus with Nick, instead of agreeing to meet him here later.

Nick started to shake his head, then caught himself. "A bit. How did you know?"

"Because your face is longer than when you're in horse form." Jamie shrugged. "I assumed either something went wrong at the saloon, or you weren't feeling yourself. I have a pain hex, if you need one."

"No. Not yet." Nick paused, and his expression eased into something like a smile. "Thank you, though."

From the outside, everything seemed ordinary at the Coven. The reporters milled about on the steps, and familiars and witches ignored them as best they could. But the moment they stepped within, Jamie knew something had changed.

Ordinarily, the MWP's headquarters was a boisterous place. Familiars flying about, arguing, or running errands; barking, laughing, and growling as they did so. Witches asking each other for hexes, or discussing cases, or even just chatting across their desks.

This morning, the air was almost eerily still. Only a few familiars moved about the corridors, and all of them seemed intent on doing their business as quickly and quietly as possible. Witches murmured to one another, but kept their voices low.

"Did someone die?" Nick asked, so only Jamie could hear.

"Not that I've heard." Jamie led the way up the nearly deserted stairs to the detectives' area. There was a surprising lack of familiars in the room, and those present seemed to be staying in human form. A thin, pale man Jamie didn't recognize drifted around the room, peering over shoulders and asking questions.

Rook and Dominic looked up at their approach. Dominic hurriedly bent back to his work, but Rook glanced in the direction of the stranger. "Who's the new fellow?" Jamie asked as soon as they were close enough.

"An observer from the Police Board," Rook murmured, as though he feared being overheard.

"A what?" Nick demanded.

"Shh! Keep your voice down, you brainless horse." Rook shot another look over his shoulder. "His name is Charles Lund. The Police Board sent him, but he's an aide to Senator Pemberton."

"Not to mention a member of Ingram's church," Dominic added. He bent over a hex, pretending it had his full attention. "He showed up this morning, talked to Ferguson behind closed doors, then announced he'd been asked by both Pemberton and the Police Board to make sure MWP resources are used, quote, 'as efficiently as possible.'"

Uncle Hurley's words came back to Jamie forcefully. Pemberton and the rest only cared about the anti-illegal hex work at the moment. If Lund found out Jamie and Nick were looking into the murders, would he be satisfied that at least it was only a single witch-familiar pair assigned to the case?

"You got my letter?" Jamie asked, as quietly as he could.

Dominic nodded without looking up. "Yes. Owen and I are both very disturbed. But we can't talk about it here."

"Agreed." Nick's voice was a low rumble. "Ingram and I have clashed in the past. I doubt a member of his flock is going to look on me kindly."

"Tonight," Dominic said. "Dinner at our apartment. Bring the wine."

"Right." Jamie nodded. Mindful of what Nick had said, he added, "We'd best leave, then. See you tonight."

When he turned back in the direction of the stairs, though, it was already too late. Lund had spotted them and made his way through the crowded desks in their direction.

"Come on," Nick said. He put a hand to Jamie's elbow, and they hurried toward the stairs, pretending not to see Lund heading their way.

They didn't quite make it. "Hello," Lund said, stepping between them and escape. "I don't recall Chief Ferguson mentioning the two of you."

He didn't hold out a hand to shake, but kept both clasped behind him, like a disapproving school teacher. Lund might have been handsome, with his thick blond hair and hazel eyes, but his mouth looked as though he spent all day sucking on lemons.

Jamie forced himself to smile. "Jamie MacDougal," he said, putting out his own hand. "We're the newest detectives, so the chief probably just forgot to mention us. My uncle is the head of the Dangerous Familiars Squad." Maybe that would make Lund leave them alone.

"I see." Lund reluctantly shook Jamie's hand, touching him only so long as basic courtesy demanded. "What assignment do you have, MacDougal?"

"Still in training," Jamie said cheerfully, as though he didn't have a brain in his head. "Whatever the other detectives tell us, mostly."

Lund's gaze shifted from Jamie to Nick. His expression grew even more sour, as though he'd smelled something unpleasant. "Is this your familiar?"

"Oh, aye," Jamie babbled. "A horse. Did you know I was a Rough Rider in Cuba? Of course, all our horses got left behind in Tampa, except for the officers' mounts."

The one time he tried to fall back on his service record, and it didn't work. "Nick, isn't it?" Lund asked. "You own a tawdry saloon on 28th Street. Now you're with the MWP as well?"

Nick's smile showed far too many teeth to be anything but menacing. "Jamie here was kind enough to let me keep it, at least long enough to find a buyer. Of course, I'll be giving it up for my witch."

"Of course," Lund said, but Jamie couldn't tell if he was convinced or not. "Good to know. It's a witch's duty to keep his familiar out of trouble."

"Excuse me, Mr. Lund?" Rook said. He bobbed his head apologetically as he approached. "I don't mean to interrupt, but as you're so interested in the illegal hexes, Detective Kopecky would like to show you something."

"A Polish hexman," Lund said with distaste. "As if all the Irish weren't bad enough." He left with Rook without bothering to say goodbye. Which was fine by Jamie.

They hurried down the stairs, before Lund could come back. Rook must have spotted Lund talking to Nick and known no good could come from it. Still… "That was quite the load of horse shit you gave Lund back there," Jamie said.

"Did you expect some other kind?"

Jamie snorted. "Very funny. Maybe you can join Rook and I in our Vaudeville act. Do you think Lund believed it?"

Nick shrugged. "I told him what he wanted to believe. That usually does the trick."

They reached the bottom of the steps and made for the big, bronze doors of the entrance. Before they reached it, the witch behind the desk in the entryway waved a hand and called, "Detective MacDougal? I've a message for you, sir."

"Who from?" Jamie asked, even as he held out his hand for the folded paper.

The witch shrugged. "No idea. Some urchin brought it in, said he'd been instructed to tell me to give it to no one but you."

The paper was nondescript, the sort of scrap that could be bought cheaply almost anywhere. Jamie unfolded it. In a blocky hand someone had written:

LAST NIGHT WAS A WARNING.
STOP NOW, OR IT WILL GET WORSE.

Chapter 20

Nick stomped up the stairs to Dominic and Rook's apartment that evening, Jamie close behind him. After Jamie received the note, Nick hadn't been willing to let the witch out of sight. He took Jamie back to his apartment, threw some ledgers at him, and told him to make himself useful. After a final admonishment not to set foot out the door, Nick retreated to the saloon until it was time to collect him for dinner.

"I think this is it," Nick said, pausing outside a door on the second floor.

"You ain't been here before?" Jamie asked in surprise.

"No." The word came out shorter than Nick had intended. "Rook knows where to find me if he needs something. You can stop giving me that pitying look right now, witch."

Before he could knock, the door swung open. Nick found himself staring down at bright red hair, accompanied by a cheeky grin. "Well, looks like the wild horse dragged himself here," Mal said. He wore a suit far too expensive for the neighborhood. The benefits of having a rich witch, no doubt. At least Mal hadn't sold himself cheap, which was more than could be said for most of the MWP familiars.

"Wine," Nick said, and thrust the bottle at Mal, before pushing past him into the apartment.

Though the place was spacious by most tenement standards, it felt cramped at the moment. Yates sat at a table, looking as out of place as it was possible to be. Cicero, in cat form, sprawled in the center of the table, ignoring Isaac who was trying to lay out plates and forks. Rook, Dominic, and Bill Quigley crowded around the stove, while Tom Halloran perched in the open window leading out onto the fire escape.

The smells wafting from the stove sent Nick's stomach to grumbling. Jamie grinned and patted his own belly. "I'm so hungry, I could eat a…" he caught himself, but not before Mal let out a bark of laughter.

"Aye, I bet you could," he said, winking at Nick. "Nothing like a bit of the old—"

"Shut it," Nick said, cheeks growing warm. Which was stupid; this lot had no right to judge him, given what most of them got up to. "Jamie got a threatening letter today."

Yates sat forward. "Really?"

"Can't we have dinner first?" Rook asked. "Cicero, move your furry ass off the table; we have to eat there."

Cicero twitched an ear in Rook's direction but didn't move. Isaac scooped him off the table and unceremoniously dumped him into Tom's lap.

"Let me pour you a drink, Nick," Quigley offered. "Beer or wine?"

"Beer." He watched Quigley pour expertly from the bucket. "Are you a witch?"

Isaac stiffened slightly, though Nick didn't know why. Quigley didn't see, too intent on his pouring to notice. "I took the tests, when I was younger. I've a bit of potential, just enough to be on the charts, but not enough to think about making a career out of. So it was off to the regular police I went. Didn't think a jot about witches for the next few years, until a fellow by the name of Tom Halloran got himself into a bit of trouble."

"More than a bit," Tom said, scratching behind Cicero's ears.

"That was the first time we encountered blood hexes," Yates put in. Apparently, he was as eager to get on with things as Nick.

Nick accepted the beer from Quigley and drifted over to the stove. "Smells good," he told Rook grudgingly. No wonder Kopecky had developed a comfortable paunch, if Rook did the cooking.

"Of course it does." Rook cast a look over his shoulder, at the other witches and familiars gathered around the apartment. "This reminds me of how everyone would get together after church, when we were little. Do you remember, Nick?"

An unexpected pang touched Nick's heart at the memory. In fair weather, everyone in the neighborhood would gather outside the church

Sunday afternoons. Set up tables laden with food, enjoy a big communal meal while children played and couples courted, and the adults exchanged gossip or discussed the news. In the rain or cold, the gathering moved indoors, rotating from house to house so no one had to play host every time.

That community had kept them afloat, after their parents died and before Nick was old enough to support his younger brother as well as himself. He couldn't help but wonder what had happened to some of them since. If he went back, who would have gotten married, or had children, or moved away, or passed on? Would they even remember him now?

"Haven't thought about that in a long time," he said.

"I miss it, sometimes." Rook glanced up. A strand of his silky black hair stuck to his brow from either steam or sweat. "But living in the barracks, with the other MWP familiars, was similar in a lot of ways. The sense we could rely on each other, even if we didn't get along all the time." Rook hesitated. "I suppose you found that at Caballus, eventually? That sense of belonging?"

Nick hadn't, not really. He did everything he could for the ferals under his protection, but there weren't any Sunday dinners. No sense that if he stumbled, someone would be there to keep him from falling too far.

His eyes strayed to Jamie. Jamie had saved his life, not once but twice. Shown up unasked on his day off, to work on the books without wanting anything in return. And last night, his concern and fear had been so damned obvious, along with the care later.

Nick had told himself they had to part ways after this was all over and their bond broken. But the thought of never seeing those particolored eyes again, never hearing Jamie's laugh, made Nick feel lonelier than he ever had in his entire life.

As if he'd heard Nick's thought, Jamie glanced up from where he'd taken a seat at the table. He flashed Nick an unselfconscious grin, and Nick found himself smiling in return.

Rook whacked Nick's arm with a wooden spoon. "Move it," he said. "Dinner's ready. Let's feast."

Jamie leaned back in his chair with a groan. Only scraps remained of the dinner: aloo gosht, corned beef, potato dumplings, salad courtesy of Yates, and apple pie. He felt like he could have closed his eyes and dozed off right there at the table.

"So what's this about a letter?" Yates asked. Jamie had the feeling he'd been waiting impatiently for everyone to have their fill.

Nick's chair creaked as he shifted in it beside Jamie. "The Wraith tried to kill me last night."

"What?" Rook yelped. "Why the devil didn't you say something earlier?"

Nick folded his arms over his chest. "Because someone didn't want to talk about any of it until after dinner. Now who was that again?"

"Enough," Dominic said. "Nick, tell us what happened. And what it has to do with this letter of Jamie's."

They took turns, Nick explaining that the Wraith had tracked him after leaving Caballus. No one asked him why he'd been out late; Jamie had the impression they assumed he'd been coming over to Jamie's apartment to begin with. Nick did nothing to disabuse them of the notion, and so Jamie didn't either.

Jamie passed around the note. "Do you think it was from the Wraith?" he asked. He'd had all afternoon alone in Nick's apartment to ponder. "Maybe he thinks we're close to catching him, and so attacked Nick to scare us off?"

"It's possible," Yates murmured. He studied the note closely, then handed it to Dominic.

"You sound doubtful," Jamie said.

Yates took off his spectacles and polished them absently with a silk handkerchief. "Dominic and I have some ideas about the bones the Wraith has been using. We don't think the Wraith is acting alone."

That didn't sound at all good. "What, you mean he ain't just some looney?"

"I'm afraid not," Dominic said. "It was your trip to the Menagerie that got us thinking. This note means your work on the case has been noticed, either when you fought the Wraith in the park, or when you visited the Menagerie. Going by what happened last night, Nick has clearly been surveilled. It's likely you have as well, Jamie."

Cicero's yellow-green eyes widened. "Or all of us."

"Let's not get too paranoid yet," Yates cautioned. "Killing Nick would have effectively removed Jamie from the case, as he'd no longer be an MWP detective."

Which was the least of Jamie's problems. He swore, drawing a startled look from Yates. "If our bond is putting Nick in danger, we should break it tonight."

He'd miss it. Miss that warmth in his chest. But anything was worth keeping Nick safe.

"No," Nick said. He put a hand to Jamie's arm; out of the corner of his eye, Jamie saw the startled looks the gesture received from everyone else.

Jamie focused on Nick's gaze, so dark he felt like he could drown in it. "I ain't going to let you get hurt."

Nick's mouth curled up into a small smile. "I appreciate the concern, but the threat means we're close. Or close enough to worry someone. We can't give up now."

"We might be close enough to worry someone, but *who?"* Jamie tore his gaze away from Nick and glanced around the room. "Surely you don't mean to imply the guards at the Menagerie have something to do with the Wraith, do you?"

Yates and Dominic exchanged a look. But it was Nick who said, "You said it yourself—the Dangerous Familiars Squad and the Wraith had the same hex. The one to force us into human shape."

Jamie wanted to argue, but wasn't certain what to say. "The squad's got nothing to do with it," he settled on at last. "Uncle Hurley might be more focused on climbing the ranks than me, but he's still a good man."

"We're not making any accusations yet," Dominic said carefully. "But after hearing that prisoners are disappearing from the Menagerie, and seeing Luther's teeth had been pulled out, it got us to thinking about the hexes scratched on bone."

Cold settled into Jamie's gut. "Saint Mary, you can't be saying what I think you're saying."

"It's possible the charms the Wraith uses were made from the body parts of familiars," Yates said. "The hexes might not even need a witch to charge them, if they could draw upon the latent magic of the dead familiar."

Jamie's dinner threatened to return the way it had come. Nick swore savagely.

"Of course—it isn't enough for witches to control our lives." He brought his fist down on the table, making the plates jump. "Now you're just killing us outright, hacking us apart—"

"Nick, *stop."* Rook shoved his chair back and stood. "No one here is doing that. We're going to put an end to it."

Nick covered his eyes with a hand. Jamie had the horrible feeling Nick was fighting back tears of rage or grief or both. Very cautiously, he put a hand to Nick's shoulder and stroked it, like he would to calm a frightened horse.

"We'll catch the bastards, Nick," he said. "I promise."

"We don't know for certain that this is what's happening." Yates spoke carefully, as though afraid of setting Nick off again. "I hope we're mistaken. But it would explain a great deal. The Wraith might be using the most primitive of all magics, lost in the mists of time. Left over from the days before we moved out of caves."

"What do you mean?" Isaac asked. His face was drawn and white, and he huddled down into his chair. Quigley cast him an anxious look, but Isaac didn't respond.

"You see it in cave paintings, like in the Cave of Altamira." Yates's silvery eyes looked even paler in the glow of the hexlights on the table. "Depictions of men donning skins, for example, then taking on the attributes of the animals they belonged to. I've heard the images interpreted as familiars in mid-transformation, and perhaps they are. But what if the skins didn't belong to hunted animals? What if they came from familiars? What if those men took the magic of the familiars and used it to give themselves animal attributes?"

"The speed of a cheetah," Jamie said, feeling as though his lips had gone numb. "The strength of a bear."

"Oh God," Cicero said. "We're all going to die."

"You ain't going to die, cat," Tom said, slipping his arm around Cicero's shoulders.

"That's why they took Luther's teeth," Jamie said. "To use in the hexes. And the other prisoners disappearing from the Menagerie..."

So there was a link between the Menagerie and the Wraith. And it was even worse than he'd ever imagined.

A growl escaped Isaac, and Rook's shoulders hunched. Nick surveyed the scene for a long moment, then wiped his hand across his face. "Halloran is right."

Rook looked at him incredulously. "What did you say?"

"This is sick, no doubt about it," Nick said. "I hope every bastard guard at the Menagerie dies slow and painful. But this won't become widespread. A few people might want to be strong, or run fast, or the rest of it. But what good does that do the average person, let alone the rich nobs on Fifth Avenue? Like it or not—and I don't—society runs on hexwork. Tell a Vanderbilt or a Carnegie that he can't have hexlights in his mansion, and his wife can't have a hexed hat to make her look ten years younger, or whatever foolishness the rich use magic for, and he won't like it. He'll like it even less when the equipment in his factories breaks, or his hotel burns down because there aren't any familiars left to charge the fire-retardant hexes."

Yates straightened his cuffs. "I can't believe I'm saying this, but I agree with Nick. It's the same reason the Heirs of Adam will never grow past a certain point. Their anti-vice campaigns are all fine and good, but outlaw magic as a whole? They might as well try to outlaw trains or electricity. It will never happen."

"Doesn't mean things will be easy," Nick cautioned. "Wholesale slaughter of familiars for body parts might not be useful, but anything short of that, to make it easier to control us…that's a different story."

"I could bring this to my uncle," Jamie offered uncertainly. "He don't have anything to do with the Menagerie directly, but he's well-respected. He could help us put a stop to it."

"No," said several voices at once. Dominic held up his hand, and the rest fell silent. "I'm not impugning your uncle's character," he said. "But we have to be very, very careful about who gets wind of this. Right now, as far as I'm concerned, the only people we can unreservedly trust with this information are the ones sitting at this table."

"So what do we do next?" Jamie asked.

"Taking the Wraith alive would be ideal," Yates said. "Assuming he could be persuaded to confess and name anyone who might have been helping him at the Menagerie. Even if he's a guard himself, he couldn't possibly remove, kill, and dismember ferals on his own."

Cicero shuddered. Tom hauled him tighter and pressed a kiss to his forehead. "Ain't no one going to lay a finger on you. I'll keep you safe."

Cicero managed a faint smile. "I know, Thomas."

Tom lifted his face from Cicero's hair. "Plain talk," he said. "Nick, Bill, and I ain't exactly small fellows. If the three of us can corner this Wraith, it won't matter what hexes he has."

Jamie shook his head. "You didn't see it. Him. He was fast. Strong. He tossed Nick like he didn't weigh anything at all."

"I'm a hexbreaker. He lays a hand on me, he'll regret it."

"Rodrigo is still watching the park," Nick said. "Along with one or two other bats he managed to talk into helping. The next time they spot the Wraith, I'll send one straight to Halloran's apartment. If he can break the Wraith's hexes, we'll have the bastard."

Tom nodded. "Aye. I'll go nowhere but the Coven and the apartment until this fellow is caught, so you can find me easy."

"But Thomas," Cicero pouted. At Tom's look, he sighed. "Oh, very well. No socializing until the Wraith is behind bars."

"Nick and Jamie are in the most danger at the moment," Dominic said. "I implore you, don't go anywhere alone if at all possible."

"Jamie's staying with me," Nick said.

Jamie bit back the impulse to say that was the first he'd heard of it. Rook gaped openly. "He is?"

"Why shouldn't he?" Nick asked, the words a challenge.

"Because you're—"

"Good," Dominic interrupted. "Then we'll all have one less thing to worry about."

The dinner party broke up after that. Jamie followed Nick down to the street. Rain had set in while they ate, a steady shower that gave no sign of stopping anytime soon. "Are you all right, staying with me?" Nick asked as they walked.

Jamie nodded. "Aye. Just a bit surprised you listened to reason, that's all."

"Reason, is it?" Nick shook his head. "Not what I'd call it."

"What would you call it, then?" Jamie asked.

"Madness," Nick said with a soft laugh. Then he took on horse form. *"Mount up—no sense in staying out in the rain any longer than we have to."*

Chapter 21

"I can't say I'm happy working with a bunch of witches," Nick said as he opened the door to his apartment. He removed his coat and shook it off in the hall, trying to avoid tracking any more rain in than he had to. "But if that's what it takes to put an end to things…"

Jamie did the same, then set about lighting the gas lamps, while Nick locked the door. If Jamie thought him foolish, relying on gas when he could have hexlights so easily now, he'd never said.

Just like he'd never taken Nick's magic without asking first. Or done any of the other selfish things Nick associated with witches.

He'd given. Lent his patience and his ear, his mind and his hands.

"It wasn't all bad, was it?" Jamie asked as the soft, warm light filled the room. "Dinner, I mean, not the discussion after."

Nick didn't want to admit it. "It wasn't awful," he temporized.

Jamie shot him a grin that said he wasn't fooled. "You can relax and let your guard down around some people, Nick. Even if they are witches."

Nick crossed the room to him. "I've let my guard down around one witch, at any rate."

"Aye." Jamie's throat worked as he swallowed. "Don't think I ain't noticed." He put a hand to Nick's chest, running his fingers lightly over the damp lapels of Nick's coat. "I swear, Nick, I won't let you down."

Hell. Nick wasn't supposed to feel like this, his insides warm and soft. Certainly he wasn't supposed to like it.

He bent and kissed Jamie. Jamie responded, hands in Nick's rain-spangled hair, tugging him closer. But the kiss itself stayed gentle, a lush slide of lip against lip, the lightest dart of tongues. Jamie's scent surrounded him and it suddenly felt like Nick would never get enough.

Drawing Jamie after him, he retreated to the bedroom. He hadn't had anyone else in this bed, preferring to keep his affairs short and casual, and separate from his day-to-day life. But Jamie had caused him to do so many other things he'd never thought he would, what was one more?

They undressed one another, taking their time, stopping to kiss and caress. When Jamie sank down on the edge of the bed to unlace his prosthetic, Nick waited until he was done, then knelt between Jamie's legs. Jamie blinked in surprise, then smiled. "Never thought I'd see you on your knees."

"To the devil with you," Nick said, but without heat. He helped Jamie shimmy out of the rest of his clothes, then leaned forward and took the erect cock waiting for him into his mouth.

Jamie groaned, his fingers tightening in Nick's hair. The salty-bitter taste of him sizzled on Nick's tongue, and he slid down, taking Jamie to the root. Jamie murmured words of encouragement, until he finally grasped Nick's hair and tugged harder. "Not yet," he gasped.

Nick drew back slowly, letting the head of Jamie's prick spring free with a wet pop. "Fuck, you're good at that," Jamie said, grabbing Nick's hand and pulling him onto the bed.

Nick stretched out by him, so their skin pressed together from chest to toes. The hard length of Jamie's cock prodded his stomach, and Nick swallowed heavily.

"Fuck me, Jamie," he whispered.

Jamie's hands and mouth stilled. He drew back a little, so he could see Nick's face. "You want me to fuck you?"

Nick nodded quickly, before he could change his mind. He half feared Jamie would ask him why. If he was going to do it with anyone, he wanted it to be with Jamie. But he wasn't certain he could say the words.

Maybe he didn't need to, because Jamie kissed him. "All right, then. Where do you keep the oil?"

Nick retrieved it. "Lay on your belly, to start," Jamie instructed. He peppered kisses across Nick's shoulders, down his spine, to his hip. "I'm going to make this so good for you," he promised, even as he spread Nick's buttocks apart.

Nick jerked at the touch of Jamie's tongue to his hole, the sensation catching him off guard. Jamie kept up his leisurely pace, taking his time, licking and probing until Nick's cock ached with need. Jamie paused just long enough to pour out some oil, then resumed, this time with the addition of a finger.

"Fur and feathers," Nick swore.

Jamie laughed. "Feels good, don't it? Just relax, sweetheart. You spend so much time taking care of everyone else. Let me take care of you, for once."

The words shouldn't have made Nick's chest feel too small for his heart. He tried to push it away, to focus on the physical sensations only, but somehow everything had gotten twisted up into a single thread.

Jamie went slow, adding fingers, finding the place inside Nick that made him groan with pleasure. Eventually, he pulled away. "Stay like that," he murmured, draping himself over Nick's back. "Right there."

Nick's fingers tensed in the pillows as Jamie began to work the head of his cock inside him. "Breathe," Jamie murmured. "Aye, there we go." His lips brushed Nick's shoulders. "Feel that? That's me in you."

"I couldn't exactly miss it," Nick said, which drew a delighted laugh from Jamie. He rocked his hips, pushing in farther, and Nick bit his lip against the stretch. But God, it did feel good, Jamie's weight on his back, prick filling him.

"Roll onto your right side," Jamie urged, tugging at him. "With me, now."

They ended up on their sides, Nick's left leg draped over Jamie's thigh, Jamie's chest pressed tight against his back. "There we go," Jamie said. "Now I can really make you feel good."

He rocked his hips in slow thrusts, while his left hand wandered over Nick's body. Playing with nipples, his cock, his balls. And oh God, it was good, sensation layered on sensation. Nick twisted his head around blindly, and Jamie shifted until their mouths met in a deep kiss.

Jamie's hold on him tightened, and his hips moved more urgently. "Touch yourself for me, sweetheart," Jamie urged. Nick did, while Jamie's clever fingers twisted and pinched his nipple, and Jamie's cock bore down on the sensitive spot inside, and Jamie's voice whispered endearments in his ear.

Nick shouted when he came. His orgasm felt dragged from his very bones, his whole body shaking with the force of it. He clenched on Jamie's cock, felt Jamie's teeth in his shoulder, muffling a groan.

Silence fell, broken only by their breathing. Jamie's hand skated up and down Nick's arm, a tender caress. Feeling discomfort for the first time, Nick shifted his hips, so Jamie's softening prick slipped out.

"How was that?" Jamie asked.

Nick rolled onto his back. "Good."

Jamie offered him a sleepy smile. His black hair was wildly mussed, his particolored eyes content. "I'm glad you liked it. I did, too." He shifted his head onto Nick's shoulder. "I like you."

"Same," Nick said, and that was the problem, wasn't it? He liked Jamie far more than was sensible. Jamie's sense of loyalty might annoy him at times, but it drew him as well. Jamie understood boundaries—he never pushed further than Nick was willing to go. He cared, desperately, about justice, and not only for Wyatt.

How would he react if he knew he was Nick's witch? That the bond was true, not just a thing of convenience?

Nick cleared his throat. Nothing had changed, and yet the thought of ending things felt like dying. "After all this is over...I'd like to keep seeing you. If you want."

Jamie's smile was bright as sunrise. "I do," he said, and leaned over to kiss Nick again.

A heavy fist pounding on the apartment door drew Nick up out of sleep. For a wild moment, he thought he'd been found out, and it was the Dangerous Familiars Squad on his doorstep. Then he heard Rook call his name, before the pounding resumed.

"What the devil?" Jamie asked, raising his head. "Is that Rook?"

"Yes." Nick rolled out of bed and pulled on his trousers. "That birdbrain better have a good reason for waking us, or I'll make a feather duster out of him."

He jerked the door open just as Rook was about to pound on it again. "Are you trying to wake the whole building?" he demanded.

Exhaustion ringed Rook's eyes and tightened his mouth. "Grab Jamie and head to Central Park. Bridge 24," he said without preamble. "Some time after the rain ended, there was another murder."

Nick's feeling of dread increased the closer they drew to the scene of the crime. In the small hours just before dawn, there was no hope of catching either cab or train, so Nick had once again taken Jamie up on his back. He had to admit, Jamie was a good rider. Not that he had any experience to compare it with, but Jamie moved with him easily, as though they were attuned to one another on some deep level.

Maybe it was the bond. If Tom broke it for them, how much would things change? Would they still be as good together, in bed and out?

What if they didn't break it after all?

The air near Bridge 24 smelled of falling leaves, and of the water from the New Reservoir. But as they drew closer, Nick scented something that didn't belong to the landscape of the park.

Blood.

"What happened to Rodrigo, or whoever was supposed to be keeping watch?" Jamie wondered aloud.

"They probably stayed in because of the rain. Hard to fly in a downpour." Of all the cursed luck.

The shine of hexlights and murmur of voices drew them on. Rook and Dominic stood on the cast iron bridge, along with Quigley. The witch who had taken over driving the MWP's wagon from Jamie perched on the driver's seat nearby.

Nick let Jamie dismount, then shifted back to human form. As they approached, Rook looked up. "Another feral," he said unhappily. "Do you know him, Nick?"

Nick stepped up to get a closer look at the body. As with the other murders, the dead man had been killed and then gutted, his own blood used to paint a hex sign on the bridge around his body.

But when he saw the man's face, Nick's blood turned to ice.

Conrad.

Somehow, Nick managed to keep his expression neutral, even though his mind raced. Had the Wraith caught up with Conrad the other night after all? But if so, where had it kept him in the meantime?

The Menagerie was somehow involved. If Conrad had stumbled into the Dangerous Familiars Squad's hands instead…

They might be on their way to Caballus at this very moment.

"I don't know him," Nick lied.

Dominic frowned slightly. "Are you certain?"

"I don't know every familiar in New York, witch," Nick snapped. The coppers might be destroying Caballus, or beating Kyle, or even invading the tenement right now for all he knew. He didn't have the time or the patience to answer questions.

"Whoa, whoa, easy now." Jamie put a hand to Nick's arm. "No reason to get mad at each other."

Nick pulled loose. "I'll get mad if I damned well want to." He was supposed to have kept Conrad safe. Just like Pia. "I don't know the man, except as a fellow feral who got murdered while we sat on our asses and talked."

"But you're not a feral, are you?" Rook shot back.

Nick's breath seemed stuck inside his lungs. He'd spent his entire life thinking of himself one way, and one way only. As a free familiar. A feral, with no witch to bind him.

Rook knew it, of course. Which was why he knew exactly where to slip in the knife.

"That was uncalled for," Jamie told Rook.

Nick turned and walked away from them all. He didn't have time to quarrel with Rook, or to feel that little flush of pleasure when Jamie took his side.

"Nick!" Jamie called. "Nick, wait up."

For a moment, Nick thought about shifting and running. Leaving Jamie behind. "I need to get back to the saloon," he said. "There are things I have to do."

Jamie's hand closed on his arm. "Nick, slow down. What's wrong?"

"A feral is dead, with his blood everywhere," Nick said. "That's what's wrong."

Jamie shook his head. "It's more than that. Are you…are you blaming yourself? Because you didn't have any way of knowing."

Conrad had been dying horribly in the park, while Nick had been in bed, taking it up the ass from a fucking *witch*.

No. Nick took a shaking breath and tried to calm himself. He wasn't going to be ashamed of anything he'd done with Jamie. "I really do have something to take care of," he said. "The sun is almost up—the Wraith won't attack in broad daylight. You go to your apartment, and I'll meet you at the Coven in two hours."

Plenty of time to warn Kyle. He'd close the saloon for the time being, so the coppers wouldn't hurt any innocent bystanders if they did decide to raid the place. The tenement could prove more challenging, but he'd think of some way to warn the inhabitants.

Some way to keep them safe, as he hadn't kept Conrad safe, or Pia. God.

His brusqueness hurt Jamie; he could see it in the crinkle of flesh around Jamie's eyes, the deepening crease between his brows. But once again, he didn't push. "All right." Jamie's hand fell to his side. "I'll see you later, then."

Nick wavered. He ducked his head quickly, brushing his lips over Jamie's. "Later," he agreed.

Then he shifted back into horse shape and cantered swiftly away, leaving Jamie standing forlornly behind.

*

Nick arrived at Caballus to find a black police wagon outside, and three burly men breaking the saloon door right off its hinges. A man with captain's bars stood to one side, a satisfied smirk on his face.

Nick could still run. Except after Nick's encounter with the Wraith, Kyle had taken to sleeping behind the bar, rather than chance walking home alone after dark.

Nick had failed Conrad and Pia, but he'd be damned if he'd let these assholes hurt Kyle.

Nick took back human form. The coppers had broken down the door and rushed inside; he could hear their shouts on the street. With a shout of his own, Nick charged in after them.

They forced Kyle to his knees, hands clasped behind his head, eyes squeezed tightly shut. One of the coppers shoved him hard in the back, and he went to the sawdust-covered floor without resistance. The copper took out his nightstick, while the captain observed the proceedings with a jaded eye.

"I want to see a warrant," Nick said, drawing their attention to himself and away from Kyle. "Right now, or get the fuck out of my saloon."

The captain looked Nick up and down insolently. "Are you the owner of this fine establishment?" he asked with deceptive lightness.

"Who the fuck are you to be asking?"

A nightstick struck the back of one leg, sending Nick to the floor. "Answer Captain O'Byrne's questions," snapped the copper who'd hit him.

O'Byrne folded his arms over his chest and looked down on Nick. "We have a witness who says you've been hiding dangerous familiars in your basement, horse."

"They're lying," Nick said.

"I don't think so," O'Byrne replied. "But I do think you're resisting arrest."

The phrase must have been a signal, because three of the big coppers moved toward Nick. Before he could try to scramble to his feet, they closed in on him, fists and clubs flying.

There was nothing for Nick to do but curl up and try to protect his head and vital organs. "I'm Jamie MacDougal's familiar!" he yelled through the pain. "He's O'Malley's nephew! Hurt me, and you'll be in trouble!"

His wild hope, that Jamie's name would stop the beating, came to nothing. A boot caught him in the side of the head, and blood poured down his face. They meant to kill him here on the floor of his own saloon.

"Enough," O'Byrne said.

A part of Nick wanted to sob with relief. But it was short lived. Hands wrestled him to his knees, wrenching his arms behind his back. Cuffs closed too tight around his wrists.

"Do a thorough search, boys," O'Byrne ordered.

Within moments, the bar's plank had been ripped down and thrown aside. Tables overturned, and chairs shattered like kindling. One of the coppers took out his nightstick and began to methodically smash every bottle, until the air reeked with spilled whiskey and gin.

Nick swallowed and forced himself to focus on O'Byrne instead of the destruction. "I'm an MWP detective," he said. His teeth had cut the inside of his lip at some point during the beating, and the taste of blood filled his mouth, but he didn't dare spit it out. "Jamie MacDougal is my witch. My badge is inside my coat, if you don't believe me."

O'Byrne jerked open Nick's coat. The lining tore as he ripped the badge free.

"Not for much longer on either count," he said. The silver badge hit the sawdust, and O'Byrne ground it beneath his heel. He leaned over, grabbed Nick by the chin, and forced his head back. "Do you imagine we don't know exactly who you are? The Inspector ain't exactly happy you tricked his nephew into bonding with you. I guess you thought it would give you cover, keep us off your back. Give you a free pass, if we caught you." O'Byrne's fingers tightened, digging into Nick's flesh mercilessly. "You were wrong. MacDougal served with Roosevelt; that alone is enough to take him a long way toward the top. Chief of Police, someday, or better. But not with a stone like you around his neck."

Nick wanted to argue. Jamie wasn't like that; he didn't care about climbing the ranks.

But he cared about being a copper. He might be willing to bend the rules, but Nick had been doing a lot more than that. When he found out Nick had been hiding fugitive ferals in his cellar…

The sound of breaking casks and shattering glass echoed up from below. Under other circumstances, Nick would have been sure they couldn't find the door. But Conrad had probably been forced to confess everything before they handed him over to the Wraith. They'd know exactly how to get into the hidden room.

Nick shut his eyes, sick with anger over the destruction of his saloon. Helpless to keep it from happening. He'd been as thorough as possible cleaning the little room in the cellar, but it might not have been enough. If they found so much as a hair belonging to Conrad, Yates's damned hexes would be able to match them. That would be all the evidence needed to send Nick right to the Menagerie.

Eventually, the sound of boots thudded on the stairs. "Empty," one of the men said. "Scrubbed down recently, if I'm any judge of things."

O'Byrne's pale skin flushed with anger, and he turned on Nick. "Do you think you're clever? Do you think a bit of soap and water will make any difference?"

Nick met his gaze squarely. "I run a clean establishment here. No idea what you're talking about."

He didn't see the blow coming. His head snapped to one side, pain blooming on his jaw. O'Byrne shook his hand as if the punch had hurt. "You use the hidden room to conceal dangerous familiars from the law. You might as well confess now. We have a witness."

Nick swallowed. "Then bring him here, so he can accuse me to my face."

The request was met with silence. Nick had been right. O'Byrne's witness was dead in Central Park. God only knew what they'd done with the puma; he was probably dead too. The coppers hadn't expected to need the ferals; they'd thought there would be plenty of evidence in the cellar.

"You haven't got anything on me," Nick said. "So why don't you just fuck on off?"

O'Byrne kicked him in the stomach. As Nick doubled over, retching, someone yanked his arms up painfully and unlocked the cuffs. A second click sounded from Kyle's direction as he was released as well.

"This ain't over, horse," O'Byrne warned. "You get clear of O'Malley's nephew, or there will be consequences. I hope you've kept the fire hexes up on your tenement here."

CHAPTER 22

"NICK WAS ACTING strange," Jamie said. "Even for him. Do you think he's all right?"

He'd gone to the Coven with Dominic and Rook, but his sense of unease had only grown throughout the ride on the El and the short walk to the MWP building. One moment, everything had seemed fine with Nick—better than fine, even. Then he'd seen the murdered feral, and a transformation came over him.

Rook shrugged irritably. "Who knows, with Nick?"

Dominic, however, gave Jamie a close look. "Do you think something's wrong?"

"What's wrong is Nick is an ass with a bad temper," Rook snapped, before Jamie could say anything. "Fur and feathers, I'd like to knock him upside the head sometimes."

Dominic sighed. "You don't have to get angry on my behalf. A few rough words from Nick won't break my heart, I promise."

"He's my brother, and he can either use a civil tone with you, or keep his mouth shut." Rook folded his arms over his chest, shoulders hunching. "Last night, I actually thought he might be getting better. Might have learned we aren't all his enemies. That we could work together. I should've known. Nick will never change."

It was still early, so few of the other detectives had come in yet. As they reached the top of the stairs, Jamie saw Chief Ferguson's door standing wide open. Neither the chief nor Athene were inside…but Lund sat behind the desk, a smirk on his face.

"Come in, gentlemen," he called.

Dominic and Rook exchanged a startled glance. Dread settled in Jamie's belly as he followed them across the room. "Where is Chief Ferguson?" Dominic asked once they reached the doorway.

Lund fixed his gaze on Jamie. "I see your charming familiar isn't with you. Don't worry—he won't be joining us."

It took a moment for the words to properly register. "What do you mean?"

Lund's smile took on a razor edge. "I was informed early this morning that a judge issued a warrant to search Caballus for dangerous ferals. It seems your familiar has been hiding them illegally from the Dangerous Familiars Squad."

Jamie shook his head vehemently. "Nick wouldn't do that."

Except of course it was *exactly* the kind of thing Nick would do.

"Another MWP familiar gone bad." Lund offered them a look of mock sorrow. "The Police Board is very disappointed. First the MWP harbored a dangerous familiar within its ranks, who proved to be responsible for the death and injury of numerous important people last year. Now an MWP familiar is caught helping other dangerous ferals evade the law."

Jamie's throat tightened. He wanted to ask about Nick, but he didn't dare betray his fear to this supercilious prick. "Where is Chief Ferguson?"

"The Police Board has removed him. I'm temporarily filling in for his position," Lund said with relish. "Until a more suitable non-witch can be found."

Rook made a small noise, quickly swallowed. Lund glanced at him. "As for you two, you're both suspended without pay. Nick is your familiar's brother, Detective Kopecky, and we have yet to rule out any sort of collusion between them."

Jamie's heart hammered in his chest. He knew he ought to be focused on the injustice of punishing Ferguson and Dominic for Nick's actions, but the only thing he could think about was Nick. Had he been arrested? Was he being dragged to the Tombs now? Or would Uncle Hurley take him straight to the Menagerie?

No. He couldn't let that happen.

"Detective MacDougal," Lund's voice cut through the haze. "I've been told to ask you to report to your uncle, say around lunch time. This business should be done with by then, and he can take your statement. We're sure you would never have participated in this willingly." He glanced in the direction of Jamie's wooden leg. "It's clear to us all the horse took advantage of you. I'm sure a better position can be found for you, once this is over."

Cold rage sluiced through fear and left Jamie clear headed. If Lund wanted to see him as some sort of passive victim, then Jamie would use that to his advantage. "Aye, sir," he grated out.

"Dismissed."

Somehow, Rook kept from exploding until they reached the street. The moment they were out of hearing of the reporters, though, he let out a blistering series of oaths. "I'm going to kill Nick!" Rook raged. "Idiot! Once I'm done, there won't be enough left of him to send to the glue factory."

"Nay." Jamie put a hand to Rook's arm. "If he's under arrest and you show up, they'll haul you in, too."

"Jamie is right," Dominic agreed unhappily. "I don't like it any more than you, but we're in enough trouble as it is." He rubbed his eyes. "The best thing we can do right now is go home and wait."

"What about the murders?" Rook asked. "To hell with that, what about *Nick?* The fool is going to get himself killed, or sent to the Menagerie, or God only knows what."

"I ain't going to let that happen," Jamie said firmly. He focused on the bond. "For right now, he's still in the direction of Caballus. I'll go straight there and talk to my uncle, or his captain, whichever is heading the raid. Get him to release Nick on my recognizance."

How he'd convince Hurley to help, he had no idea. He didn't even know what sort of evidence they might have against Nick. If it was just someone else's word against Nick's, they could surely find enough people to testify to Nick's character and have the charges dropped.

But if it was more…

No. He couldn't think about that. Just like he couldn't think about the painful twinge deep inside, that Nick hadn't trusted him enough to tell him about any of this.

"Just wait for me," he said, dropping his hand back to his side. "With any luck, Nick and I will both join you later. I'll hold him myself, while you kick his arse."

Rook didn't look happy, but after a moment managed a shaky smile. "Deal."

Jamie's relief at finding no police outside of Caballus ended when he got a glimpse inside.

Everything that could be broken had been, from the piano against the wall, to the booze, to the chairs and tables. The air reeked of spilled whiskey.

For once heedless of the *Familiars Only* sign, Jamie stepped through the broken door. Nick sat at the only table not on its side, his head in his hands. At the sound of Jamie's footstep, he looked up.

One eye had swelled nearly shut, and his lower lip was split. Blood from a cut on his scalp slicked one side of his face. But even worse was his expression of defeat.

Fury and the need to comfort battled in Jamie's chest. "Saint Mary, Nick—" he started as he hurried across the room.

Nick held up his hand. "No closer."

Jamie froze, swaying in place. "Nick?" He licked dry lips. "Did…did Uncle Hurley do this?"

Hurley couldn't have. Not this. Not this destruction. Not beating his familiar until he bled.

Nick shrugged. "His captain did. O'Byrne."

Jamie took a deep breath, trying to think through rage. "I'll make this right. Once Uncle Hurley knows, he'll have O'Byrne out on his ear."

Nick's laugh was bitter. "I doubt that."

"You're angry. Of course you are—look at this." Jamie shook his head in disgust. What had been done here was deliberate, petty destruction, for no reason other than to try and put Nick in his place. "I'm going to do everything I can to help. But at least they didn't arrest you. That means they didn't find anything." Relief loosened the tight muscles in Jamie's back. Nick hadn't been doing anything illegal after all. "I told that arsehole Lund you were innocent."

Nick's brows drew together. "Lund?"

Jamie nodded. "You have to come back to the Coven right away. The warrant against you was used as an excuse to seize control of the MWP. Chief Ferguson is out, your brother and Dominic are suspended, and Lund is in charge. But you're innocent, they couldn't arrest you, so that means we can put an end to this."

Nick shook his head. "Don't you understand yet? I'm not innocent, Jamie!"

Jamie had thought it himself, back at the Coven. But the reality hurt anyway. "You've been hiding dangerous familiars," he said, the air thick in his lungs. "How long?"

"As long as we've been together."

"And you never…you never told me?" Jamie flung up his arms in despair. "Don't you trust me?"

"Why would I trust you?" Nick demanded. "You're a witch."

He felt as if Nick had punched him in the gut. "You...you don't mean that."

"Why wouldn't I?"

"Because we've moved past that!" Jamie shouted. "Because I love you!"

They stared at one another for a long moment. Nick's throat worked as he swallowed. "I met Wyatt...because he was helping me smuggle fugitives out of the state."

Jamie's heart stuttered. No. Not this. Nick knew how he felt. He wouldn't have lied about Wyatt.

"It ain't true," he managed to say.

Nick avoided his gaze. "I'm sorry, Jamie. I couldn't take the risk."

All the grief and the guilt, the wondering what Wyatt would have thought, where he'd been...and Nick had stood by silent. Keeping the answers to himself.

"You son of a bitch," Jamie managed to say through the haze of grief and rage filming his eyes.

Nick flinched, as if Jamie had struck him. "I didn't lie about anything I thought could help bring his killer to justice." As though that would somehow make it all better. "I never knew anything personal, or where he lived." Nick wet his lips. "He was one of my contacts. He would take dangerous familiars out of my hands, on to the next stop."

"That's why he was in New York?"

Nick shrugged. "I don't know why he was in New York. But that's what he dedicated himself to once he was here."

Jamie touched Wyatt's pendant where it hung beneath his shirt. Had he ever really known either of the men he'd given his heart to?

"You used me to get into the MWP," Jamie said, and was amazed his voice didn't break. "You lied about Wyatt. You slept with me, knowing I was a copper, knowing I could lose my job if you were caught with fugitives in your basement. Did you hope to use my connection with Hurley to save yourself, or sabotage the squad's work?" His eyes burned. "How could you do this to me? I thought you—"

The words caught in his throat. Because of course Nick had never made any declarations of love. Never made any promises. And if Jamie had expected them, the more fool he.

"Jamie—"

"What I thought I had with you, what I thought I had with Wyatt...

none of it was ever real at all." Jamie became aware he still clutched the pendant through the front of his shirt. He forced his hand to relax, took one step back, then another, until he'd reached the door. "I don't want to ever see you again. I wish to God I'd never met either of you in the first place."

Nick sat alone in the ruins of his life.

All his hard work had come to nothing more than a wrecked bar and a wrecked heart.

He'd never regretted lying to a witch. This wasn't supposed to have been any different. But the look of betrayal on Jamie's face had seared itself into Nick's very soul.

Telling Jamie the truth about his connection to Wyatt hadn't been an option before. Not with the fugitives in his cellar, relying on Nick's silence to keep them safe. The risk had just been too great.

He'd seen Jamie grieving the man, and he'd kept his mouth shut, and a part of him still didn't know what he might have done differently. Maybe the day they'd gone to the Menagerie, he should have acted on his impulse to bare his soul. Jamie wouldn't have turned him in, he knew that now.

He'd known it then. But he'd stayed silent, and pretended fear was really caution. And now he'd not only earned Jamie's hatred, but tainted Jamie's memories of Wyatt without ever having meant to.

God.

At least Jamie would still have a career, now that he'd severed ties with Nick. He could go on with his life.

O'Malley wouldn't forgive Nick, not for Jamie and not for escaping his grasp this morning. The anti-fire hexes might keep the coppers from burning down the tenement, but O'Malley would find some way of making Nick pay. A knife in the kidney some dark night. A slip onto the tracks of the El.

Nick had no one to blame for any of it but himself. He'd known from the start he shouldn't get involved with Jamie. Jamie of the kind eyes and boyish smile. Jamie, who brought him doughnuts for breakfast, and helped him with the books, and made love to him with such care.

His throat tightened. He'd told Jamie up front he wouldn't be broken by any rough rider. But that had turned out to be just one more thing Nick was wrong about.

How long would Jamie wait to have their bond severed? Or, if there was trouble at the MWP, would he even be allowed to contact Tom?

Nick forced himself to his feet, ignoring the aches in his body. At least the fucking coppers hadn't broken any bones. Of course, for all he knew, that was just because they'd meant to render him down for parts once he was arrested, and didn't want to damage anything useful.

Anger was fuel, and he clung to it as he put back the still-serviceable tables and chairs, and set the others aside for repair or scrap. His entire stock of booze was gone; it would cost a pretty penny to replace, and he had no idea how he'd come up with the funds. Jamie would help him take a look at the books—

Nick closed his eyes against the stab of renewed pain. He and Jamie would never have worked.

But oh God, he'd wanted them to.

There came a soft knock on the door. Nick opened his eyes and turned. For a moment, he didn't recognize the familiar hovering uncertainly in the doorway. Then the pale golden eyes came back to him. This was the familiar he'd seen at Ingram's sermon that day he and Jamie went to the park to talk to Bess. The day the rain had trapped them in the Cave, and Jamie had grinned and asked if he let witches fuck him.

It felt as though it had happened a thousand years ago, or to someone else altogether.

"Yes?" Nick asked, more harshly than he'd intended. The familiar shrank back, eyes darting around at the wreckage nervously. "Sorry," he said, holding out his hands before the young man could get too spooked. "There's been a bit of trouble this morning. Nothing I couldn't handle. What can I do for you?"

"My name is Simon." The familiar swallowed. "I…I need your help."

"Finally fed up with Ingram's hate?" Nick asked sympathetically.

A nod. "It…I can't sleep any more. I can barely eat. I don't want God to hate me."

"God doesn't hate you." Nick indicated a chair. "Have a seat. Let me see if I can find you something to eat."

Simon shook his head. "No. That is, I-I can't. I have a brother, who wants to leave too, but he's afraid. I thought…I thought if he could see you, see how strong you are, he wouldn't be so frightened."

Weariness settled over Nick like a blanket. He longed to lie down and sleep for days, weeks, years. He didn't want to wake up until the wound left behind by Jamie's loss had scarred over, turned silvery with age.

But he couldn't. The only thing he could do was try to help whatever feral turned up on his doorstep, for as long as he could. "All right," he said. "Tell me when and where."

Chapter 23

Jamie went to Central Park for lack of anywhere else to go.

A mix of anger and grief thrummed through his veins, though he wasn't certain who he was angriest with. Hurley, for not even bothering to let Jamie know the squad was on the way to arrest his familiar? O'Byrne, for destroying Caballus and beating Nick? Nick, for lying to Jamie, using him?

Wyatt, for dying and leaving him behind with so many questions?

Maybe it was himself he ought to be maddest at. Everyone had warned him about Nick. Rook had told him upfront that if things came down to it, Nick would only ever see him as a witch. But Jamie had dismissed all of it. He'd handed over his heart to Nick, and now it was broken. It shouldn't have come as a surprise.

Wyatt, though...

He'd been here in New York, working with Nick and against the law. If Jamie hadn't been a copper, if Hurley hadn't headed up the Dangerous Familiars Squad, might Wyatt have come to him?

Uncle Hurley would be expecting him in an hour or so, but Jamie couldn't imagine walking into Hurley's office now. Hearing Nick's name from his lips.

He'd told himself that, despite his recent doubts, Hurley was still a good man. But his officers had wrecked everything in Caballus and beaten Nick bloody. And Hurley hadn't even warned Jamie. Hadn't even had the guts or the courtesy to let him know his familiar was hiding criminal fugitives. Did he think Jamie would have warned Nick the squad was coming?

Would Jamie have warned Nick?

Of course he would have. He hadn't even been really surprised when he found out what Nick was accused of doing. Only hurt that Nick hadn't confided in him.

This was what love did to a man. He'd been a good copper—a good solider. Followed orders, done what he was told. Bent the rules from time to time, but certainly never broken them outright.

Nick had thrown all of that into chaos. He lived on his own terms, and to hell with anyone who didn't like it. At his side, Jamie had started to change without even realizing it. Agreeing to the deceit of their temporary bond, because it was the only way for Wyatt to get justice. Meeting in secret with other familiars and witches, to keep Lund and the Police Board from finding out what they learned.

Going against orders, or around them. Lying to the warden of the Menagerie, lying to Lund, because doing things the right way…was no longer the right thing to do.

Jamie stopped walking. The wind was cold on his bare face, but he welcomed it.

Nick and Wyatt had worked outside the law. But he knew both men; knew they believed entirely in the rightness of their cause. Yet neither had trusted Jamie to do the right thing.

Whatever that even was.

If Wyatt had come to him, told him everything…what would he have done?

Of course, Jamie still didn't know the entire story. How Wyatt had survived Cuba. Why Eddie hadn't. Why Wyatt hadn't reported back to the unit, or a commander, and just let everyone think he was dead too.

If only they'd been able to find out where Wyatt had been staying. Surely there would have been some clue amongst his things.

Two women passed Jamie, both holding binoculars and chatting animatedly. Jamie tipped his hat absently as they went by. "A Pine Siskin the other morning…" one was saying.

Jamie shook his head. Except for the middle of the night, every time they'd been in the park there'd been at least one bird watcher about. These folks were obsessed.

Wait.

"Excuse me, ladies?" Jamie called, before he could let himself either hope or despair. "May I ask you something about bird watching?"

They paused and gave him curious looks. "What would you like to know?" one asked. "I can recommend binocular manufacturers, if you need guidance. What one really needs to look for in a set is—"

"No, no," interrupted the other. "You're getting ahead of yourself, Mina. To start with, you need a small journal which can withstand a bit of rain, in order to keep the list of birds you've correctly identified."

"Er, aye," Jamie said. "What I really need to know is whether either of you ladies, or any other, ah, enthusiasts have seen an eagle flying over the park recently."

"As a matter of fact, we have." They exchanged a look. "There was a great deal of speculation as to whether the creature was a familiar or a wild bird, actually, as eagles aren't terribly common in the city. Either way, it hasn't been seen for some time."

Jamie's heart contracted almost painfully. "Did anyone notice if it seemed to go anywhere in particular?"

"Yes." The other woman nodded. "The creature was spotted outside of the park a few times. Mr. Greene said he saw it alight several times atop Madison Square Garden. As it isn't nesting season, we took that to be evidence it wasn't an ordinary eagle after all."

"Familiars don't count on one's life list," the other put in sadly.

Had Jamie heard right? "Madison Square Garden?"

"Yes. He said it seemed to be fond of the top of the tower, just below the statue of Diana the Huntress."

Everything seemed to snap into place. "Saint Mary," Jamie said, touching the pendant nestled against his skin, "I'm an idiot."

Accessing the top of the tower wouldn't have been easy for a man with both legs—which no doubt was why Wyatt had chosen it. The confused Madison Square Garden staff tried to dissuade Jamie, but for once he followed Hurley's advice and relied on his badge and a great deal of bluster. In the end, he found himself thirty-two stories above the ground, in a tiny room half open to the sky, just under the gilded statue of Diana that served as a weathervane.

The space should have been deserted. There was no reason for anyone to come there, save for maintenance of the statue. But the space held a few small comforts: bedding, shaving kit, and a packet of letters wrapped in oilskin.

Jamie slumped against the wall, muscles trembling from the exertion it had taken to get up here. His left knee throbbed with pain, and the muscles of his whole leg burned. But it had been worth it.

This was where Wyatt had spent the last few months of his life. He'd sat in this same space, stared out over the city, and thought…what?

About familiars. About the Pemberton Act and those it affected. About Nick, probably.

Had he ever thought about Jamie?

Once he'd caught his breath, Jamie unfolded the packet, and sorted through the letters. Most of them proved to be from Wyatt's time in Cuba: correspondence with old friends in Arizona, where he and Eddie had lived. But the final one was from Wyatt rather than to him.

Jamie MacDougal was written on the envelope in Wyatt's rough hand.

For a long moment, Jamie did nothing but stare at it. Proof that Wyatt had been thinking about him after all. That he hadn't been forgotten.

That, maybe…he'd been forgiven? For not being there when Wyatt had surely needed him the most. For not saving Eddie.

For, ultimately, not saving Wyatt.

His hands shook so badly he could barely unfold the letter. He took a deep breath, told himself not to break down no matter what it said. Then he began to read.

My dearest Jamie,

I write this letter without knowing if I'll ever get the courage to send it. A part of me believes you'd understand all the actions I've undertaken…and a part of me fears you'd never forgive me for them.

"For what?" Jamie murmured to no one but the wind. Or perhaps the statue above. "Christ, Wyatt, what did you do?"

I'm trying to imagine your reaction to even receiving this. A letter from a dead man. As the Goddess is my witness, Jamie, I never meant for you to think I'd died. After you were hurt, I got down on my knees every moonrise and gave thanks to the Huntress your life had been spared. Eddie and I talked about what we'd do once the war was over. He suggested we go to New York City, to find you…and my brother.

I know I told you about my family, when you asked about the pendant around my neck. We were raised in a faith that believed familiars to be abominations.

I'm writing around the thing I really need to tell you. The thing I don't want to remember. What happened in Cuba, after you were hurt.

You know the basics; Roosevelt wasn't shy about trumpeting our accomplishments. But after the Spanish surrendered, word came that they needed

Eddie and me for a special mission. Many units had lost their witch and familiar pairs, so we assumed it was some sort of temporary reassignment.

It wasn't. An American civilian met us. He told us he was with the government—though what part he never said—and a member of the congregation I'd been raised in. The Heirs of Adam.

Jamie went cold. The Heirs of Adam? Ingram's group?

In the government, and a follower of Ingram's. Wyatt couldn't be referring to Lund, could he?

The government, or whatever part of it he worked for, was searching for something hidden high in the mountains. Somewhere accessible only to a winged familiar. According to legend, a conquistador known for his cruelty had used hexes to torment and enslave Indians throughout South America. In particular, he had learned of a way to turn the workings of the hexes inscribed on their plazas and temples, meant to protect their people, against them.

His use of magic was overlooked, at least until the native population had been decimated. After, the Inquisition entered the New World in force, and forbid all hexes, put to death all familiars. The conquistador was enraged, and hid away high atop a mountain, until he died…of what the stories didn't say.

I think you'll agree it all sounds like a bunch of hogwash. But Eddie and I were soldiers; we went where we were ordered. I'll spare you the grueling details, but the story turned out to be true, at least in one particular. High up, where only wings could take you, there was a cave. Something that might have been a man a long time ago. And a journal containing hexes like none neither Eddie nor I had ever seen. Things drawn in blood, meant to corrupt and destroy.

Jamie's breath caught. No. It couldn't be.

We returned with the book, as ordered, though neither of us was entirely easy about bringing such hexes back into the world. Better they should be left forgotten. When we next met with the man, no one else was there from the army. Only detectives hired to provide for his security. That should have been a warning sign, but…we weren't looking for warning signs. We didn't think we needed to.

They shot Eddie first. From behind, like fucking cowards. I wouldn't have survived if not for the hex in my pendant. It gave me just enough of a chance to take to the air. One of their bullets hit me and I fell into the jungle.

Saint Mary, Holy Familiar of Christ. Jamie read the paragraph again, then again. Eddie hadn't just died in action, or on a special mission.

He'd been murdered. On the orders of a representative of their own government.

Cuban villagers found me. Otherwise, I would never have survived. When I'd healed enough to fly again, I knew I needed to go back to the army. Report in.

Except I didn't know if any of the commanders had been in on it. I didn't want to think so. But with Eddie dead, and assuming they thought I was dead too, I decided not to chance it.

I was broken inside, Jamie. Losing Eddie hurt, and I mean physically as well as emotionally. I felt like my heart was ripped out, like there was a ball of ice in my chest. I can't describe it to you adequately. Maybe if you ever bond, you'll understand.

Jamie closed his eyes. It didn't seem fair his bond with Nick should feel so warm. If only…

But no. He forced his eyes open again and went back to reading.

So I made my way back to America. To New York. I thought maybe I'd find you. But the Pemberton Act had just passed, and suddenly my very existence was illegal without a witch to watch over me. It was too soon after losing Eddie. I couldn't bear it.

I was nervous for another reason, too. Someone out there has those hexes, Jamie. The ones Eddie and I delivered into his hands. I'm scared as hell to find out what he intends to do with them.

I can't help but think they want a war against familiars. Not a real war, of course. But I've heard rumors, that other old, forgotten hexes have been used recently. By theriarchists, they say, and maybe that's even true. But a bunch of penniless radicals didn't fund expeditions to find ancient hexes. I can't help but wonder if someone put them in their hands deliberately. To give those in charge an enemy to point at. An excuse to further their own power.

Wyatt hadn't shared this with Nick, that was for damned sure. It didn't sound like the sort of speculation Nick would be inclined to keep to himself, even amidst all the other lies.

When I heard your uncle was the head of the Dangerous Familiars Squad, I was even more confused. Maybe I should have come to you anyway. I don't know.

In the end, I got involved in things I can't tell you about. I met a familiar I think you'd like, though. I can't name him safely here, just in case, but he's something. Angry at the world, and witches in particular, but I think you could get through to him.

I think he needs someone to get through to him.

Jamie swallowed against the tightness in his throat. Nick. He meant Nick.

I found my brother and have a meeting with him tomorrow. Maybe he'll know what the Heirs of Adam had to do with what happened in Cuba. If I can, I'll talk him into leaving the church.

After that, I'll have to decide what to do with this letter. If it's safe to send. I want to see you again, more than you could possibly know.

I miss you.

Yours always,

Wyatt

Jamie blinked rapidly, fighting back tears. But it was too much, and in the end, he curled up on the blankets, pressed his face into them, and sobbed. For himself, for Eddie, and most of all for Wyatt.

Wyatt, who had still loved him. Wyatt, who had died in fear and pain, alone and without anyone at his side. Thoughts Jamie had kept at bay broke free, along with the grief he'd suppressed so he could focus on finding the killer, and he howled his anguish to the wind and the empty sky.

Eventually, the storm passed, and he lay spent, feeling hollowed out. He wished he could go back and change things, make it so Wyatt and Nick would have trusted him, relied on him.

But he couldn't. All he could do was decide what to do next.

He picked the letter up from where he'd let it fall and read through it again. It was possible the anonymous man from the government had been Lund, but as the letter didn't name him, it would be hard to prove. Either way, the Heirs of Adam were involved somehow. Was Ingram at the heart of this?

Wyatt had been going to meet with his brother, who was still part of Ingram's church. Was that where he'd been ambushed? Or had the reunion simply put him within the Wraith's sights?

Jamie's head ached. All of these connections needed to be investigated…but he didn't have the authority, the standing, to force anyone else to listen. Ferguson might have done so, but he was gone now, and the entire MWP under the watchful eye of a man who belonged to Ingram's church.

Who might have killed Eddie, and tried to kill Wyatt.

Clock towers chimed across the city, marking the noon hour. Uncle Hurley was expecting him.

Could Hurley help?

Jamie squeezed his eyes shut. O'Byrne had wrecked Caballus. Hurt Nick. He didn't want to talk calmly to his uncle—he wanted to scream his lungs bloody. Demand O'Byrne be kicked out into the street.

The arrest Jamie had seen, when Hurley had been present, hadn't been violent. O'Byrne was surely abusing his authority without Hurley's knowledge. Once Hurley knew the truth, he'd keep it from happening ever again.

Yes, maybe Hurley had become too focused on pleasing his superiors in exchange for promotion. But he cared about Jamie. About Muriel and Fan, and their children. He might have lost sight of the reason he'd joined the force to start with, but this was something different altogether. This was a possible conspiracy that had already resulted in a score of deaths, if Wyatt was right about the connection with the theriarchists. Hurley wouldn't ignore that, or else he wasn't the man Jamie had always thought him to be.

The mayor might not listen to Jamie MacDougal, MWP detective. But he'd listen to Inspector Hurley O'Malley, head of the Dangerous Familiars Squad. If he didn't, they'd go to Roosevelt. If nothing else, this letter proved Wyatt hadn't vanished due to cowardice. Surely the governor would believe the word of two of his former soldiers, plus the man who'd saved his life while he was on the Police Board.

It wasn't much of a plan, but it would have to do. Aching inside and out, Jamie dragged himself to his feet and set about the long, slow descent back to the ground.

Chapter 24

Nick stood outside the church, watching from across the street for a time. The place wasn't lacking in finery—the Heirs of Adam might be backward puritans, but they had money. No wonder men like Senator Pemberton so eagerly climbed into bed with them.

From what he could see, the church was deserted this time of day. No one went in or out of the large wooden doors, or rang the bells in the tower. But still he hesitated, until he was forced to admit that he simply didn't want to go inside alone.

Stupidly, he wished Jamie were with him. But he wasn't, and never could be again. Nick thrust the treacherous thought aside, squared his shoulders, and stomped across the street and up the stairs.

He slipped inside as quietly as he could, just in case. The nave was draped in shadow, illuminated only by a single candelabrum. It flung flickering shadows across the plain wooden cross dominating the wall behind the pulpit.

"Hello?" Nick called. His voice echoed.

"Here." Simon was visible only as a shadow in a doorway to the side. He wore a bulky overcoat, as if chilled even inside the building.

No one else seemed to be with him. Nick cocked his head cautiously. "Where's your brother?"

"Downstairs. The reverend has a…a room below the church. My brother is a dangerous familiar. He's kept locked up, so he can't hurt the rest of the congregation."

Horror crept up Nick's spine. "Fur and feathers."

"Ingram thinks I've proved myself." Simon glanced fearfully over his shoulder. "But my brother…I thought I knew where the key was, but it's gone. I need your help. You're strong—you might be able to break the chains."

Nick wavered. There was no point in calling the coppers. Hell, given the Pemberton Act, the poor soul trapped in the basement might even be registered as under the church's supervision. Nick didn't want to go any deeper into the building, certainly not that far from a door, but he couldn't very well leave a familiar to suffer when he had a chance to fix things.

"Lead the way," Nick said.

Simon nodded and hurried back through the door. Nick followed, listening intently. But there was nothing. No sound of an ambush.

Maybe he was insane to have expected one. Ingram preached on the sidewalk and riled up the reform papers, but his congregation were the sort to write angry letters to their congressmen, not engage in violence themselves. That was for the coppers to do on their behalf.

The door led to a short hall, with stairs at the end. At the bottom of the stairs was a heavy steel door that would have been more at home in a prison than a church. The hairs on the back of Nick's neck stood up.

Simon opened the door, barred from the outside. The smell of old blood spilled out to greet them.

What the hell was Ingram doing down here?

A lone gaslight illuminated what looked like an abattoir. Rusty restraints hung from the walls, and a steel table dominated the room. Dried blood spattered the gray stones of walls and floors.

A puma lay unmoving on the table. Nick swore and rushed to its side.

It was dead, and had been for some time. Nick frowned, recognition plucking at his thoughts. Too late, he realized it was the feral who had stayed in his cellar, before leaving with Conrad.

He spun to the door, even as it slammed shut behind him. Simon was still inside with him, though. Only he'd thrown off his overcoat, revealing black clothes and a frayed black cloak. Hex-marked bones hung across his chest, and he lifted a headdress crowned with ram's horns.

The Wraith.

It took Jamie longer than it should have to reach the offices of the Dangerous Familiars Squad. He used a pain hex on his knee, but the cheap hex served only to blunt the discomfort to a dull ache. By the time Jamie arrived, the place looked nearly deserted. Maybe there'd been a second raid, or a new report of a familiar breaking the Pemberton Act.

The same aide as before sat outside Hurley's office. "Your uncle is waiting for you," he said with enough of a chill to his voice to let Jamie know his tardiness wasn't appreciated. "Go right inside."

Hurley sat behind his desk, puffing on a cigar. The standing ashtray at this elbow was heaped with ash, and a haze hung in the room, as if he'd been smoking relentlessly all morning. "Jamie," he said, and for once it was no affectionate welcome. Rather, the tone was the one Hurley had taken when he and Muriel misbehaved as children.

Jamie's spine stiffened. "Sir," he said, carefully. "I'm sorry I'm late. But—"

"Not yet." Hurley held up a hand. "I need to speak my piece first. I'm very disappointed in you, lad. Very disappointed indeed."

"As I am in you," Jamie snapped. "Your Captain O'Byrne came to arrest my familiar, and you didn't even bother to warn me beforehand. That ain't all—O'Byrne and your men wrecked Caballus and beat Nick."

He'd expected the last to shake his uncle's confidence. Instead, Hurley said, "If you'd told me exactly who you'd picked for your familiar to start with, I could have warned you off. I assumed you had the good sense to choose one of the unbonded familiars in the MWP. Instead, I had to hear the truth from Reverend Ingram. Came around asking if I knew my own nephew had bonded with the feral troublemaker from Caballus." Hurley shook his head in disgust. "I've never been so embarrassed. Why didn't you tell me?"

Jamie stiffened. "For one thing, you never asked about him. Not even his name. You talked like you thought familiars are just, I don't know, pets. Go pick one out from the newest litter, as if they don't have any say in the matter. I tried to explain to you how it works, but you wouldn't listen."

Hurley's face darkened. "They ain't like us. But you're right—I should have paid more attention, so I could have told you not to bond with the horse. Maybe this is all my fault."

"Told me?" Jamie's hands curled into fists. "I'm sick of people acting like I can't think for myself. That losing a leg means I can't make decisions like an adult."

"And no wonder, given the decisions you've made!" Hurley surged to his feet. "You almost threw away your career for a lowlife feral who stirs up trouble at best, and abets fugitives from justice at the worst. That would have been bad enough, but he's been whispering poison in your ear against me. Why else would you have ignored my advice to let the feral murders go and concentrate on the illegal hex campaign?"

"Because it was the right thing to do!" Saint Mary, how could Hurley not understand? "Did you expect I'd turn a blind eye for the sake of a promotion? Of gaining the notice of the right kind of people?" Jamie took a deep breath, fighting for calm. "Maybe you can look at the murders and just see dead criminals. Dead ferals no one cares about. But it's part of something a lot bigger."

Maybe he'd finally gotten through, because Hurley paled slightly. "What do you mean, something bigger?"

"A conspiracy. The kind that's already ended in more death and mayhem than it had to." Jamie took the letter from his coat and held it out. "This letter was written by Wyatt, the eagle I served with in Cuba. He and his witch were betrayed, his witch killed, and it has something to do with what's happening now in New York."

Hurley stared at the letter as though it could burn him. Jamie stepped closer, and he finally took it, though he didn't open it. "I see. Who else knows about this letter?"

"No one. I thought you'd be in the best position to help out."

Hurley nodded. "Good lad. I'll read it when I have a moment, and we'll meet later, once I've had some time to think."

Jamie shifted nervously. "Uncle Hurley, I'd really rather you—"

"Jamie!" Nick's voice shouted in his head. *"I need—"*

Jamie almost fell, grabbing the back of a chair for support. "Nick?" he said aloud. "Nick, what is it? What's wrong?"

Only silence answered him.

Dread poured through Jamie's veins. "Something's wrong. Nick's in danger. I have to go." He turned to the door, only to find the aide blocking his way. "Excuse me."

The aide glanced past him at Hurley, and didn't move.

"Out of the way." Jamie didn't have time for patience. "My familiar's in some kind of trouble, damn it. I have to get to him."

"I'm sorry, Jamie lad," Hurley said heavily behind him. "I can't let you do that."

Nick didn't waste time denying what was before his very eyes. He charged across the room even as the headdress settled into place, fist cocked. He glimpsed an expression of surprise on the Wraith's face, even as he buried his fist into Simon's gut.

The Wraith hadn't had time to activate any of his hexes, and crashed into the door. The room wasn't near big enough, but Nick shifted into horse form anyway. If he had only a few seconds, best to use those to get what help he could.

Even if it was from the man whose heart he'd broken only a few hours ago.

"Jamie! I need—"

The electric shock of the hex forcing him into human form blazed through him, breaking the connection. He went to his knees, and all the pains from the earlier beating howled their protest. A metallic taste filled his mouth.

The Wraith gripped a new addition to his collection of bones. With a sick twist of his gut, Nick recognized it as the canine of some large cat. A lion.

They'd pulled Luther's teeth.

The fang cracked as the hex carved into it activated. The Wraith seized Nick by the collar and back of his shirt, and hurled him into the wall. Bloodied restraints rang as Nick slid dazed to the floor.

He wouldn't be the first feral to die here. Not by a long shot. The Wraith had been making his gruesome charms in this very space, amidst blood and death and screams.

Ingram knew. Somehow, the Heirs of Adam were a part of this mess. Ingram preached against magic, then allowed ferals to be butchered for their power in his own basement.

Rage burst through Nick, propelling him to his feet. He grabbed one of the chains and swung it, just as the Wraith reached him.

The heavy iron shackle on the end smashed into the Wraith's face, splitting open his cheek and gouging his brow. Nick followed it up with a vicious kick to the shin, sending him staggering.

It wasn't much of an opening, but it was enough. Nick ran for the door, and nearly sobbed with relief when it swung open at his touch. The hex the Wraith had used on him still clung to his skin; he wouldn't be able to take horse form and call for help. Assuming Jamie would even answer.

Nick just had to stay alive for a little while longer. If he could reach the street, the Wraith would never dare attack him in broad daylight, in the midst of a host of witnesses.

Nick raced up the stairs, taking them two at once. As he burst out onto the upstairs landing, a dark figure stepped out from the shadows. He barely had the time to recognize Ingram, before a hex was pressed to his neck.

"Sleep!" Ingram ordered.

Nick staggered. But he was a big man; it would take more than an ordinary sleeping hex to put him down. Still, it made his legs clumsy, and the hallway seemed to stretch before him, unfairly adding distance between him and safety.

Ingram swore and snatched another hex from inside his coat. For a moment, he seemed to pause, concentrating on the square of paper.

Just as witches did when charging hexes.

"You...you fuckin' hypo...hypocrite," Nick managed through numb lips.

"Even the tools of the devil may serve the Lord's purpose," Ingram said. "Now, sleep, damn you."

The second hex took effect. Nick found himself lying on the floor. Colors swirled in his vision as he fought to keep his eyes open.

He couldn't fall asleep. If he succumbed, he was dead.

The last thing he saw was the shadow of the Wraith looming up behind Ingram.

"Jamie," he mumbled. "I'm so sorry."

Then the world swirled away and vanished into darkness.

Jamie turned slowly to face his uncle. Hurley still stood on the other side of the desk, looking as exhausted as Jamie had ever seen him. "What do you mean?" Jamie asked. "Never mind. I'm going, and you can't stop me."

The aide drew a revolver and leveled it silently at Jamie's chest.

"Sit down, Jamie," Hurley said. "Thanks to that damned familiar of yours, you're in over your head. Just let me take care of things."

Jamie's heart thumped painfully against his ribs. Fear for Nick twined with slow building horror as he sank into the chair. "Take care of things?"

Hurley rubbed at his face tiredly. "I've always done my best to guide you. But I made a mistake, getting you in with Roosevelt. Sending you to Cuba. I thought...I thought you'd serve and come home, covered in glory, proud but unchanged. Instead, you almost died."

Jamie's fingers curled around the armrests of the chair, squeezing hard. "That don't mean you have to look out for me now, like I'm a child."

"I have to make things right for you."

"Where is Nick?"

"I don't know." Hurley sat down at last. "I sent O'Byrne to arrest the horse this morning. Once he was out of the way, you would no longer be a detective. You wouldn't have the authority to investigate things better left alone. But the damned familiar was one step ahead of us. Other measures had to be taken." Hurley leaned back in his chair. "Don't worry about the details. Just let it happen. Then you'll be free."

Horror swamped Jamie. *Free.*

They meant to kill Nick. Not only that—Hurley *wanted* Nick dead.

The man Jamie had looked up to his whole life. Who had roughhoused with him as a child, and taught him how to ride when he was older. Who had impressed the need for duty on Jamie, for sticking up for family and fellow coppers.

Just looking at him made Jamie ill. The weight of betrayal pressed down on his heart like a stone. "Holy Familiar of Christ. You're in on it, ain't you? You've been in on it all along."

Irritation flickered across Hurley's face. "Whatever I've done, it's all been for you and Muriel."

"Been for us!" Jamie started to rise, then stopped when the aide shifted his grip on the gun. "Killing innocent people? Murdering Wyatt? Threatening Nick?"

Hurley shook his head. "I ain't killed anyone, lad. I told you, the day you came looking for the photograph, to leave things alone. I tried again when I learned our allies had failed to kill your familiar, warning you to leave off before it was too late."

"You sent the threatening letter." Jamie shook his head numbly. "You knew about the Wraith. You…oh God. The Wraith tried to kill Nick to get me off the case, didn't he? As a favor to you?"

"If Nick died, you'd no longer be a detective. I didn't like the idea of demoting you, but you had attracted the wrong sort of attention." Hurley looked away. "If you're going to catch the notice of powerful men, you've got to do it for the right reasons. Otherwise…let's just say the men involved have the ability to crush simple Irish coppers like us without so much as a thought. The horse managed to escape, so I sent the anonymous note, warning you away." He seemed to remember he held a different letter in his hand. "Speaking of notes."

Jamie cried out as Hurley swung open the pot-bellied stove. He tried to grab for it, but the aide seized him by the shoulder and shoved him down into the chair. Hurley tossed the letter into the stove and watched it begin to curl into ashes, before closing the door again.

Wyatt's letter. The only evidence Jamie had of a conspiracy. Gone.

His throat tightened. He'd failed Wyatt all over again. Taken the one thing Wyatt meant to entrust to him, and handed it over to the wrong man.

"I don't know you," he said in a low voice. "You ain't the man who raised me. Who taught me to be proud of being a copper."

"Don't you see? This is the only way to keep you safe." Hurley leaned forward, peering into Jamie's face, as if willing him to understand. "These men don't play games. At first, I agreed to go along with certain things because of the money. The promotion. The medals. But if I tried to get out now...well, they wouldn't kill me, at least, not at first. They'd start with Muriel. Then you. Then the boys. Only after they'd made enough of an example would they come for me." Hurley took a shaking breath. "I almost lost you once already. I can't...I can't go through that again."

Sickness tightened Jamie's throat. Bad enough Jamie had failed Wyatt one last time. He'd failed Nick as well. Now Nick would pay for it with his life.

He shouldn't have walked out on Nick. He should have fought harder for what they had.

Beautiful, angry Nick who cut through the world like a meteor hurtling through space. Who hadn't laid the burden of hero on Jamie's shoulders, but who had never pitied him, either. Nick had accepted him for who he was, and that was that.

Nick wouldn't just sit here and crumble. He'd kick and bite until his last breath, the kind of bronco no man could ever tame by force.

Time to be like Nick, then.

With a shout of rage, Jamie grabbed up the standing ashtray and swung it at the aide behind him.

The man didn't have time to react before getting a face full of ashes. He shouted, scrabbling at his eyes in an attempt to clear his vision. Hurley cried out in protest, but Jamie swung the stand again, and caught the side of his uncle's head. Hurley sagged, not unconscious but clearly dazed.

Before either could recover, he hurried out the door, pausing only long enough to jam the ashtray against the door latch. It wouldn't hold them long, but Jamie only needed enough time to get out of the building.

He wouldn't get far with his knee protesting every step. Jamie ducked out a side door, rather than the main one onto the street. As he'd hoped, it led to the small stables and courtyard where the squad kept their wagon. The wagon and two of the horses were gone, but a bay gelding raised its head when Jamie limped into the stable.

A few minutes later, the side door burst open, and Hurley and the aide ran out. But Jamie was already in the saddle. He set his heels and flew past them and onto the street at a gallop.

"All right, Nick," he said grimly. "I'm coming for you. So don't you dare give up before I get there."

Chapter 25

The horse had been trained for police work, and knew how to get through crowds. It bore Jamie in and out of traffic, barely slowing until they reached Caballus.

The bond burning in his chest told him Nick had moved in the direction of Central Park. Although the Wraith had never struck in daylight before, Jamie couldn't chance that this one time would prove the exception. Even though he wanted nothing more than to gallop straight to Nick's side, if the Wraith was somehow involved, he needed help.

The MWP was too far away, and in the wrong direction. Which left only one option.

To his surprise, a group of ferals had gathered and were busy putting the saloon to rights. When Jamie stepped inside Caballus, everyone froze, and he found himself the focus of a lot of very unfriendly gazes.

"You," said one of the ferals, a handsome dark-haired man with the golden eyes of a cat. "You're Nick's witch."

"Jamie!" Rook appeared from the crowd, clutching a dustpan full of shattered glass. "Where the hell have you been? Where is Nick? Dominic and I got tired of waiting, and Kyle said the Dangerous Familiars Squad raided the place, and—"

"Let him tell us," Dominic ordered. He held a broom in his hands, which he leaned on now. "Jamie?"

Jamie swallowed. "Nick's in trouble. The Dangerous Familiars Squad—and my uncle—are involved." Saint Mary, didn't it hurt to say that. "The Wraith might be too. Nick tried to call for help, but he was cut off. He's still alive, but I don't know how long they mean to keep him that way."

Kyle's eyes widened in alarm.. "Nick made sure the coppers focused on him, instead of me. I got away with not so much as a bruise earlier, while they beat him. If there's any way I can help, tell me and I'll do it."

His words opened a floodgate. "Nick doctored my little girl, when I was sure she was going to die from the croup, and didn't even ask for payment," said another feral.

"When I broke my arm and couldn't work for a month, Nick didn't ask for rent, let me pay it back as I could."

"I was running from someone who'd used a hex on me, to see if I was unbonded, and Nick punched the bastard in the face and brought me here."

More and more voices rose up in a clamor. When it didn't seem as though they'd let up, Rook climbed on top of a chair and waved his arms. "Quiet!" Silence fell, and Rook turned to Jamie expectantly.

"Nick needs us," Jamie said, feeling a bit awkward. "I know he'd never ask any one of you to put yourselves in danger—"

"The daft tit," Estelle muttered.

"—and I don't want anyone who can't fight to come. I won't lie—people could get hurt. Killed even. Or sent to jail." Jamie drew a deep breath. "I ain't known Nick as long as most of you. But one thing I've learned, is that he's worth fighting for. Who's with me?"

A cacophony of shouts, hoots, and barks rang out, half the ferals shifting into animal form on the spot. "Avians!" Rook called. "Spread the word!" He pointed to an owl. "You there—go to the MWP and ask for Tom Halloran. Tell him he's needed in Central Park, as fast as he can get there."

Which likely wouldn't be fast enough. As much as Jamie would have preferred to face the Wraith with a hexbreaker, time wasn't on their side.

Within half a minute, the bird familiars took to the wing. The rest looked expectantly at Jamie.

"Well?" Kyle asked.

"Follow me, then," Jamie said. He walked outside to his stolen horse. As he mounted, Rook approached.

"Thank you," Rook said. "I'm glad you didn't listen to me, that first day."

Jamie picked up the reins. "You are? Because I doubt Nick feels that way right now."

Rook snorted. "As much as he'd like to deny it, I know my brother. He's out of his head in love with you."

Jamie didn't think he'd ever experienced such a balance of terror and joy all at the same time. He swallowed, then guided his horse onto the street. "For Nick!" he shouted.

"For Nick!" yelled those ferals still in human form. Then Jamie set his heels to the horse's flanks and they were off.

Nick regained consciousness only slowly. His mouth tasted like the bottom of an old boot, and a fierce headache pulsed behind his eyes. The sound of rushing water filled his ears, as though a waterfall lay just a little way off. The air smelled of steel and cool, wet stone.

He blinked, then lifted his head. Sunlight streamed through four windows, two to either side of the strange room he was in. The rectangular chamber was made from gray stone, and arched high over his head. In front of him—and behind, most likely—water poured in through high, arched culverts, onto a ledge, then fell smoothly into a pool that filled the lower part of the structure.

He was near the center of the room, suspended above the water on an octagonal metal grate. Someone had tied him to one of four large valves, no doubt meant to control the flow of water either in or out of the building. To either side, a stair ran up to a balcony overlooking the whole operation. Directly across from him, a smaller spiral stair plunged down, vanishing beneath the surface of the water. Large metal doors opened off the balcony to the left, leading to the outside judging by the windows flanking them.

It took his sluggish brain a long moment to realize where he must be. He was in one of the Gate Houses—the north one, judging by the size—of the reservoir in Central Park.

If the Wraith had brought him here, rather than killing him in the church…it meant he was about to become a sacrifice.

Nick jerked wildly on his bonds, but they were too tight. With his arms tied behind him, he couldn't shift without dislocating his shoulders and possibly worse.

Had Jamie heard his aborted call for help? And if he had, would he even come after the way Nick had lied to him about Wyatt?

Nick sagged against the valve. He should have at least told Jamie he loved him, with every fucking fiber of his being. Jamie might not have forgiven him, but at least he would have known.

He should have trusted Jamie. Should have told him, about Wyatt if nothing else. And maybe they still wouldn't have found a way forward together, but at least they would have had a chance. Maybe Jamie would still love him.

A shadow detached from the balcony to Nick's right. Nick started badly—the Wraith had been there all along. Watching him regain consciousness. Hood and face mask now in place, he walked down the stairs toward Nick. An obsidian knife glittered in his hand.

Nick yanked against the bonds again, but they didn't yield. "Simon, that's your name, isn't it?" he asked as the figure walked implacably toward him. "Simon, you don't have to do this."

The metal doors swung open, then shut again. "You're wrong about that," Ingram said. He clasped his hands behind him, looking smugly down on them from the balcony. "I've explained it all to him very carefully. Only by doing this, by making the necessary sacrifices, can he be purified."

Sacrifice. Oh hell. What had the scribbling in the Blockhouse said? "It is the blood that maketh an atonement for the soul."

"Indeed it is," Ingram agreed. "Once this is ended and you are dead, the blood Simon has spilled will wash the Sin of the Serpent from his soul."

"What the hell are you ranting about?" Nick asked. "Sin of the Serpent?"

"The animal nature he has been afflicted with." Ingram smiled. "God will honor his sacrifices and make him entirely human."

"Liar." Nick stared at Ingram instead of the approaching Wraith, but projected his words. "I saw you. You're a witch. You used magic."

Ingram's expression twisted. "Another sin Simon must atone for. His magic tempted me off the righteous path."

Bile rose in Nick's throat. That was the sort of wretched excuse men like Ingram used to justify whatever abuses they chose to indulge in. "You're fucking sick." Nick spat at him, but didn't come close to his target. "This poor deluded fool might believe all the bullshit about sin and repentance, but you surely don't, preacher-man. What is all this really for? You're using the murders to weaken the Great Hex somehow, but I can't see how that helps your righteous cause."

Ingram cocked his head and studied Nick thoughtfully. "Since it's your death that will complete the pattern, perhaps you have the right to know. The sites of the killings, of the blood hexes, have been chosen very carefully. Once your blood finishes the spell, the Great Hex will not be destroyed—it will be inverted. It will sicken the air, blight the plants, and poison the water."

Ice slicked Nick's veins. "Poison the water. The reservoir."

"Indeed."

"You maniac! Millions will die!" Nick struggled again, but the bonds held firm. "Why would you do something like that?"

"Oh, but it won't be blamed on me." Ingram grinned savagely, as if Nick's distress filled him with delight. "Sufficient evidence will be left behind to pin it on the theriarchists. With so many innocent lives lost, people will finally see familiars and magic for the dangers they are."

If Ingram succeeded blaming the theriarchists, the crackdown on familiars wouldn't be confined to New York. The entire nation would panic. Once the likes of Pemberton and his cronies finished, familiars wouldn't have any rights left.

"It's all about power," Nick said. "Just like always. You can't even come up with anything original, can you? Pick a group, demonize them, and use the resulting fear to pass whatever laws you like. Your pal Pemberton will look like a prophet who tried to keep everyone safe, but was thwarted by those who willfully ignored the signs until it was too late. He'll be in the governor's mansion by the next election cycle."

"We're thinking the White House." Ingram gestured to the Wraith. "Now, I believe we've talked long enough. End this."

"You don't have to do this, Simon," Nick said as the dark figure crossed the last few feet between them. "He's lying to you. You don't have to be ashamed to be a familiar."

"Don't waste your breath," Ingram called. "He began this venture by killing his own brother."

Fur and feathers, no. "Wyatt?"

"The eagle knew too much about things our allies don't want made public. And was an excellent test of Simon's loyalty. Two birds with one stone, as it were." Ingram chuckled at his own wit. "Though only one bird, in this case."

Nick swallowed convulsively as the Wraith knelt in front of him. "What about Pia? Why kill her?"

"She'd joined our church recently. Unfortunately, she saw some things she wasn't meant to, and hoped to blackmail me to solve her money troubles." Ingram shook his head in mock sorrow. "I blame her death on you, actually. You made her just confident enough that she never totally accepted my authority. You have an unfortunate way of inspiring familiars, of luring them from the righteous path. Once you're dead, they will see the light and flock to my side, begging for forgiveness." He paused. "Those who survive, at any rate."

The Wraith put the edge of the knife to Nick's throat. Nick stared defiantly at where he imagined Simon's eyes to be.

God, he hoped Rook and Dominic looked out for Jamie. The people he loved most in the world, and the one's he'd pushed away hardest, like a fool.

The metal doors burst inward.

Jamie leaned low over the neck of his stolen horse, pounding up the Bridle Path in the direction the bond told him led to Nick. A host of ferals raced around him, or flew in the air. Dominic clung to the mane of a horse feral beside him, his eyes wide as if he expected to fall off at any moment.

As they rounded the curve of the reservoir, Jamie shouted, "The North Gate House! He has to be inside!"

Rook flicked a wing in acknowledgement and increased his pace, leaving the terrestrial ferals behind. The other birds followed him like a small storm. To his shock, Jamie realized they numbered far, far more than there had been when they'd left Caballus. Had the ferals of the park joined them? How far had word spread among the feral community?

He didn't just have a mob now. He had a small army.

"Rook says there are guards in front of the Gate House," Dominic called. "Damn it. It's the Dangerous Familiars Squad."

Jamie pressed his lips together. No wonder the station had been all but deserted when he'd gone to see Hurley.

He'd thought Hurley had betrayed him as completely as possible, but he hadn't even known just how deep his uncle's treachery ran. While arranging to meet Jamie, Hurley had sent his squad here, whether at someone else's behest or not, to preside over Nick's murder. He'd known all along that Nick would die, and where, and hadn't spoken a word of it to Jamie.

A few of the ferals peeled off, not willing to face the Dangerous Familiars Squad. But more poured in, avians carrying the word to colonies, to the streets, to workshops: *Nick needs our help.*

If they lived through this, Jamie was never going to stop telling Nick how fucking proud he was of him. Everything Nick had done, all the years of hard work and pushing back against anyone who tried to hurt familiars, and here was the result. All these ferals, ready and willing to return the favor and risk their lives.

Of course, that assumed Jamie didn't end up in jail for inciting a riot against the police.

"Don't slow down!" Jamie shouted. "Overwhelm them! It's our only chance."

"You go inside for Nick." Dominic clung grimly to the horse feral beneath him. "We'll handle the rest."

The Dangerous Familiars Squad drew together in a nervous knot at the sight of so many converging on them. "Stop, or we'll shoot!" called their captain. "Men, get ready to—argh!"

A flock of birds fell on them, too many and too fast for them to take aim. Herons stabbed with their vicious beaks, and a swan chased one of the larger officers away, using its great wings like clubs. A hawk Jamie thought might have been Bess sank her talons into the hand of a man who'd drawn his revolver. He shrieked and spun, trying desperately to shake her off. The gun discharged, hitting one of his fellow squad members.

Then the rest of the mob was on them, some in animal form, others shifting to human to use makeshift weapons: bricks, branches, whatever they had picked up on the way. The officers started to fight back, laying about with nightclubs, and within minutes blood soaked into the bare earth.

But their line had crumbled, leaving a gap. A last man leapt out of the way to avoid being ridden down, and then Jamie was through.

He slid off the horse, swearing as his leg nearly went out from under him in his haste. Drawing his revolver, he hurled open the iron doors with all the force he could muster.

Chapter 26

The first thing he saw was Nick, tied to one of the big valves. Light reflected from the rippling water below, and the inflow cascaded through the great pipes with a low roar. The Wraith crouched in front of Nick, knife in hand. Ingram stood on the balcony just in front of the door, already turning as Jamie came inside.

"Put your hands up!" Jamie ordered, training the gun on Ingram.

Rook shot in like a black arrow, making for the Wraith. The dark figure swiped the knife at him, then started up the stairs for Jamie. Rather than wheel back for another pass, Rook dropped to the metal grate beside Nick and shifted into human form.

"Order the Wraith off," Jamie said, jabbing the gun at Ingram.

"Jamie, look out!" Nick called. "Ingram is a witch."

Ingram sprang at him, and Jamie glimpsed a hex paper in his hand. Jamie fired; the shot missed, but forced Ingram back.

"Stop him," Ingram ordered.

The Wraith was still a few stairs below the balcony. He lunged forward, the obsidian blade gleaming, too fast and strong for Jamie to escape. It slammed into his left calf.

"Wrong leg," Jamie said, and twisted hard.

Surprise loosened the Wraith's hold, and the knife tore free of his grip. The hilt stuck out to the side, pinning Jamie's trousers to his wooden leg.

The Wraith didn't hesitate for more than an instant. He grabbed one of the hexed bones dangling from his costume. It cracked. Before Jamie could scramble out of the way, the Wraith bounded up the last steps and wrapped his arms around Jamie's chest.

The Wraith's strength was immense, fueled by the dead familiar whose essence he'd stolen. Jamie's ribs creaked under the pressure. He fought, kicking and clawing, but the Wraith seemed unmoved, his grip inexorably tightening.

"Let go of my witch!" Nick roared.

The Wraith jolted as Nick's weight landed on his back, trying to pry him loose from Jamie. For a moment, the three of them balanced precariously at the very top of the stairs.

Then gravity took over, and they tumbled back in a heap, with Nick on the bottom. Jamie fell head over heels, slid across a body or perhaps two, then struck the metal grate near the valve where Nick had been tied. Pain spiked through his body, and he'd lost his revolver during the fall. Instinct shouted at him to move, so he grabbed for the railing to pull himself up. Rook seized one arm and heaved him to his feet, then took on bird form once again.

The Wraith staggered up. Somehow, Nick had already made it to his feet, though the sight of him stabbed Jamie with a mixture of relief and fear. Bruises bloomed on his face, and he moved with a stiffness that spoke of more injuries beneath his clothing.

But he was alive, and that was all that mattered. Now Jamie just had to keep him that way.

"You!" Jamie yelled at the Wraith. He bent down and yanked the knife free from his leg. Waving it in front of him, he said, "Surrender, or I'll gut you the way you gutted Wyatt."

"My brother was a blasphemer," the Wraith said.

Wyatt's letter had spoken of meeting his brother. But Jamie had assumed that was a pretext on the part of the Heirs of Adam. Not that the Wraith actually was Wyatt's brother.

Shock slowed Jamie's reactions. The Wraith charged him—only to get a face full of black wings from Rook. When the Wraith stepped back, Nick struck him from behind, driving a fist deep into a kidney.

The Wraith went into the railing near Jamie. Jamie stabbed at him, but the Wraith was too fast. He caught Jamie's wrist with one hand, using the taloned glove on the other to slash at his abdomen. Jamie twisted away, but still felt a sting as skin parted across his belly.

Nick slammed into the Wraith, smashing him hard into the railing. The Wraith let go of Jamie, but before he could grab the railing, Nick heaved him up—and over.

There came a loud splash as he struck the water below.

Rook shifted back to human form. "That won't keep him for long—there are stairs leading back up on the other side."

"Then let's get out of here," Jamie said.

"Ingram already ran." Rook glanced at Nick as they hastened up the stairs as quickly as Jamie was able to hobble. "Are you all right?"

"Right enough." Nick clasped Rook's arm. "Thanks for coming for me."

Rook shrugged awkwardly. "Well, you're my brother. Even if you are a literal horse's ass."

The sunlight outside was almost painfully bright after the shadowed interior of the Gate House. "Who the hell are all these people?" Nick asked.

"Your rescue party," Rook said. "Except…oh."

Jamie shaded his eyes, blinking rapidly. The struggle outside had ended, police standing to one side and ferals to the other, staring at each other with unconcealed hostility. In the center was Uncle Hurley, his gun trained on none other than Ingram. The reverend stood very still, his hands raised.

"Jamie," Hurley called. "Are you all right, lad?"

Jamie's throat constricted. Hurley had come to save him. Even if that meant changing sides and endangering everything his uncle had worked so hard for.

"Aye," Jamie said, "but the Wraith—"

Ingram dove at Hurley, slapping the hex paper he'd held concealed in his hand against Hurley's neck. "Die."

Hurley dropped his revolver, clutching at his throat. His face purpled; he began to gag and choke.

"Uncle!" Jamie cried.

Ingram bolted. He got no more than three steps before a shot rang out from one of the policemen. The reverend collapsed into the dust, body twitching spasmodically.

Jamie limped to Hurley's side, but Dominic got there first. He snatched up the hex Ingram had dropped. "A hex altered to be poison," he said. Dropping it, he pulled out his hexman's wallet. "Rook!"

Rook crouched by him. "Don't worry, Jamie. Dominic always carries his hexman's tools with him. He can make an antidote."

Dominic's hands flew over a scrap of paper, even as Rook uncapped various inks and handed him what he needed before he even had to ask.

"Cure," Dominic barked as he slapped the hex onto Hurley's forehead.

Hurley's breathing eased, and some of the color returned to his face. "He won't feel good for a few days, but he'll live," Dominic said.

Nick's hand closed on Jamie's shoulder. Jamie turned into him, found himself hauled into an embrace. He breathed deep, savoring Nick's sweat.

"You came for me," Nick said.

Jamie clung to him. "Of course I did. I love you."

"I thought you hated me." Nick's arms tightened. "I couldn't have blamed you, after my lies." He took a shuddering breath. "Just so there's no more deception between us…you're my witch."

"Well, aye. How do you think I found you?" Then the implication of Nick's words caught up. Jamie drew back, just far enough to look into Nick's eyes. "Wait. You mean, *your* witch?"

Nick nodded. "Yes. I lied about that because…because I was afraid the MWP would force me to stay if they knew."

"I'd never let them do that to you."

"I know that now. I'm so sorry I didn't tell you earlier." Nick leaned in and kissed him softly. "I love you, Jamie MacDougal."

A horrible scream sounded from within the Gate House.

Jamie and Nick broke apart with a start. "What was that?" Jamie asked.

Nick nodded in the direction of Ingram's body. "He died." Nick couldn't bring himself to be even the slightest bit sorry. "That was the bond breaking."

"Wait. The Wraith was his familiar?" Jamie's mouth gaped. "That fucking hypocrite!"

"Men like him often are," Nick said. But an idea had started to congeal in the back of his mind. "If we can subdue Simon—the Wraith—for even a few seconds, we can use a hex to force him into animal shape. Given the sorts of things he said earlier, I have a feeling he hasn't been anything but human for a long time."

"Forcing him to change will shock him, the way it did Velma?" Jamie guessed.

Nick grinned, feeling obscurely proud. "I always knew you weren't just a pretty face, witch."

"We'll go in first and try to restrain him," said Kyle. He'd drawn close enough to overhear; the other ferals had gathered behind him.

Nick would never have imagined a mob of ferals would rally to his defense. Just looking out over the gathering left him with a strange feeling in his belly, part embarrassment and part pride. "You all came to rescue me. At risk to yourselves."

"Someone needed to save your ass." Kyle shrugged. "We couldn't exactly leave it for the witches to do, now could we?"

Nick held out his hand, and Kyle clasped it. "Thanks, Kyle." He swallowed. "Thanks to all of you. Now, let's go show this Wraith he can't just kill ferals and hope to get away with it, eh?"

"Sentimental as ever, I see," said Rook. "All right, you heard the plan, straight from the horse's mouth."

"Maybe you should've let the Wraith kill me, so I wouldn't have to put up with this nonsense," Nick muttered. But he couldn't help but feel a surge of affection.

"Love you, too, horse," Rook said. Then he flashed into crow form and glided through the open doors into the Gate House, the other ferals right behind him.

"Here," Dominic said, pressing a hex into Jamie's hand. "This should do it."

Jamie nodded. "Nick, do I have your permission…?"

"Do it." He felt the tug behind his breastbone, magic siphoning through the bond, into Jamie, and filling the hex.

When they reached the balcony just inside the Gate House doors, several other ferals had gotten there before them. They'd paused on the stairs, a murmur going through them as they got their first look at the Wraith.

He should have been a bedraggled figure, leaning heavily on the railing, one hand clutching his chest from the pain of the broken bond, his cloak hanging sodden with water around him. But some aura of primal terror yet hung around him, from the bones to the ram's horns, to the darkness of the concealing mask beneath the hood.

As they entered, he straightened slowly. Though it was impossible to tell for certain, Nick felt the Wraith's wrathful gaze fix on him.

"You," the Wraith grated out. "This is all your fault. Now I'll never enter the Gates of Heaven." He curled one gloved hand around a hexed bone, and it cracked with a dry snap. "But I'm going to take you all to Hell with me."

The Wraith exploded into motion. Before the ferals could even react, he was amongst them: heaving them over the railing into the water, slashing claws across vulnerable skin, and knocking them aside with brutal punches. Bones cracked. The cries of pain and anger nearly drowned out the rush of water.

Nick charged. There wasn't enough room to take on his horse shape, so he readied his fists. "Swarm him!" he yelled. "He can't fight us all at once, no matter how strong he is!"

Kyle jumped the Wraith from behind, locking his arms around the killer's neck. A badger sank teeth into one black-clad leg and refused to let go. A bulldog took the badger's lead, and did the same to the Wraith's near arm. The hex-woven cloth might be impervious to bullets, but fangs seemed to be another matter altogether.

The Wraith bellowed in fury and pain, dragging them after him as he struggled toward the stairs. He swung his free hand at Nick; Nick ducked, then grasped his wrist. They wrestled for a moment, Nick clinging with both hands, using his whole body to brace against the Wraith's immense strength. "Jamie, now!"

Jamie slapped the hex down on the arm Nick clung to. "Be bound to your animal form," he ordered.

The Wraith shrieked as if he'd been stabbed. His entire body convulsed, and Nick hastily released him, as did the other ferals.

It should have been quick. A flash of light or a puff of smoke, and they should have found themselves facing whatever animal form the Wraith possessed.

Instead, he thrashed and fell to his knees, body distorting strangely, even as the hexed bones strung all about his costume began to glow with a terrible red light.

"That...that ain't supposed to happen," Jamie said.

The Wraith began to shift, but not into a single animal. His body swelled, the steel stairs groaning under the sudden weight. The horns now sprouted from the head of a ram, eyes wild and tongue lolling from a frothing mouth. A lion's head pushed out beside it, fighting for space on its shoulders. Legs sprouted where there should be no legs, and eyes blinked from scaled elbows, or the sides of a long crocodile tail. Patches of fur struggled with scales and feathers, and a malformed wing jutted from its back.

Nick retreated, his stomach churning at the wrongness of the abomination in front of him. A dozen eyes swiveled in his direction. Red mouths full of teeth gaped, and with a blast of necrotic breath, the chimera roared.

"Run!" Jamie shouted.

The thing in front of him was unspeakably wrong in every way.

Somehow, the hex he'd used must have reacted with the hexed bones the Wraith and Ingram had torn from dying familiars. The stolen power had awoken all at once, coalesced, and turned the Wraith's body into a mishmash of a dozen different creatures.

The chimera roared again, even as ferals fled past Jamie. Eyes maddened by pain and horror fixed on him, and the chimera lurched forward on mismatched limbs.

"Come on," Nick said. He grabbed Jamie's arm, hauling him bodily up the stairs. "On my back, now!"

Jamie didn't question, only locked his arms around Nick's shoulders. Nick heaved Jamie onto his back, shifting as he did so, and Jamie found himself sprawled awkwardly over the warhorse's withers.

The chimera howled behind them, and there came the rending shriek of metal. Nick had fallen straight into a gallop, and they broke through the iron doors and into the free air. Nick didn't stop until he'd put distance between them and the Gate House. Then he turned, agile despite his great size, and faced the enemy.

"What's going on?" Hurley called in a scratchy voice. He was on his feet near Dominic, though he didn't look good. "Jamie, what—"

The front of the Gate House exploded as the chimera burst through the stone wall, its bulk too vast to fit through the doorway.

Some of the police screamed and fled. "Fire!" Hurley ordered. "Kill it!"

The remainder of the Dangerous Familiars Squad formed up, guns drawn. The chimera jerked and shrieked in pain, but their bullets seemed to do no more damage than they would have against a bull elephant. Enraged, it lowered two of its heads and rushed them. The lion bit and tore, the ram smashed, and claw-tipped limbs grabbed and ripped. The chimera batted a man with its crocodile tail, sending him flying into the reservoir, his scream echoing across the placid waters.

Jamie stared with a mixture of fear and horror pumping through his veins. "How can we fight something like that?" It was impossible; the thing was too huge, too terrible. It would swat even a horse of Nick's size aside like a gnat.

"It has to have a vulnerable point. Somewhere." But Nick didn't seem at all certain of that.

"Where? We could cut off a head or two and not kill it. It has a dozen eyes—we can't put them all out. Chop off a couple of legs, and it has five more." A coppery tang coated the back of Jamie's throat.

"I'd bet it only has one heart," Nick said.

Oh hell. Was he right? Despite all the monstrous outgrowths, the thing did seem to have a single torso. But how could they hope to reach it through the waving heads and arms, the blinking eyes? Even if they could, none of the other guns had done any damage. Jamie still had the Wraith's knife, but the blade wasn't long enough to pierce the thick bands of muscle across its misshapen chest.

"We need something long. Like a spear." Nick paused. *"Or a lance."*

No convenient lances lay within reach. Only rubble from the shattered Gate House: broken stone and twisted metal.

Metal.

"There!" Jamie shouted, pointing.

A straight length of steel that had been part of a railing lay a few feet away. One end had snapped free of a weld, but the other twisted into a jagged point.

"What do you need?" Dominic called. Dust covered him, but he seemed otherwise unharmed so far.

"That steel rod. We're going to try something." Something absolutely insane, but it wasn't as though any of them had other options at the moment.

Nick bore him to the rubble pile, while Dominic hefted the steel rod into reach. Jamie gripped it like a lance, so that the jagged point bit the air a few feet in front of Nick. The end wanted to tip down, and Jamie struggled to brace it as best he could.

Rook landed beside them. "Are you crazy?" He grabbed a handful of Nick's mane. "This is insane, even for you, Nick. It'll never work. You're both going to get killed."

Jamie licked dry lips, tasted the dust from the collapsed wall on his skin. "Do you have a better idea?"

At the shore of the reservoir, the chimera raged. Bodies lay strewn in its wake, and the longer they delayed, the more there would be.

Dominic put a hand to Rook's shoulder. "Let them try," he said softly. Then he looked at Jamie. "Good luck."

"Thanks."

Rook withdrew. Jamie swallowed and gripped Nick as tight as he could with his knees. "You ready, horse?"

"Whenever you are, witch."

"Then let's go."

Nick's powerful muscles surged beneath him, propelling them forward. Rook was right, Jamie thought, as he leaned low over Nick's mane. This was madness. There were too many heads, too many teeth, too many claws. He couldn't even see the chimera's chest through the misshapen horror of limbs and eyes and mouths. The lance might pierce its flank, but without an incredible stroke of luck, they wouldn't find its heart.

Nick's hooves struck the ground like thunder, each great stride carrying them closer. They had to try, before more died. The Wraith had already killed too many. Left behind too much grief. They had to do this for the familiars, for the dead.

For Wyatt.

Jamie's hand closed on the pendant beneath his shirt. *"A little something extra,"* Wyatt had said, in a jungle thousands of miles away, *"just in case."*

"Nick! I need your magic!" Jamie shouted over the pounding of hooves.

Nick didn't question. *"Use it."*

Jamie felt the hex on the pendant catch and fill with magic. Even though he didn't know what it would do, he said, "Diana, guard and guide me!"

A great light welled between his fingers—then burst forth, seeming to flood the air before them. It took on the shape of a great, golden arrow shrieking straight at the chimera.

Perhaps it was only the wind, or only a strand of Nick's mane, but Jamie felt the brush of feathers against his cheek. As though for a moment another flew beside them.

The arrow of light struck the chimera, blinding its many eyes with its brilliance. The creature howled and roared through its mouths, rearing back in pain, clawing at its weeping eyes. The movement exposed its malformed chest.

Nick didn't slow in his charge, all the weight and force he and Jamie could bring to bear slamming the point of the steel rod through muscle, between ribs, and straight into the chimera's heart.

A deafening scream shook the air around them. The steel bar ripped loose from Jamie's hands, taking skin with it. Then the massive body was gone, just a dark figure falling with them, into the waters of the reservoir.

The cold water shocked Jamie as it closed over his head. He took an inadvertent gasp, and it flooded his mouth. For a moment, everything was thrashing limbs and darkness, the weight of the wooden leg dragging him down toward the bottom.

Then a warm body bumped into his. Strong teeth closed on his collar, hauling him up until his face broke the surface. Jamie coughed and choked, but managed to grab hold of Nick's mane. Nick let him go, and he flung an arm over the arch of Nick's neck, hanging on while he swam to the water's edge.

The remaining ferals and police waited for them. Jamie crawled out first, and Dominic hastened to wrap a dry coat around him. Nick stumbled up after him, then shifted back into human form. Rook flung his arms around Nick with a squawk. "Stubborn horse."

Nick returned the hug, then turned toward Jamie. "About time I saved your life for once," he said with a crooked grin.

"Ah, sweetheart," Jamie said as he slipped into Nick's warm embrace. "I owe you for a lot more than that."

CHAPTER 27

A FEW WEEKS later, Nick stood behind the restored bar of Caballus, as night began to fall beyond the big glass window. Sunday meant the saloon stayed closed, and he'd spent the afternoon and evening alone with his thoughts.

Nick ran a damp rag across the plank. Maybe he ought to consider investing in a real bar some time. Though it would just be one more thing to replace if the coppers decided to pay him another visit. That didn't seem likely at the moment—the Dangerous Familiars Squad was in utter disgrace, and rumor had it they'd be disbanded altogether. But the Pemberton Act was still on the books. Whatever time they'd gained by defeating Ingram and the Wraith, it was only a temporary reprieve.

In the meanwhile, Nick was back behind the bar. And Jamie was back with the MWP.

Nick had done his best not to think of the witch since he'd last seen him, shortly after the battle at the Gate House. Despite his foray into law enforcement, Nick had always known it would never last. He'd turned in his familiar's badge and returned to the bar. Where he could look after the feral community, as best he could.

Or maybe, given the rescue they'd mounted for him, where they could look after each other.

Still, Jamie's absence in his life left behind a hole that felt as though it could never be filled. Nick's heart ached with a pain no hex could ease. He wanted Jamie more than he would have thought possible: in his bed, in his bar, in his life.

Even though the case had ended rather decisively, Nick hadn't been able to bring himself to visit the hexbreaker. The bond, his last link with the witch he loved, still burned behind his heart.

Someday it would vanish. Jamie would go to Halloran, and that would be that. He'd move on, find another familiar, and Nick…

Would survive. Somehow.

The bell above the door rang, but the figure in the doorway didn't come in. "Stop letting in the cold air," Nick said. "Do you think coal grows on…"

He trailed off. In the doorway stood Jamie, watching him with hopeful eyes. "I wasn't sure if I should come in," Jamie said, indicating the *Familiars Only* sign.

Nick nodded mutely. When Jamie frowned in confusion, he said. "Come in. God, Jamie. You're always welcome here."

He met Jamie halfway across the room. Jamie's arms locked around him, and Nick crushed the smaller man to his chest. Jamie smelled of cold air and smoke, of sandalwood and warmth.

He smelled like coming home.

"Missed you too," Jamie said, when Nick finally let him go. His eyes went to the wall behind the bar, and he grinned. "Nice headline."

Nick flushed. But when some of his regulars had tacked up the front page of the Herald, the morning after they'd killed the chimera, he'd grumbled…but left it up.

HEROIC HORSE SAVES CITY

MWP's Newest Detectives Stop Poison Plot

"Just doing our job," says Witch Detective MacDougal

"I didn't put that there," Nick said.

Jamie rolled his eyes. "Oh aye, it was the faeries as did it."

Nick swatted him on the rear. "To what do I owe the pleasure of this visit?"

Jamie sobered. "I meant to come sooner. But I had things to deal with…arrangements to make…"

Nick winced. He let go of Jamie and retreated behind the bar. Pulling out two glasses, he poured a generous measure of whiskey into each.

"I'm sorry about your uncle," he said.

Between the case he and Jamie had built, and what O'Malley had confessed, there had been no question as to what Ingram had planned for the city. It had broken the influence of the Heirs of Adam, and even though some of Ingram's parishioners continued to congregate in his church, the newspapers had turned against them. The links between the Dangerous Familiars Squad, the Menagerie, the butchery in the church basement, and the murderous Wraith were undeniable. Once the municipal witches had the information they needed, they'd been able to confirm the alterations to the Great Hex—as well as set about restoring it back to its original purpose.

O'Malley had confessed to everything he could, even though it put him behind bars for his involvement. But it seemed he'd still feared the powerful men he'd warned Jamie about. The ones who had sought out the hexes the Wraith had used, who had killed Eddie.

Nick was certain Pemberton was involved up to his neck. Lund too, for that matter. But O'Malley had refused to say anything. Perhaps he would have changed his mind eventually, but he'd been found hanging in his cell last week.

"I got your letter," Jamie said. "It meant the world to me. I just didn't have time to write back for a few days, and then I decided I'd rather talk to you face to face anyway." He took a sip of his whiskey. "Muriel thinks Uncle Hurley was murdered."

"But you don't?" Nick asked, surprised.

Jamie shook his head. "Nay. He wanted to keep us safe, above all else. He kept his mouth shut on certain matters long enough to reassure anyone watching that he hadn't told us what he knew. Then he killed himself, so no one could use Muriel and me against him, or him against us."

Nick wasn't particularly sorry to see the end of O'Malley, but he hated the sadness in Jamie's eyes. "I'm sorry," he said again, and put his hand on Jamie's.

Jamie turned his palm up, and their fingers curled together. "Aye. So am I."

They sat in silence for a long moment. "So what's next for you?" Nick asked at last. "I suppose you wanted to talk about breaking the bond?"

The words scraped coming out of his throat. But Jamie needed to get on with his life. It was the only way.

"Not exactly." Jamie swallowed nervously. "Actually, I wondered if you…if you had any interest in leaving it intact?"

"I want to." Nick stared down at their joined hands. "But I can't go back to the MWP. The feral community, the work I do here…it has to come first, Jamie."

"I know. That's why I quit the force."

Nick looked up in shock, met Jamie's particolored gaze. "You…you quit?"

"Aye. Turned in my badge yesterday. Then spent last night trying to work up the courage to come see you." Jamie smiled ruefully.

"But…why?" Nick asked. "I thought the Police Board had been forced to reinstate Ferguson. That's what Rook said, anyway. Things ought to get better at the MWP, at least for a while. Why not stay?"

"Because you were right," Jamie said with a shrug. "About everything. About how society treats familiars like they ain't people. Like they've got nothing better to do than work for some witch, or be harassed by the coppers, or locked up in jail even when they ain't done anything but try to live free."

"I…I'm glad."

"You were wrong about one thing, though," Jamie added.

Nick arched a brow. "Oh? And what was that?"

Jamie's expression softened. "You don't have to do this alone. I want to stay with you, Nick. I want to help you, any way I can. Whether that's behind the bar, or doing your books, or helping out with magic here and there. Even if you decide you'd rather break the bond, I still want to stay with you, as your lover if not your witch."

Nick stared at him, unable to get the words past the fullness of his heart. He swallowed hard, twice. "I'd rather you were both."

Jamie's grin almost blinded with its brightness. "Then that's what I'll be."

Nick didn't want to say anything to spoil the moment. But this would never work without honesty between them. "It won't be easy. Pemberton managed to stay free of the scandal. The Dangerous Familiars Squad is out of favor, but the Act is still in place. They'll start trying to enforce it again soon enough."

"Don't forget about all the ancient hexes Pemberton, or someone like him, seems intent on digging up," Jamie said.

"I couldn't if I tried," Nick muttered. "This work…it's a hard road to walk even when you don't have blood hexes and religious lunatics in the mix. Whoever is ultimately behind all this, be it Pemberton or someone else, they're not going to just go away."

"I know." Jamie's particolored eyes softened. "But we're not alone, Nick. Rook and Dominic, Quigley, Isaac, Cicero, and all the rest are on the lookout now. Thanks to Wyatt, we know there's something big happening. And when the time comes, we'll fight it. Together."

Nick put aside his whiskey and drew Jamie to him. "I like the sound of that."

Jamie arched a brow. "Fighting?"

"No," Nick said, and kissed him softly. "Together."

Share Your Experience

If you enjoyed this book, please consider leaving a review on the site where you purchased it, or on Goodreads.

Thank you for your support of independent authors!

END NOTE

THANK YOU FOR reading *Hexslayer.* If you would like to discuss it with other fans of the series, please feel free to join my Facebook group, Widdershins Knows Its Own.

The Midnight Assassin (also known as the "Servant Girl Annihilator") was an American serial killer who murdered eight people in Austin, Texas between 1884 and 1885. Though largely forgotten now, the attempts of the authorities to find and stop the killer were national news in the day.

What Jamie refers to as "soldier's heart" was one of the names given to what we now call PTSD. Psychiatric studies were in their infancy—or perhaps their fetus-hood—in the 1800s, but symptoms of PTSD were noticed and recorded as early as 1678 by Swiss military physicians.

Speaking of psychology, Nick refers briefly to Richard von Krafft-Ebing, author of the groundbreaking *Psychopathia Sexualis.* Krafft-Ebing was one of the doctors first to write seriously about homosexual and bisexual behavior, and though he considered any non-procreative sex to be "perverse," he also argued that sexual orientation was determined before birth. As a result, his work was used to support decriminalization of non-heterosexual behavior. The Hexworld version of *Psychopathia Sexualis* presumably added familiars to the list of those whose sexuality was studied.

Theodore Roosevelt stands out as one of the more colorful figures in American history, and—like most of us—was an extraordinarily complex human being, for both good and ill. Oceans of ink have been spilled over the Spanish-American War, but *Rough Riders* by Mark Lee Gardener and *The War Lovers* by Evan Thomas are excellent places to start. Roosevelt, a highly accomplished writer, himself produced the first book on the war titled simply *The Rough Riders.* Long out of copyright, it can be downloaded freely on the internet.

Sunken Meadow Island is no more, as the channels between it and Randalls Island were filled in. There was never a prison on the island, but it seemed like an innocuous place to put the Menagerie.

While much of Central Park remains the same now as in 1899, some features mentioned here have been lost or altered. The Cave was a natural grotto within the Ramble. Its relative privacy attracted people looking to put it to the same use as Nick and Jamie did, and frustrated authorities had the Cave sealed off in the 1930s. The Croton Waterworks and Old Receiving Reservoir have been largely filled in to create the Great Lawn; all that remains now is Turtle Pond, just below Belvedere Castle. As for Belvedere Castle, it was originally an open air structure, having doors and windows installed when it became a weather monitoring station in 1919.

Huge thanks to the readers who joined me for dinner and dessert during my research trip to Central Park. I'm so glad you could make it, and I hope you find the Mr. Quinn/Niles Whyborne secret baby/left at the altar fanfic of your dreams.

About The Author

Jordan L. Hawk grew up in North Carolina and forgot to ever leave. Childhood tales of mountain ghosts and mysterious creatures gave her a life-long love of things that go bump in the night. When she isn't writing, she brews her own beer and tries to keep her cats from destroying the house. Her best-selling Whyborne & Griffin series (beginning with *Widdershins*) can be found in print, ebook, and audiobook.

If you're interested in receiving Jordan's newsletter and being the first to know when new books are released, plus getting sneak peeks at upcoming novels, please sign up at her website jordanlhawk.com.